T0284289

PENGUIN BOOKS

VEINS OF POWER

Mica De Leon is the author of two novels published by Penguin Random House SEA. Her first novel, *Love on the Second Read*, is a rom-com set in the Philippines about two Filipino book editors. Her second was *Winds of War*, the first novel of the Seedmage Cycle—an epic, high fantasy trilogy.

She is a Filipino author of swoony romance comedy novels and epic fantasy novels, and she has won the Don Carlos Palanca Awards for Literature in 2019 and 2022 for her essays on romance, feminism, history, fantasy, and the Filipino identity. She is also the managing editor of one of the leading publishing houses in the Philippines and has produced over 200 books in her ten years there.

She likes walking on the beach, dogs, cats, swoony and spicy romance novels, epic, sci-fi-fantasy novels, Brandon Sanderson's Cosmere books, Pierce Brown's *Red Rising*, and Taylor Swift. She is trying (and failing) to catch up on the Cosmere books.

Connect with her on Instagram and TikTok: @micadeleonwrites.

Also by Mica De Leon

Veins of Power

Seedmage Cycle Book 2

Mica De Leon

PENGUIN BOOKS
An imprint of Penguin Random House

PENGUIN BOOKS

Penguin Books is an imprint of the Penguin Random House group of
companies whose addresses can be found at
global.penguinrandomhouse.com

Published by Penguin Random House SEA Pte Ltd
40 Penjuru Lane, #03-12, Block 2
Singapore 609216

First published in Penguin Books by Penguin Random House SEA 2024

ISBN 9789815144291

Typeset in Garamond by MAP Systems, Bengaluru, India

www.penguin.sg

For you,
may your duty to your heart exceed all else.

Love is never the death of duty.
Duty is borne from it.

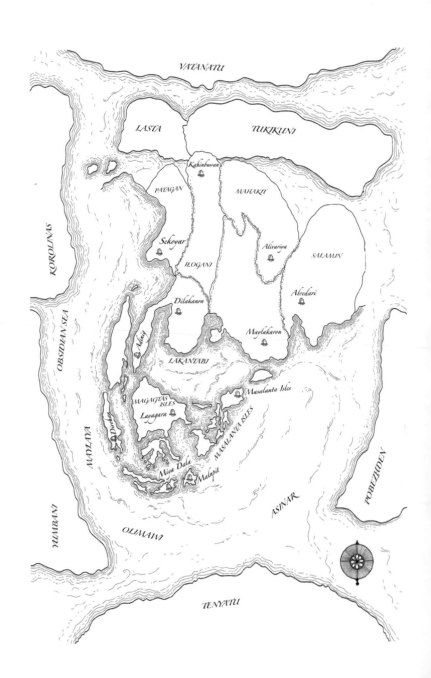

Notes

- **KAYUMALON:** A powerful kingdom with ten provinces, occupied by various noble houses (the leaders of which are from the direct bloodline of Maragtas the Conqueror), Dayo servants, and strangelord (non-human) races.
- **KAYUMAN :** The common language and the people of the Kayumalon kingdom.
- **DATUS:** The leaders of the ten great noble Houses of Kayumalon are called this.
- **DAYO:** The people who are the serving class in the Kayuman society. Identified by their pale skin. They are manual labourers and work on plantations to cultivate the seeds from which the oils that allow seedmages to harness their magic are made.
- **STRANGELORDS:** There are four strangelord races:
  - **Dalaket:** The tree folk
  - **Tikalbang:** Horse-humanoids, akin to centaurs
  - **Asinari:** The merfolk
  - **Asuwan:** The undying
- **REDS:** Soldiers of the Kalasag Army of Kayumalon who've sworn fealty to the monarch.

- **THE SEVEN SKYWORLD GODS:** They are also known as seedgods (which then use humans as vessels to exist in the earthly realm). They are essentially pieces of one big god who was broken apart. The seven gods are as follows:
  - **Dirigma:** Red moon
  - **Haliya:** Orange moon
  - **Sinag:** Yellow moon
  - **Tala:** Green moon
  - **Asin:** Blue moon
  - **Buwan:** Indigo moon
  - **Bihag:** Violet moon
- **SEEDMAGES:** Those who can harness the divine power using seedoil.
- **THE MAGIC SYSTEMS:** There are three magic systems used by the mages. They are listed below:
  - **Vitaulurgy:** The main magic system that reaches for the origins of seedmagic from which theochemy and germachemy branch out.
  - **Theochemy:** The (unstudied) magic used to fuse souls with a seedgod.
  - **Germachemy:** The magic that seedmages can harness using seedshooters. The different powers correspond to their respective colours listed below:
    - Red: Increases adrenaline
    - Orange: Increases and strengthens muscle mass
    - Yellow: Releases pheromones that serve different purposes

- Green: Allows you to manipulate other's vision by interfering with light
- Blue: Used to invoke darker mood, can be used as a depressant
- Indigo: Helps repair cells and accelerates healing
- Violet: Increases muscle and skin elasticity

Dramatis Personae

KAYUMALON

THE HOUSES OF KAYUMALON

There are four great houses; House Maylakan, House Laya, House Payapas, and House Layon—and several minor houses that serve the Datus as bannermen.

THE GREAT KAYUMAN HOUSES

HOUSE MAYLAKAN
(LAKANLUPA)

KALEM MAYLAKAN: The king preceding Duma

DUMA MAYLAKAN: The current monarch

LIGAYA LAYA-MAYLAKAN: The current queen and wife of Duma Maylakan

DAKILA MAYLAKAN (*Talim*): The second-born prince, allegedly the queen's bastard

DANGAL MAYLAKAN: The first-born prince, child of Duma and Ligaya

MAYIN: Half-Kayuman and half-Dayo girl living on Masalanta Island and a godvessel to the East Wind Goddess

LUTYO: The King's henchman and godvessel to the Death God

HOUSE LAYA
(MAYLAYA)

PATAS LAYA: Also known as the Obsidian Datu

DIWA LAYON-LAYA: Wife of Patas Laya

KALEM LAYA: Patas and Diwa's son and godvessel to the Earth God

BATAS LAYA: Younger brother of Patas Laya

HOUSE LAYON
(MARAGTAS ISLES)

MARALITA LAYON: A member of the Kalasag Army, works under Dakila's command

THE LESSER KAYUMAN HOUSES
HOUSE TALIM

PANDAY TALIM: Kalem's aide and bodyguard

THE SEED GODS

DIAN: A yellow maya, East Wind Goddess

DAMU: An indigo turtle, Earth God

SITAN: A violet-black raven, Death God

THE SPIDER'S SEED GODS

LAMIG: A blue-white spider, Frost God
GINAW: A rabbit, Snow God
HALIYA: An owl, Cold God
AHON: A whale, Tide God

MASALANTA ISLAND

TIYAGO MASALANTA: A Dayo labourer working on the Masalanta seedplantation

FERIDINAN MASALANTA: Brother of Tiyago, a Dayo labourer working on the Masalanta seedplantation

REJEENA MASALANTA: A Dayo labourer working on the seedplantation

GALENYA: Healer working on the Masalanta seedplantation
YIN'S FATHER: An ex-military Kayuman, now working as foreman on the Masalanta seedplantation

TUKIKUNI

THE SPIDER EMPRESS

THE SPIDER'S CHILDREN

JINWUN

SEYO

HANABI

HONGSU

GAMU

JIJIN

JEONJUN: A foot soldier in the Tukikuni army
GONCHUN: JinWun's husband

ASINAR

SEDHAJ MALIK: Datu of the Asinari merfolk
NAJIMA SAFIR-MALIK: Wife of Sedhaj Malik

Prologue

Lutyo

The Wind Goddess hid in mountains that would not bend to her winds. The rest of the island worshipped her anyway.

The Death God kept watch over her from a distance, watched the island turn her into legend and myth in the flesh. More Reds did try to take back the island after their first attack and her retaliation, but the Dayo somehow kept them at bay using the abandoned ships and by keeping the dead bodies scattered on the beach. A warning for all who would threaten the Dayo of Masalanta—this was the fate that awaited them at the hands of the Dayo's patron goddess. Soon, Masalanta Island became the Dayo runaways' safe haven and every day, the Dayo population living on the island grew—and with their numbers came the bravado to challenge the powers that be.

They made a sport of it, hunting down and executing their Kayuman oppressors and then executing their captives at midnight in the Wind Goddess' name and offering her gifts, praises, and supplication.

She tried to stop them, but she just ended up being forced to use her magic anyway to drive away the Reds that got past the ships and bodies. Eventually, her visits to the village grew far apart, and, soon, she stopped seeing them at all. But the legend of the Wind Goddess of the mountain stuck, and her protection stayed with the island even when she didn't heed her people's cries for help.

The Berdugo Rebels, the Kayuman had begun to call them—'berdugo' meaning 'butcher' in the arcane language—not knowing that these Dayo were simply lucky to have the protection of a Wind Goddess.

'*Is this part of your plan?*' the Shadow's raven, Sitan, asked, fluttering around his head as he watched the girl from the shadows of the thicket of trees surrounding the dead atis tree where her blade had once been. She was just coming up from foraging for food, including bird eggs.

To say that this was planned was overestimating his own faith in . . . fate, and fate had been cruel to him from the second he was born. He knew who this girl was the first time he found her at his master's behest—he felt it from the invisible tug of the King's command on his soul through Sitan's blade, his blade—but he saw an opportunity there to hit his master where it hurt the most and took it.

He had a godvessel's blade, Dian's blade, that he couldn't use on himself, and he found a direct descendant of the King, of the Maragtas lineage of Kayumalon kings—a Dayo princess no less. He'd be overestimating himself if he didn't admit that all he had was hope that the girl would use the blade to harm herself if he left it where she could find it. All he had to do was let the pieces fall where they would.

But the hand of fate be damned—what he hoped would happen happened. The Dayo princess used the blade to harm herself, and it was by his hand that this new goddess was made.

His master should have commanded Lutyo to kill the girl at the get go. That was his mistake, but maybe the King had too much faith in his shadow slave or at least in the chains that bound the Shadow to him. Whatever reason the King had to delay—creating political leverage against his son and biggest political rival, keeping a potential Dayo rebellion figurehead under wraps, preventing the creation of a martyr, or not having the political acumen to see the forest for the trees—it didn't matter to the Shadow because, now, the King could not compel him to kill this girl even if he tried. The girl's magic equalled and therefore cancelled his out.

For things to turn out the way they did on Masalanta Island and trigger the inevitable chain of events that would certainly rock Kayumalon's veins of power, now the Shadow may let himself think that he was a lucky man indeed.

Lutyo had never seen himself a lucky man, but for once in his long, miserable life, things were turning out in his favour—even the ones he hadn't set into motion himself. The Tukikuni's march south. The destruction and slaughter of House Payapa, the frost in the north, the famine in the south, the budding Dayo rebellion and the resulting labour shortage, the seed trade war between balangays, the rift within the Maragtas lineage—all of it had in some small way contributed to his goal: destroy his master and set himself free.

At the very least, he had found a way to defy his master in this small way.

The gods must have a sense of humour. Even now, the very bloodline—the bloodline of the gods, as the legends

would say of the Maragtas kings—that gave the King his
position, his power was the very thing that made him weaker
by the day. Yet, this also meant that Lutyo was under the
power of a frail, feeble man.

And this frail, feeble man had given him a new command
so sinister, it made Lutyo sick to his stomach just thinking
about what he would be compelled to do next. After all these
years of doing the vilest things for this man, he still couldn't
get himself used to the wanton murder of innocents—not
even the people who fashioned themselves as datus and
monarchs of their own lands.

'You've got to admit that there's some poetic justice in this.' He
couldn't hide the humour in his voice. Already, he could feel
the power pulse from her, that magnetic energy that pushed
at his magic but pulled at his mortal body. *'Or at least a punchline
to a joke.'*

'Or irony.'

*'I could never tell the difference. Father didn't spring for the full
Kolehiyo experience for me.'* Unlike his son and his wife's bastard.

**'He's going to want this girl dead one of these days.
How are you going to tell the old man?'**

'Easy. I just tell him and then sit back and enjoy the show.' He
squinted to see if there were telltale signs of the yellow magic
in her veins. He smiled, tracing the faint yellow lines under
her pale skin, up her arms, her collarbones, her cheeks, and
then her eyes, golden even in the waning morningstarlight.
It took his breath away. Dayo seedmages could never hide
the magic running through their veins under their pale skins.
'A Dayo Maragtas princess that I can't kill? This will crush him.'

'Clever.'

'You know how much pleasure I get from thwarting his will.'

'And what about the Tukikuni general?'

What about her?

'You think she'd do as you planned?'

His gambit on the Tukikuni general was like his gamble with this Maragtas princess. He could only prod the pieces into place, the rest he left unto fate—no, fate was an unreliable god. He put his faith in the very mortal desperation of the enslaved for freedom and the lengths they would go to get it.

I think she will use my gambit to her advantage.

In fact, he knew the Fire Godvessel had already set something in motion. On his last excursion to Tukikuni, he'd seen armies marching toward the Kayumalon borders.

'Was it justified? What we did in that village?'

It was not, Sitan. Nothing I do with your magic is ever justified. No mortal should ever have this power. Not me, especially.

'So you want her to take it?'

I do want to see her kill my master. That would be . . . ironic? Poetic justice? Whatever. Imagine the King dead at the hands of the girl he couldn't compel me to kill.' He scoffed and then shook his head at the thought. *I am tempted to say that I planned this all along, but really all I did was create another god to equal my power, a god that's indebted to me.*'

That gave the raven pause, and Sitan projected a dark energy on the Shadow at this implication, at the loophole in the magic system of the godvessel that he wanted to use, at a future that awaited them both should the Shadow's intention come to fruition.

The raven went quiet, pensive, and perched on the Shadow's shoulder. They watched the girl go through the motions of preparing dinner, setting up the cooking implements over a fire, and watching and waiting for whatever food she was able to cook until it was ready to eat. Most days, it was fruit, herbs, or root crops. Sometimes, eggs of random birds. Never meat, he noticed.

'Maybe it won't be so bad, me and you parting. She seems like the kind who wouldn't let anyone control her.'

'Does she?'

She stopped stirring the pot in front of her, pulled her knees up to her chest, and rested her chin on top of her knees, eyes on the fire but her gaze far away.

'Yeah . . .' Lutyo said it with too much conviction, as if he was convincing the Death God of his own fortitude. *People like her and me, people who come into power we can't use for our own benefit, we know desperation. We know the struggle for control over a life that everyone wants to claim for themselves. She'll fight for her autonomy. She'll fight to keep her independence.'*

And then, she buried her face in the crook between her knees, her shoulder trembling, her hold on her legs tightening like she was fighting to make herself smaller than she actually was.

He'd never noticed it when he first found her, how small she was, how frail she seemed, how vulnerable her big, golden eyes looked—like daylight paving the way for the coming of the seven moonslight, painting the world like an everchanging canvas.

Suddenly, his mind went to the child hiding under the floorboards of his family home, trembling in fear, yet glaring back at Lutyo like he stood a fighting chance against a Death God. A casualty of this secret war the King was waging on invisible enemies. So, Lutyo gave him real enemies, a real war within and without their borders. This was only the beginning of his vengeance, the beginning of his road to his own demise.

The winds blew a cold breath across the clearing, frost forming on the blades of leaves and the trunks of trees, the space devoid of warmth that he'd come to associate with this island, this summer country, this girl with the magic of the east winds. He tapped the hilt of the girl's blade and felt its magic pulse under his gloved hand. He had found the girl's blade in one of the Dalaket shipwrecks dotting the waters around the island. She didn't even know what this blade meant to her life. How could she? She was just lucky that the blade wasn't the kind that would actually kill her. What would have happened had the blade been found by someone else? Someone much more insidious than him?

He imagined feeling kinship with her through this unholy, unfair bond with him that he had forced on her without her knowing.

Alone, lonely, and loathing himself for what he had been doing all his life—executing innocent and guilty alike—the Death God decided it was time to atone for his sins.

ACT ONE

Chapter 1

Kalem

Kalem was uncomfortable sleeping in his own bed in his father's Castel embassy. It felt like a stranger's bed with its crisp, clean sheets, its smooth mattress, its newness. In the decade of living and studying in Kolehiyo, Kalem had grown accustomed to the dungeonesque feel of his dormitory room in the school, the lumpy mattress that knew the shape of his back, and the scent of seedmagic, crisp and sweet and spicy in the air, the sound of students and researchers rushing about outside, the nearness to the Alaala Archives, and so much knowledge. How would he feel when he returned to Maylaya, an ocean away from this island city, after being so far from home for so long?

He sat up and leaned against the headboard. The Dalaket twins, Sibila and Setefan, had generally kept his room the way he left it as a young boy when he first came to the city with his father at the start of his first-ever term at Kolehiyo. It was jarring to be here, a cold disparity between the boy he had been and the man that he was.

'Do you feel like there's something amiss?' the Earth God said in that invisible, otherworldly voice of his. *'Like when you know you've forgotten something very important on the way out the door but can't remember what it is?'*

It surprised Kalem just how articulate the Earth God was, how he liked to juxtapose what he saw against more abstract things that he knew. It shouldn't be surprising, given that the god was an abstract thing itself. He learned that the god wouldn't be able to read his thoughts, that the way it communicated was predicated on Kalem focusing on the god as if he were straddling two realms—mortal and abstract. A part of him, the part he dreaded to entertain, told him this must be the beginning of the seedsickness. He tried not to grimace. *'I'm not sure I know what you mean, Damu.'*

Turtle-shaped mist appeared before his eyes, swimming about as if it was underwater. *'It's probably just nothing. I'm probably just getting used to having a body.'*

'My body, you mean?'

The turtle stopped swimming and hovered before Kalem's face, its face and aura pensive. *'Our body now, I suppose.'*

Kalem scowled, not out of confusion or the bizarreness of talking to sentient mist but more out of the absurdity of his faith, his belief, wavering now, of all times. He still couldn't—didn't—believe that this thing floating idly in front of his face was a god. Magic was magic until scholars much smarter and wiser than himself understood it better. Then magic became science, germachemy, and eventually practical technology. The parts they hadn't understood yet, the parts scholars had relegated to faith and religion *for now*, those remained magic—seedmagic, the magic of the seedgods.

This discovery, though, Kalem's discovery of the godvessel, was just the proof he needed to prove his original thesis that germachemy was simply a branch of a more all-encompassing source of power. If only he could dedicate his life to its study again.

'Are you really a god?' Kalem asked impulsively, years of his study and work, of wrangling with his faith, desperately hanging on to five simple words for dear life.

'I don't know. Depends on what your people mean by "god", I guess.'

'I don't believe in my people's gods.'

'Well, what do you think is a god?'

Kalem turned to the open window, seven moons dotted the night sky amid a sea of stars. He remembered his mother on nights like these when the sky was clear, when nothing obstructed the moonslight, when the night reached the seam by which it gave way to day, when the twin citadels of Maylaya reluctantly began to let go of yesterday. His mother would hold him and tell him stories of the sky gods racing against each other across the Skyworld.

The turtle stared at him, and Kalem realized why he didn't believe it was a god. *'My mother taught me a game when I was a boy, the Skyworld game.'* He paused, remembering the song his mother sang to him the night the voices came to her first, and then sang it to the turtle.

'It's sung in the old tongue. It's the story of the sky gods chasing each other across the sky.'

'I don't see how this explains what you think gods are.'

'*Gods are cruel, mysterious, infinite beings that play with people's finite lives,*' Kalem began, and when he did, he realized he couldn't stop. He didn't get to his own faith in gods—or the lack of it—on a whim. He'd given it much thought back when he needed the magic of the gods and none answered. His mother was gone. *Believing in them is an acceptance of subservience to nebulous beings who treat life so flippantly. They are contradictions of what they stand for, of what roles theologies and religion assign to them. If gods are supposed to be infinite, perfect, divine, then why are they so . . . imperfect, so ineffectual, so very mundane?*' He trailed off, turning the words on his tongue like the first bite of hot *pandesal* on a cold morning. Funny how not wanting to believe was complementary to actually believing. How could he have not realized this earlier? Annoyance and frustration festered in him, looking for a way out, for any other host who'd bear the weight with him, willing or not.

'**I don't think I am ineffectual. You have my power to do with as you wish.**'

'*Why can't you use it yourself?*'

'**I don't know, but I think it's because I'm not of this realm.**'

'*How convenient.*'

'**Fine. If I am not a god, then what am I? And what does that make you?**'

Kalem bit the inside of his cheek. He couldn't help thinking that the answer to this should be easy.

He got out of bed, put on a long-sleeved shirt to cover his tattoos—a habit he wasn't planning on letting go of even after he left the Kolehiyo—and went out to take a walk in the estate's sprawling garden.

He was man, mortal, Kayuman. He was a datu's son. Most of his adult life he'd studied arcane seedmagic relentlessly. He couldn't help thinking that he'd wasted his life. This was what he wanted, right? He wanted to be proven wrong about the gods. He wanted to know that they could save his father, that they could have saved his mother, that they could save him. Now, the voice was speaking to him clearly, articulately, shrewdly. Was this the beginning of the madness? Was this how it began for his mother and father? Not with screaming, contradicting voices, but with one voice speaking so reasonably?

He didn't bother with shoes on the way out, wanting to feel the cold dew on the grass under his soles. He walked through the main hallway embellished with art, tapestries, and weapons hung there by his ancestors, tokens of past lives, past glories of people who had Kalem's blood but had not lived long enough to know him. This was not the entirety of the collection. The rest of these objects, the best, the bad, and the forgotten, were tucked away in their homeland, a sea away, hidden and pretending to be gone, like most family histories. Castel was not an island that accepted weakness so easily. Kalem made an effort not to look at the ones on the wall, though his eyes caught glimpses every so often—the statue approximating a Goddess of Fertility owned by an infertile queen who bore ten heirs, the sword of the first Maylaya Datu, the one who bowed to the conqueror, the patterned tapestries of every banner paying allegiance to House Laya.

By the time he stepped on the grass outside the indigo mansion with silver, black, and white pagoda-tipped rooftops, he felt small next to such grand heritage.

The turtle followed him quietly as he made his way to a garden of young mango trees around an old mango tree that crested a hill. A stone bench sat there, lonely and neglected. **'You walk these halls like you don't belong here. Isn't this your home?'**

Kalem frowned at the turtle. He was too observant. Too articulate. Too insightful. *'It is my ancestors' house.'*

'Your mother, the one who taught you the game, she lived here, too, then?'

'They kept her alive here for as long as they could. All her healers live in this city.' He wished his mother had died back home, if only so she would have been surrounded by people she loved in her final days.

Kalem sat under the mango tree and leaned back against the rough trunk, staring up at the canopy of green leaves and branches that were heavy with clumps of yellow fruit. He inhaled the sweet scent of ripe mango. It reminded him of yellow magic, the deceptively delicious aroma of sex and summer and awakenings. He liked this tree, for it didn't pretend to be more than it was. Its simplicity was its magic. He closed his eyes and let the scent and cool night winds lull him to sleep. The turtle would not let him.

'Where is she?'

'She's gone. Her ashes are buried under this tree.' Sometimes, he imagined that the mangoes of this tree were sweeter because of her, and the winds whistling through its branches was her singing the Skyworld song, chasing summer and spring like a game.

'She's gone and you're still here. Does it bother you that you will not die because of what you've done?'

Kalem opened his eyes sharply and shot the turtle a look. Right. He never asked what their bond entailed. Immortality then, must be one such condition.

'You mean our bond makes me immortal?'

'Only if your body is not destroyed. But if nothing happens to you, you will live forever as long as you have me.'

'You said I have your power to do with as I wish. Explain that to me.'

The god froze, he did not have a human face, but Kalem could tell by his aura that he was confused, surprised, and curious—the way one would feel after remembering a memory thought lost to him. **'I think . . . I feel . . . my magic is of the earth, of growth and regrowth, of cultivation. I just know it. I think knowing is an approximation of human instinct for me.'**

Kalem touched the ground with his bare hands, dew-soaked earth smearing his tattooed skin. He pushed down, gritting his teeth, willing something to happen. Nothing. He looked up at the turtle again, eyes waiting for instruction. *'What am I doing wrong?'*

'You're thinking yourself separate from the earth.' The god's tone was still curious, still surprised as if he'd found coins he thought he'd lost in his pocket.

Kalem breathed in deeply and then expelled the air out. He felt the dirt between his fingers, the ground beneath his soles, roots reaching outward, branches reaching up. He felt himself a part of the world, a small detail in a painting. His veins lit indigo under black tattoos. His eyes widened, and he pulled back from the earth as it overtook him.

'Do not be afraid of yourself.'

Kalem was panting before he realized that he was. He must have been holding his breath the entire time, but then he felt his body get lost in one world and then found in another; finite and infinite. He took off his shirt, got on all fours, and touched the ground again, this time determined to fade into the earth. His veins lit indigo again, his body, his consciousness disintegrating into the ground. Every grain of dirt, every rock, every stone, every gem, every speck of ash and crumbled bone that made up his body felt a rush of magic flowing through.

'That's it. You are the earth.'

Soon, his eyes glowed indigo, too, and the grass around him grew taller, the mangoes hanging from the tree grew much bigger and heavier, such that many plummeted to the ground. Even the dirt felt richer on his skin.

He felt, too, the rustle of footsteps approaching, and Kalem reluctantly pulled away from the magic, feeling as though he was tearing himself apart.

He leaned back against the tree trunk, controlling his breath and racing heartbeat, and watched as a figure in elaborate sleepwear approach him from the dirt patch that led to the mansion. He put his shirt back on to hide the vein stains, past stains from constantly overusing indigo magic thankfully hiding the glow. His uncle—tall, lanky, and sharp-faced—smiled at him as he neared, hands clasped behind his back.

In many ways, Batas Laya resembled his older brother, and in other ways—the ones that mattered—he did not. There was something about second siblings that looked at their elders with such disdain, as if a privilege, a gods-given right, had been plucked from them in their mother's womb.

Batas Laya carried himself with the poise of a man who wanted to seem bigger than himself. He must have relished the idea of looming over Kalem who was sitting stooped and panting under the mango tree, muddy and barefoot in his plain grey shirt and even more plain fading sleeping pants, all his tattoos hidden, as if in shame, under his spartan clothes. Kalem looked wretched next to the man standing over him. Kalem glanced around him, the grass overgrown, ground crooked with snarled roots, the floor scattered with ripe mangoes resigned to their rotting fates.

'The embassy's servants have let this place go. Look at this mess,' Lord Batas said, sitting on the stone bench next to the tree. He covered his arms, too, likely to hide that he did not have as many tattoos as his brother, but he kept the front of his shirt open to display his house sigil and position. He was someone important in a Great House of Kayumalon, the tattoos said, just not the most important.

'Sibila and Setefan manage the embassy just fine, Uncle. I asked them not to touch this spot.' The last part was a lie, of course, but he wasn't telling this man about the power he'd stumbled upon.

But the man was a master, who had won many a war with words, and Kalem knew that his uncle could tell that he was lying. 'A pity then to waste such a nice corner of our home here. It would do us no good if visitors and rivals saw this.'

'Let them see. I have nothing to hide.' He narrowed his eyes at the sharp-faced man, who was looking out at the city beyond the walls. His uncle was testing him, gauging where he'd falter so he could take over.

'I think we do. Your father is growing weaker and weaker by the day.'

'Greater men have given up more to the passage of time and aged in worse ways than my father. Only lesser men worry about it, Uncle.'

His uncle's lips pressed into a thin line, head turning to Kalem. Kalem had his uncle's full attention. 'I am told by my son that you left Kolehiyo in disgrace.'

'Your son worries too much about things that shouldn't concern him.'

'Why do you antagonize me, nephew? Have I done something wrong?'

'With respect, I came out here to sleep, Uncle, which as you can see I am not doing.' He dusted his palms on his pants, waiting, hoping the man would take that as a sign to leave. He didn't, so Kalem said, 'Uncle, just please tell me why you came to see me at this hour.'

The affable pretence was gone. 'No patience for subtleties, have you, boy? You won't survive court politics, let alone the Congress, if you don't play nice.'

'And you think playing nice with *you* will help me, Uncle?'

'It never hurts to have an elder, wiser counsel on your side.'

'Weren't you just concerned about ageing, Uncle?'

'Don't play games with me, boy.'

'I'm not. You've been playing games way before you humiliated my mother in court.'

Batas Laya stood so he was looming over Kalem again. 'That crazy wench doesn't belong in court and neither do you!'

Kalem stood, the magic in his veins reacting to his mood, the earth vibrating subtly under their feet. He shouldn't have let the man provoke him, shouldn't have let his emotions come out like this. If anything, in the wars fought with words, everything he said was weapon and ammunition that could be used against him. 'No one believed you then. And godsdamn, no one believes you now!' The veins on his cheek glowed indigo, forcing the older man to back away, threatened. Kalem moved to grab the man by the collar but decided against it. Calmly, he said, 'Even if I do step into the title earlier than intended, mark my words, you will be the last person I seek to give me truthful counsel.' He turned to leave but stopped to say, 'My father is strong and healthy, Uncle. His reign will last.'

He left the older man stunned on the hill where his mother was buried and walked back to his father's house, feeling like a fool for letting lesser men provoke him.

* * *

As he stepped through the door, cries of pain sent cold shivers down his spine. He ran into the house, up the stairs, and into his father's room. Panday, Narra, his father's Tikbalang aide and bodyguard, and the Dalaket twins, Sibila and Setefan, ran in after him.

His heart sank at the sight of his father convulsing in pain, and his mind went to the part of his memories that had haunted his dreams for so long. Blood and spittle and sweat and tears, his mother screaming and screaming about the voices at war in her head. His mother scratching and clawing at her skin, trying to get to invisible aches underneath. The madness, the mind giving in to sickness, was the thing that rattled him then. It rattled him now into forgetting everything he'd learned about seedmagic. How could a mind succumb like this to invisible aches? This could not happen to his mother. His father. Him.

Narra pushed him aside to hold his father down, barking commands, 'Master Kalem, Panday, help me hold down the Datu. Sibila, ropes, hot water, and towels. Setefan, get Master Makabago. Now!'

Stefan ran out the room, and Panday rushed forward to hold down the Obsidian Datu's feet. Kalem followed—mind blank, head hazy and confused—and held down his father by the shoulder, staring down into blank, bloodshot eyes; white, foaming mouth; and veins stained black on cheeks. People hovered around the doorway, and he recognized one smug face to be his uncle's, watching, staying back. All he had to do was stand back.

Narra dug into a bedside drawer and took out a vial of indigo seedshooter, then went to the bed to force open the Datu's mouth and empty the vial into it. His father choked and screamed and cried, indigo liquid trailing down the side of his lips, mouth foaming, and teeth gritting. His skin was hot like a furnace, and Kalem shuffled through pages in his mind, trying to remember the lessons and remedies he'd painstakingly memorized in school. But healers were taught not to heal themselves or the people they loved— their judgment could be clouded and biased. The words, shifting and warping, were indecipherable. Sibila returned and handed the rope to Narra who tied down the Datu's limbs to the four posts of the bed. The hero of the Obsidian War, the Datu of Maylaya, Kalem's father, reduced to a man who had to be tied down to his own bed so he wouldn't hurt himself. Panday and Narra stepped away, watching, waiting, like this wasn't the first time this had happened.

'It's getting worse,' he heard Panday say, his voice muffled, like an echo spoken underwater.

The convulsions neither stopped nor slowed down. Still, his father writhed in bed, and Kalem looked to Narra as if to ask him to do something, anything.

Narra turned to Sibila, 'Master Makabago?'

She closed her eyes for a second, the air around her undulating for a moment, tugging at the invisible line that connected the Dalaket twins to each other, before speaking again, 'Setefan just got to Kolehiyo. He is waking up the germachemist now.'

Kalem didn't let go of his father. He didn't have precedent to react calmly, in the same way Narra and Panday were doing, to see his father like this. He doubted, however, if he could be that calm, even if he knew it had gotten this bad.

In helpless desperation, Kalem felt his tears fall on his cheek. This couldn't be it. This wasn't where his father ended. Nothing he'd discovered or learned or done in the past could stop this. Nothing he knew could help alleviate his father's pain. He could do nothing.

The Earth God hovered near him, twisting in the air and trailing ribbons of glowing mist where it swam. Faith is medicine that the desperate turn to when magic or science proves insufficient.

So, he held his father, put his head on his father's heart, weighing the Datu's body down, and called to his god.

Kalem's veins glowed indigo and magic flowed out of him in tendrils of glowing mist. His father breathed in, making his own veins glow under his brown, tattooed, withered skin. The convulsions slowed. They turned into panting, then into slow, restless breaths. He lay still on the bed, and Kalem rose to see that his father had fallen asleep.

He looked at the people in the room. Sometime in the middle of the mess, Master Makabago had joined them with Setefan. They were staring at him with wonder and pity and fear. And if he looked close enough, he thought he saw some reverence. But Master Makabago was suspicious, his eyes demanding an explanation.

Nothing in Kalem's mind, nothing in his studies could explain what he had just done. He had been an arrogant fool who was so deeply absorbed by his studies that he had ignored his own limitations. It hurt him, it killed him that he'd wasted his life studying what could not be understood completely, trying to pin down the divine with mortal devices. He was a fool, a fool who watched his mother die, who watched his father barely survive death. He was still that helpless boy.

Only the stories his mother told him could explain this. Gods were real, if only in this moment, when even magic could not explain reality.

'Gods explain what cannot be explained by reason. Infinities understand what cannot be understood by the finite,' Kalem said, humbled, to the god swimming close to his face, crying like the child he had been the day his mother died, feeling Damu's infinity flowing through his veins, the disparities finding and blurring the fault line where the boy he had been ended, and the man he now was began. *'And I am . . . finite.'*

Chapter 2

Yin

Freedom unchained was wild, and Yin saw herself as just that. A creature of the wild.

She didn't wander out of her mountain, didn't follow the path back to her old, ruined home, didn't let her mind wander back to the past, to what could have been, to what should be.

No, she wasn't ready for that yet.

Even when she was among people, she didn't know where to place herself. She was pale like a Dayo, but Kayuman blood flowed through her veins. She'd been lost all her life. She didn't belong to anyone, so she decided she belonged to herself and therefore kept to herself in the silent sanctuary of her mountain.

Of course that wasn't completely true. She wasn't alone in the mountains. Belonging to herself, meant belonging to her god, to the Wind Goddess Dian. And she was glad to have the voice in her head for company even when it pestered her constantly about leaving the island.

'Yin, are we ever flying off this mountain again?'

'*Soon, Dian,*' she answered nonchalantly for the nth time that day. She was strolling through the forest, looking for dinner before the seven moons ushered in the night.

'**You never use our powers. Why can't we fly again? I'm a bird. I need to flyyyy!**' Dian complained, floating in place as Yin continued to walk forward. She'd decided to find eggs today to go with the mangoes hanging from the whispering tree. She could also do away with the mangoes if she found something else, anything else really. Meat ideally.

She heard rustling in the thicket of trees ahead, perhaps the sound of wings flapping. The Wind Goddess followed her, still waiting for an answer, so without thinking, she said, '*Maybe there are others like you that you can talk to.*'

The bird hovered again, as if pausing to think, and then it grew in size, its splendid wings growing outward, the glittering mist shimmering in the waning morningstarlight. '**YES! That's it! There are others like me!**' Dian flew forward and blocked Yin's path. '**We need to leave the island and find them.**'

She walked past the glittering body of the bird. '*Soon, Dian.*'

'**What are we waiting for? Didn't you always want to fly? You have my power to do it. What's stopping you?**'

She looked over her shoulder and narrowed her eyes suspiciously at the bird. '*How did you know that? Can you read minds, too?*'

'**No, but you were prepared to leave that day on the beach. I don't understand why you didn't.**'

Yin didn't answer the bird as she forged ahead, looking for the tree where she heard the flapping of wings. The Wind Goddess continued to pester Yin, flapping her wings, growing and shrinking in size, blocking the way with her glittering incorporeal body. Yin stopped at the base of a tree where she saw a bird's nest perched on the crook of two branches and began to climb it.

She knew the answer to the question. She had stayed because she was protecting her people and this island from the Reds, who could still retaliate after her attack. She had stayed because she was waiting. Her father, her real father, was looking for her. She had learned that when you are lost, the sensible thing to do is to stay put and wait for somebody to find you. So, she was staying put and waiting.

The bird flew over her face just as she reached the first branch, startling her into almost losing her hold on the tree. The winds instinctively caught her and pushed her up to sit on the tree branch. *'What if he never finds you, Yin? What if he's not looking for you? What if he's dead?'*

Yin frowned at the Wind Goddess and waved her away like smoke. *'He'll find me.'*

'He'll find me,' she said this time in her own tongue, more to convince herself that she wasn't holding on to false hope.

'I found you,' a man's voice, hollow and sharp like a crow's, called from below the tree. He was wearing a black cape over a splendid, black, double-breasted jacket with onyx trimmings similar to the Reds' uniforms. Sleeves and black boots hid every inch of his skin. His black trousers were held down by a black leather belt from which a blade—her blade—hung. She was only just realizing that she had never recovered her blade after the Reds took it from her on one of their ships. He slid the hood of his cloak back to reveal his face, marred by veins stained black and faintly glowing from subtle magic. His short black hair was neatly slicked back. His black eyes were like a pair of onyx stones in the waning light.

He was Dayo like her.

'Will you come down or would you rather I join you up there, little bird?'

Yin shrank back into the tree. She hadn't seen another person in months and here was a Dayo in Reds' uniform smiling up at her like an old friend.

'I'm coming up then,' he said, pulling himself up lithely from one branch to the next, black cloak billowing behind him like a raven's wings, till he was sitting next to her, the branch creaking under their combined weight.

Yin sprang upward, calling the winds to carry her away from the man, who merely sprang after her. For a second, she thought the man had morphed into a cloud of shadow mists as he flew off the tree to join Yin midair, but when she looked again, the man was shaped like a man—who was made entirely of smoke!

'Stay away!' she screamed at him, pushing the winds so he drifted far from her. The shape of his body flickered like smoke in the winds but reformed into the shape of a man.

'I have a rule. I won't attack unless I'm attacked first,' he said, smiling, smoke billowing out of him. 'And you attacked first.'

The smoke swirled around her like a hurricane, tainting her veins black, holding her in place. The winds came to her rescue, blowing the smoke off her so she could flee from the mysterious man.

She flew over the village, passing the large, dead Kanlungan tree, which had once served as the central piece of the town's plaza. The Dayo people stopped in awe to watch her fly away, chased down by a black cloud. In her peripheral vision, she thought she saw a body that looked a lot like her father's, hanging from the tree. But no, no it can't be him. *It isn't him.* Reluctant to take a better look, she turned her face away as she flew past it, trying to get as far away as possible from the tree. The black cloud matched her speed, morphing into the shape of the mysterious man's upper body, the smoke forming part of his black cape. 'Stop! I just want to talk to you!'

Yin flew downwards, through rows of dwarfed yellow seed trees, swerving between the branches in the hopes of losing her tail. The cloud of smoke merely rolled over the trees, leaving them dead in his wake. Yin shot upwards again, flying higher and higher and higher till she hit a cloud and came out on the other side wet, cold mist soaking her patterned halter dress and red scarf, and drenching her pale skin. The smoke spread like black ink across the clouds. He reached upward to envelop Yin in its black mass, crawling up her feet, knees, and waist.

Yin raised both arms and called more winds and clouds, casting a greyness over the entire island, but the black cloud of smoke would not let her go. When it was up to her neck, she screamed, 'Stop!'

The black mass stopped enveloping her into its body and reformed into the shape of the mysterious man, who was clinging to her just as she was clinging to him. 'I want to talk.'

'About what?' she said, preparing to push him off her.

She felt his sigh. 'I didn't want to have to do this, but—' A blade appeared within the cloud, glowing golden in the dark. She closed her eyes, waiting for it to stab her.

But the blade didn't move. A wave of electricity surged through her body, streaming out of her like thin strings of glittering mist all connected to the blade.

'Take us back to the tree,' the man whispered into her ear, and though she didn't want to obey, she felt herself commanding the winds to take them back to her tree.

They landed in the clearing around the dead atis tree. Reforming into a man of flesh and bone, he let go of her, putting the blade back into the sheath hanging from his belt. She drew away from him but found that she couldn't run very far.

'No use running. You're tethered to me while I hold your blade. I'll just call you back from wherever you run off to,' he said, sitting down on the grass. 'Do I have to command you to sit and talk to me?'

Yin gritted her teeth, glaring and preparing to call the winds again. His hand reached the blade's hilt, and she felt herself freeze on the spot. There was no fighting it. So begrudgingly, she nodded and sat in front of him.

'What do you want?' she snapped.

'The magic of this dagger, which you've claimed,' he said, unclasping the top two rows of buttons of his uniform, revealing pale, untattooed skin adorned by veins stained black.

Yin's eyes darted to the blade on his belt, then she stared up at him, confused.

'You stabbed yourself with the seedblade, right?' He said it like it was the most obvious thing in the world.

She narrowed her eyes at him. 'You mean to kill me?'

He shook his head. 'I can't even if I tried.' He ran a gloved hand through his hair.

She folded her arms across her chest, feeling the pull of the invisible magical cords that tethered her to him. 'How are you supposed to take the magic from me then, if you can't kill me?'

His eyes went to the hilt of Yin's blade, his expression conflicted, as if the next thing he was about to say was going to cause him serious pain. He grinned, shrugging off the conflict like it was a decision he'd rather leave for another day. 'I don't have my blade. Besides, between the two of us, you're the one more likely to hurt me.'

'What does that mean? Why should I trust you?'

'You shouldn't,' he said, patting the blade. 'Don't trust anyone who tries to control you.' With his eyes closed, he drew in a deep breath and then exhaled slowly, like he was trying to let go of a load weighing down his shoulders.

Yin eyed the blade on his belt again. She could reach for it, get on all fours, and bring her hand over his lap. It would be easy.

With his eyes still closed, he grabbed her wrist halfway to the hilt on his belt. 'You're an impulsive one, aren't you, little bird?'

She pulled her hand away roughly. 'Can't blame me for trying.'

'No, no, I can't.' He opened his eyes again and watched her pull her knees up to her chest. 'Do you have a name, little bird?'

'Of course I do. What kind of person doesn't have one?'

'Someone who wasn't supposed to be born,' he said, smirking bitterly. 'Don't be difficult. I don't have a lot of time. If I'm compelled to leave before I give you back your dagger, you'll have a far worse master than me.'

Yin looked up from her knees. 'You're bound to someone else?'

'The worst one, I'm afraid.' He tilted his head as if studying her face. 'Your name?'

'You first.'

He rolled his eyes. 'Fine. Lutyo.'

She hesitated, watching him, wary of his hand on her blade. 'Yin, my name is Yin.'

'There, that wasn't so hard, was it?' He sat up straight and leaned toward her. 'This is an odd place to find a Dayo halfling from an ancient bloodline. What are you doing here, little bird?'

Her heart skipped a beat. *Was it that obvious who—what I was? What was possibly giving me away?*

'Why do you need to know, Lutyo?'

'Look, I'm trying to give you free will, but you're really making it difficult to resist using the bond on you.'

'You'd be no better than your master if you did that, and I can tell that you don't want that.'

He grinned and shook his head. 'You're right. I don't want that, but I'll do it if I have to.' He raised both eyebrows, threatening to command her.

'Do it. I dare you,' she said, calling his bluff.

He stared her down. She matched his glare, her yellow eyes locking with his obsidian ones. He blinked, pulled back his head, and huffed. 'Fine, woman! Seedgods bind with specific ancient magic bloodlines. You're obviously only half-Dayo. Like me. You obviously have the magic to get away from here so why are you still here?'

'I'll tell you if you give me back my blade.'

'This is not a negotiation, little bird.'

'I'm turning it into one.'

'I have half a mind to give your blade to my master.'

'You wouldn't.' She narrowed her eyes at him, pausing to watch him squirm.

He rolled his eyes. 'Why must you make this so difficult?'

She found it ironic that the man who could make her do whatever he wanted was so easy to sway. 'I feel like this isn't something I should tell just anybody. Why do you need to know?'

'I want to save you.'

'You're kidding.'

'I am not, but it seems like you don't need it. Answer my question. Why are you still here? What are you waiting for?'

She held out a hand. 'Blade first.'

He scowled, unclasped the blade from his belt, and raised it between them. 'Now, will you just please answer the question, woman?'

She took the blade from his hand before he could pull it back.

'I have nowhere else to go . . .' she said, shrugging and eliciting a groan out of him.

As her hand gripped the hilt, she felt the tether of magic let go of her, and she knew the only person who could compel her to do her bidding was herself.

He stared at her, looking both annoyed and enthralled by her.

'You are . . . vexing, do you know that, little bird?' he said, but he was smiling at her. 'No one talks to me the way you do.'

'I'm generally alone on this mountain. So no one generally talks to me at all. Except the seedgoddess,' she said.

He let out a laugh and shook his head, then suddenly paused as if listening. She knew that look, those subtle shifts on his face. He was speaking to his god.

'I have to go,' he said, standing up mechanically, body transforming into a cloud of smoke that drifted up and away from her and the island.

Yin watched him go, stunned by the man's sudden departure, until he was out of sight and the grey clouds parted to give way to the moonslight.

That was when it dawned on her. He was like her. A Dayo mage. A Kayuman-Dayo halfling with the magic of the gods. That very revelation alone should have scared her, should have shown her how much more dangerous the rest of the world was, should have convinced her of the threat to her life, to her kind.

Instead, it just made her feel less alone and that made all the difference in the world.

Chapter 3

Kalem

Parties were never fun affairs among the upper echelons of Kayuman society. One held at the King's embassy in Castel would surely be the worst of them.

Kalem had not attended a function like this since his undergraduate years, but he could tell that nothing had changed since then. It wasn't fun for him as a boy. It would certainly be no fun for him now that he was a man, one that was about to come into power.

Maylakandito Manor was a tiered palace with red pagoda roofs cascading over every floor. The manor towered over the island like a sky god descended to earth. It was located on the northernmost tip of the island, surrounded by miles and miles of sprawling orchards and gardens, separated from the rest of the island by a black wall ten times the height of a Tikbalang. The hallway leading from the main door to the grand hall was flanked by bas-relief sculptures, telling the tales of the Maragtas kings—from the first king of Kayumalon, Datu Maragtas the Conqueror, to the thirteenth, Kalem II the Warrior. The current and fourteenth king, Datu Duma III, was yet to be added to this gallery.

'Kalem, maybe you should take off your jacket,' Panday said, trailing behind him, standing right outside the main hall where the party was already well underway. 'Never trust a man who hides his skin,' he added, quoting an old saying among the Kayuman.

'He's right, Master Kalem,' said Narra, his father's tall, black-maned Tikbalang aide. 'You represent Maylaya as son and future datu. The rest of the empire must see that.'

Kalem hesitated, pulling the edges of his jacket closer over his chest. He'd hidden his tattoos for a decade, as was the practice among scholars of Kolehiyo. In all cases, scholarship must remain neutral.

His father placed a comforting hand on his shoulder. 'It's all right, son. You can show your skin at the next gathering.' He wore a jacket himself, to hide his blackened veins caused by seedsickness. Yet, he stood tall, his back straight and shoulders squared, like he was going into a fight. But he was covering his skin. Hiding weakness was a weakness in itself among the Kayuman.

The man had had the worst blight attack Kalem had seen and here he was, standing as if he was on his ship again, about to go to war in the Obsidian Sea. Kalem's new magic could not heal the seedsickness completely, at least not the parts that the sickness had already ravaged beyond repair. He'd tried the magic over and over again, but no matter how many times he tried, the most it did was alleviate the pain of the blight somehow, perhaps dull the voices or the agony of being eaten alive from the inside by magic that cannot be contained in a mortal body. Whatever the seedsickness was, it was embedded in the very complicated fabric of a person's life, a person's body, and could not be reached so easily. What Kalem could do wasn't complete healing, but it was a start.

Kalem felt a pang of guilt in his chest. Why was he so hesitant to show his ink? He wasn't a scholar anymore. He couldn't be that person anymore. He had promised his father he would try. He was born with this duty. Sighing, he pulled off his jacket and handed it to Panday, exposing the tattoos he's had since he was a child. It told his story—that he was a direct descendant of the Maragtas kings, that he was the son of the Obsidian Datu, and that he was the next Datu of Maylaya. A new tattoo, one that had been added during his first years in Kolehiyo, was darker and smaller than the others. It was stamped next to his house's turtle sigil. It was the symbol for germachemy, an upturned leaf filled with the patterns of seven seeds and veins. He was most proud of that one. It was the one he wasn't born into, the one he had earned with his own hard work.

'There, that wasn't so hard, was it?' Panday said, folding the jacket over his arm. 'Your face is already scaring off the ladies. You gotta show some ink to—'

'That's enough, Panday,' Narra said sternly. 'Practice a modicum of respect here at least. It's a formal event.'

'Not too formal, I hope,' Kalem said, nodding to his father who smiled proudly. 'Are you sure you're all right, Father?'

His father nodded but didn't say any more before leading the way into the hall. Kalem sensed some hesitation there, but he saw relief in his father's determined albeit slower stride forward. Whether it was from Kalem's magic or his presence here with his father, it didn't matter. He had made his father happy. And that meant everything.

* * *

Kalem had never cared much for pageantry, even from before he'd gone to Kolehiyo. So, his heart wasn't in it when he and his father did the rounds of meeting and mingling with friends and rivals.

It seemed everyone was making a show of their wealth, magic, and power. The Kayuman lords—at least the ones with magic—let their veins glow blue or yellow under their black tattoos. They wore their finest jewellery and their most resplendent patterns. The men wore their ceremonial swords on their belts and clothes that exposed their glorious tattoos—some even going in *bahag,* patterned loincloths that fell to their knees, instead of trousers. The women wore their most expensive vest over wrap-around *saya* skirts in the patterns of the houses they represented.

Even with the pageantry making the hall look chaotic, Kalem could see the divides between factions—the Kayuman lords and the strangelords. The strangelords—the collective word used for the people of Kayumalon who were not strictly human—kept mostly to themselves. The Tikbalang, horse humanoids in armour and splendid patterns, towered over everyone, intimidating with their perpetual demeanour of a warrior in a battlefield. The Dalaket tree folk were not far behind in height. Their tree-like bodies trailing the scent of their bark and leaves in their wake; their black, beady eyes from within the hollows of their trunks, looking out at everyone with suspicion. The Asinari merfolk glittered in their wispy clothes and pearl jewellery, their scales shining in all the colours of the rainbow under the many lights of the glowlamps. Only the Asuwan undead did not participate in this competition of splendour. Instead, they stewed in their chosen corners, their grey skin looking like it was decaying in this light.

Kalem noticed that while the northern Kayuman lords stayed close to the King's still empty throne, signalling where their loyalties lay, the strangelords drifted toward his father as he entered the room.

Kalem felt oddly overdressed in this crowd and was glad he had taken off his jacket at least. His father didn't seem affected by the pageantry. Lesser lords treated him with some degree of reverence, cautious about rival houses, while house datus treated him with the kind of respect that was usually reserved for the King himself.

The King had not yet joined the party, but it was important to notice who was there and who was not. There had been some rumours about the King's waning health, and he wouldn't exactly be helping his case if he didn't show up here.

The Kayumalon government wasn't an absolute monarchy—at least it hadn't been for decades, not since Kalem the Wise, four sovereigns ago. The throne relegated a lot of its executive powers to the Congress of Datus, which had ten seats for the leaders of the ten major provinces of Kayumalon, including the King's seat of power, which was a role traditionally fulfilled by his heir-apparent so that the King could not influence or impede the Congress' collective votes.

Datus usually sent advisers and bannermen to represent them, their interests, and their house on regular days in

Congress, and the ten datus were only summoned to Castel to cast votes in person on matters as grave as installing a new member on one of the ten seats, waging war on another country, and deciding on the monarch's line of succession if ever there were any doubt. It was rare then to see all the datus and their bannermen in the same room. This party was the best and only opportunity for the datus to lobby for individual causes, make allies, and mend rivalries—if that was at all possible—before the actual Congress tomorrow.

The vote on whether to wage war against the Tukikuni was contentious and had many implications for the future of the country. With the Payapas gone and the King's son, Dangal Maylakan, nowhere to be found, their votes went to their closest living blood relatives from the Maragtas bloodline or they went back to the King to dispense as he pleased—an executive power that his eldest son and heir, Dangal Maylakan, had been trying to divest to the Congress for years. At the very least, before his sudden departure, he succeeded in preventing the King from choosing a replacement for the Payapa seat until after this congregation.

Kalem remembered a late night conversation with his father over blue seedwine so strong, that his father had let go of his inhibitions and secrets. His father, Datu Patas, had been talking to Dangal about a gambit he was about to play in Congress, a way to use the law in his favour, but Kalem had had too much of the wine as well, and he had wondered if his father had always had the political acumen to play such gambits or if it was a skill he learned from scheming with the King's son and heir.

Meanwhile, the three Dalaket lords of the north wavered between war and diplomacy, as their borders abutted the

Tukikuni borders, to prevent as much damage as possible. The Tikbalang Datu, Datu Sentori Sekoya, remained neutral and insisted on keeping his vote to himself until Congress reconvened. The last remaining northern Kayuman seat, Lakanlupa, was held by the King himself. With Dangal missing and the King's other son, Dakila, swearing off any government position after enlisting into the Kalasag Corps, the seat defaulted back to the King. So, the vote was up to the four southern lords, Datus Panganay Layag of Maragtas Islands, Stark Natera of Olimawi, Sedhaj Malik of Asinar, and his father Patas Laya of Maylaya. There was little question as to how the southern block would vote. The southerners had always presented a united front in most votes and they all looked to Kalem's father for leadership.

If his father's gambit worked, this vote would not only decide the fate of the war against the Tukikuni but also decide who would lead the country moving forward.

Based on the talk Kalem had overheard, the King seemed indifferent about going to war, but he could benefit from getting another opportunity to prove his mettle, an opportunity he had lost when Kalem's father won the Obsidian War.

Kalem spotted Master Makabago on the balcony, pointedly avoiding everyone trying to engage him in small talk.

Meanwhile, his father was introducing him to every lord and lady who came to him and made particular notice of girls and boys who were close to his age, like he was not about to plunge the entire country into an extended war.

'Kalem, this is Ibon Layon, daughter of Datu Agila of Lakantabi,' his father said about a girl older than him, with skin the colour of wet sand. 'Kalem, this young lady is Bulaklak Ylang-Ylang of Lakanlupa,' he said about a teenage girl with skin still red from her new tattoos. 'Kalem, this is Hayag Dalisay from home, north of the Ading Twin Citadels,' he said about a girl around Kalem's age with sharp eyes and dark circular-patterned tattoos all over her body, ending in patterned vines along her chin. This one had been brought forward by his own Uncle Batas and his wife Lady Bilad. His father took his time introducing this girl and pointedly mentioned that Hayag was a daughter of a bannerman who was cousin to his brother's wife.

'Father, don't you have better things to do than introduce me to potential spouses?' Kalem said when the last had girl left—some didn't even need introduction. They came up to Kalem without being urged to do so.

'Your future happiness is more important to me, son,' his father said, nodding at the Asinari Datu and his wife, who were walking up to them.

'No, I mean, shouldn't you be lobbying like the rest of them?' Kalem forced a smile as the Asinari approached.

'Why? The vote is yet to be decided. There's nothing more I can do.'

'Seems like you hold two-fifths of the vote.'

'I have one vote, Kalem.'

'But—'

His father shot him a look just as Datu Sedhaj Malik came up to his father and pulled him into an affable embrace. 'Tides take you, old man. It's been too long!'

'Tides take you, Sed,' his father answered the grinning merman with green, glossy scales, beady, black eyes, and fins along his limbs and the back of his head. He wore a bahag and a sash with blue and silver patterns of his house. A tall mermaid with iridescent indigo scales and silver seaweed hair stood next to him in a thin, flimsy halter dress with the same patterns. She was looking at Kalem curiously, as if studying his face, trying to pinpoint where she had seen him before. 'Tides take you, too, Lady Najima. This is my son, Kalem.'

'I know, Patas. I've heard much about his . . . theologies at Kolehiyo from my children,' Najima said, still staring at Kalem.

'I studied germachemy, Lady Najima. I leave the theologies with the philosophers and the Alagadan priests,' Kalem answered, a little too defensive than he had intended to be.

'Religion and seedmagic are often confused to be one and the same,' Najima said, sliding her arm into her husband's.

Kalem fought the urge to frown and ended up grinning weirdly instead. 'So are religion and theology, it seems,' he said before he could stop himself. His father eyed him, brows raised as if asking him what he was trying to do, but he looked more bemused than mad. Najima merely smiled while Sedhaj burst out laughing.

'I hope I see the day you take your place in Congress,' Sedhaj said, his belly jiggling with laughter. 'You'll definitely make court feel less like drudgery.' Sedhaj was the one datu who came to Castel to cast even the minor votes personally. It was no secret that the true datu was his wife.

'Now, now, husband, don't tease Master Kalem,' Najima said, then directed the conversation to his father. 'Patas, I've been hearing . . . rumours. About the King's health. About the prince and an illegitimate child.'

Kalem heard Panday stumble, and when he turned around to check what had happened, Narra was already helping Panday get back up on his feet. Kalem tilted his head, frowning, asking him if he was all right. Panday waved him off. Kalem turned his attention back in time to see his father tilting his chin up a little saying, ' . . . all is well. Nothing has changed.'

'The prince's absence indicates otherwise,' Najima pressed on.

'On the contrary, the prince's absence will more likely be in our favour, Najima. Have I ever given you reason to doubt?'

Najima cast a dubious look at Kalem, but that was enough of an answer for him to understand what she actually meant to say. She did not trust Kalem. 'Of course not, Patas. We need to talk about the Asuwan. In private, if you please.'

His father was about to answer when Kalem cut him off. 'Father, do you mind if I step out on the balcony for a while? I think I saw my old master there.'

Patas paused, the look on his face saying that he didn't have to go, that he should be part of this conversation, but Kalem understood the doubt cast by his presence there. 'Of course, son,' Patas said, as he and Narra walked toward a secluded conclave at the side with the Asinari.

Kalem faced Panday. 'What was that about, Panday?' he asked, leading the way to the balcony.

'What was what?' Panday said, feigning innocence. 'I'm supposed to be invisible here.'

'You're not doing a very good job,' Kalem said, searching up and down the balcony lit by glowlamps hanging from ornate posts.

'It's nothing, Kalem. Just clumsy,' Panday said, trailing behind him still. 'Why did you leave? Your father will tell you what they talked about anyway. You might as well have listened in.'

His friend was anything but clumsy. 'She wouldn't have been as honest as she needed to be if I were there.'

'She's going to have to learn to trust you if you're to be datu.'

'That's just it. She doesn't trust me. I've done nothing for her to trust me.' Kalem spotted Master Makabago in his Kolehiyo robes—black lined with silver—on the far side of the balcony, smoking a pipe that was glowing blue in the night. Kalem slowly walked up to him, unsure if he would be a welcome intruder to his master's peace, but when Makabago finally noticed him he waved him over. Kalem strode to him with short, eager steps. Panday stood to the side, out of earshot of the pair, to give them privacy.

'Master Makabago,' Kalem said, feeling awkward with his tattoos exposed and wishing he'd taken his jacket back from Panday.

'Kalem,' his master said, the pipe hanging from between his teeth. He blew out smoke. 'Glad to see your tattoos out.'

'I can't say I'll ever get comfortable with them being seen.'

'No one ever gets comfortable with unearned ink. Hide them, expose them. You simply live with them.' He took another drag and then exhaled luxuriously, the blue smoke drifting into the night. 'You've come to talk about your discovery? I must admit that I am eager to read your paper about it. I hope you'll make time to pursue it even with your . . . new duties.'

Kalem placed his elbows on the railing. The city was alive tonight. In the lead up to the Congress of Datus, the Reaping ritual happened within the span of a day, but the celebrations, events, contests, and parties lasted longer. The cheers from the arena reverberated all the way to the balcony, and a light from the park danced as the rest of the city celebrated without their lords. The Reaping was a gruesome ritual of the Alagadan faith that Kalem hated, but he'd come to learn that people needed faith to cling to when life felt unstable. There must be some truth to that. The Earth God hovering in his peripheral vision proved that.

Still, he felt that he needed to be out there, that he didn't belong in a place like this, flaunting his ink like it was his gods-given right.

'I'm confused, Master. I thought—I had hoped that my father would focus on training me in court when I returned. Instead, he's introducing me to brides and grooms . . .' Kalem gestured at his house's tattoo on his chest.

Master Makabago took a long drag from his pipe and blew out a cool blue mist. He seemed tentative, a teacher deciding if this was a lesson a student needed to learn on his own or if it must be said out loud for him to know it. 'Don't you see, Kalem?' he finally said, smoke trailing out of his nostrils. 'He's trying to give you more reason to do your duty.'

'What reason could that be, Master?'

'Love, I suppose. He's always preached about that,' the master answered a little too melodramatically, his veins glowing blue from the cigarette, relaxing him. 'Same thing that happened to him when you were born.'

Kalem snorted. 'I thought love was the death of duty.'

Master Makabago shook his head then tapped the chamber of the pot off the side of the railing, letting the seed grinds fall to the ground below. 'What is duty if it's not born out of love?' He pocketed the pipe and moved to lead Kalem back into the party.

Kalem stopped him. 'What if I can't do it, Master? What if I choose to do it and fail anyway?'

'What the turtle lacks in physical prowess, it makes up for in other ways. You're smart. You'll know what to do when the time comes.' A burst of trumpets and drums came from the main hall. 'Fair warning, son, the King's court is the tiger's den. Trust those seeking the same ends as you as much as you would those who oppose it. You never know whose stripes are true.'

He turned toward the doorway, eyes on the grand procession walking to the throne on the far side of the room. Next to the King, who stood tall despite the subtle tremors of his hand, was a man in all black, his skin covered so that no tattoo was visible.

From the corner of Kalem's eye, he caught a glimpse of Dakila bowing to the King just as the procession passed him, before backing away from the crown. The other prince was nowhere to be seen.

Makabago pulled Kalem's attention back to the procession. 'Ah, see, here comes the old, crusty tiger himself.'

Chapter 4

Yin

Yin had supposed that a short life spent on the run would have made it easy for her to move on. Yet here she was, stuck on this island, waiting on a promise not even directly given to her.

When Lutyo chased her around the island, she got her first glimpse of the village in weeks. It was a quick look, but it struck her that life had moved on so fast. It's like they'd purposely left her behind. She'd been working up the nerve to go back to the village to salvage what she could from her home and Galenya's house, afraid that she'd run into one of the villagers—especially Tiyago.

In the end, she decided to wait till the village was asleep and then flew in quietly at midnight. She hovered over the village, close enough to watch the people there work but far enough for them to mistake her as light motes in the sky. The Dayo had cleared the debris, washed out the blood on the floors, and taken down the Dayo bodies hanging from the gnarled branches of the Kanlungan plaza tree—dead and charred black after the fire that took it, a claw reaching for the moons in night sky. Now, weeks after her attack and after she became the Masalanta Dayos' reluctant goddess and protector, the mangled bodies of their former masters—Kayuman soldiers and noblemen alike stripped of their uniforms and resplendent patterned sashes and scarves as well as their dignity—hung from the branches. One body stood out amid the Kayuman masters, the body bearing the decaying face of the man who haunted her dreams and who had been her father figure for as long as she could remember. But they wouldn't do that, would they? Knowing who he was to her, their goddess, their protector?

'I don't suppose you've brought us here to say goodbye to your friends,' Dian said, perching on her shoulder as a small glittering, maya bird.

'They're not my friends,' Yin said, spotting Tiyago among a group of labourers coming from the fields and orchards, his bright auburn red hair a beacon far below. He was still that beautiful boy she'd admired from afar for so long, the same boy who had invited her to become his friend when he didn't know who she was—what she was.

This time, her heart didn't flutter, her stomach didn't stir. Instead, she felt a cold flash sparking from the base of her spine and surging all over her body. She couldn't stand to remember that look of despair, distant and confused, on his face when he had seen what she was and what he could get from her.

He tilted his head skywards, and although she was sure she was too far away to be seen, he seemed to look directly at her. She'd never noticed it before, but he always seemed to know when someone was watching him, when *she* was watching him. As if he expected everyone to be looking at him.

Crestfallen and irascible, she tore her gaze from the beautiful boy and flew away.

* * *

The seven moons dotted a field of stars in the night sky, casting an eerie, almost sinister light on the ground. It was the kind of night when one closed the shutters, lest the moonlight turn into nightmares.

Yin landed stealthily on an empty dirt path between stone houses. Though quiet, the village was not completely asleep yet. Many of the younger villagers had stayed up to party in the plaza under the tree. Now that the masters were gone, there was nothing stopping the Dayo from doing whatever they wanted. And it seemed there were more Dayos living on this island than before the Kayuman masters left. She could hear the frenetic music of *kulintangs*, *kudyapi*, and *dabakan* all the way here at the outskirts of the village where the ruins of her home stood.

She stared at the house, feeling an emptiness inside. She had hoped that this would be her last home, an end to a life of running, a life that seemed to surge past her faster than she could turn each experience into a memory and compartmentalize it in her mind. Her life up to this point felt like one big ongoing story that refused to stay in the past.

She couldn't move on because she was still here, still living in that one memory. And her greatest fear was that it would never stop.

'Every time I think we're going to leave, you prove me wrong. Now we're back where you started.'

'Where I started?' The goddess had made it clear that they existed as one in this realm.

'This isn't where I started, Dian,' she said, still just standing outside the house, its bundled-up yellow straw roof shingles blown off the top, exposing its inside to the elements. The windows on all sides were either lost or in the process of coming off their hinges. Moss and vines were starting to grow over the stone walls, and the door was gone. Through the open doorway, she saw the small fire pit around which orange and black clay pots lay in broken pieces on the floor.

She closed her eyes and the bramble and overgrowth and moss peeled away from the house, the roof returned, the fire started in her mind. She remembered the scent of freshly cooked white rice mingling with the perpetual nectarine scent of seed berries. She remembered plucking leaves off kangkong stalks harvested from their humble garden and dropping them into a pot of fish, tomatoes, *labanos*, tamarind rind, and sliced green mangoes, and her father coming home from the orchards, clothes covered in seeddust. She could almost taste the sour–sweet soup of sinigang in her mouth.

When she opened her eyes again, the bird was standing a head taller than her on the ground in front of her. She stepped back, startled. *'Didn't we talk about personal space?'*

'Your person is my person, Yin,' the bird said, shrinking back to her small, maya size. **'You were just standing there in the middle of the dirt path, and I was getting bored.'**

Yin walked ahead towards the ruins of her old house, the forest around them humming with the sounds of the night— night owls and bats and the buzzing of nocturnal insects. *'You know, for an eternal immortal being, you are terribly impatient.'*

*'Well, you're exceptionally slow even for a human.
You have the winds at your beck and call, but you hide
in the mountains like a mouse scared of a little rain.'*
The bird fluttered around her head like a mosquito. It
reminded her of a Kayuman legend that Galenya had told
her. Legend has it that the Kayuman soldier Lamoc and his
followers had failed to protect their master from his killer,
who escaped and hid away in an untraceable cave. And so,
to avenge their master, they spent their lives searching every
earhole, looking for the assassin. It was supposed to explain
why mosquitoes buzz in people's ears. Yin waved her hands
around her head as if trying to swat an actual mosquito,
her gaze drifting momentarily from the path ahead as she
approached her house.

When she turned her attention back to the path, a figure
with blazing red hair was walking toward her, and without
thinking, she practically dove into the open doorway of her
house and rolled into a standing position in the middle of the
hollow structure.

'Yin?' the voice called from outside the house.

Yin froze in place, looking around for a way out, panic
rising like bile in her throat, realizing too late that she'd
trapped herself by coming in here instead of running back
up into her mountain.

'Yin? It's you, isn't it?' Tiyago called, almost at the door

Frantic, Yin scanned the empty room for hiding
spots. It was like a whirlwind had descended specifically
onto the house. The plain yellow *banig*—a sleeping mat
made of *abaca* and straw, with the black and red striped
patterns—lay crumpled in a corner. Jars and bottles of

preserved fruits lay shattered on the floor, their contents
black and rotting. The large stone vase where her father
would keep white rice was upturned and emptied. Her father's
and her clothes were dirty and strewn about on the ground.
Shadows splayed across the dark corner at the foot of the
bed, unreachable to the eerie moonslight above.

The goddess fluttered at the edge of her vision, Tiyago's
heavy footsteps coming closer and closer.

And then she stopped.

'What am I doing? I can fly,' she said, shaking her head
and preparing to leap onto a gust of wind she summoned.

Just as her feet left the ground, a gloved hand grabbed
her by the waist and pulled her into the shadows, which
enveloped her like a cloud of black smoke.

She gasped, but a gloved hand covered her mouth, pulling
her closer, her back landing softly the person behind her.

'Shhh . . .' Lutyo whispered in her ear, his breath grazing
her cheek. 'The shadows will hide us.'

Tiyago burst through the door, his red hair gleaming like
fire in the light streaming through the doorway. He scanned
the dark room, frowning in confusion.

Though she could not see Lutyo's hands on her, he held
her tight, her body barely hidden within the shadow's edge.
From where she stood, she watched Tiyago search the house
and pick through the debris, as if searching for proof that what
he saw wasn't just a figment of his imagination. He stopped in
front of the dark corner, staring at it with his eyes narrowed
and his brows furrowed, the way one might look at a dirt path
in a forest that had always been there and now wasn't.

It had been weeks since she'd looked at Tiyago from this
close. A pink scar ran across the beautiful boy's face, the bags

under his eyes seemed heavy, burdened, and his once bright red hair was the colour of rust. He'd changed so much in the weeks following the attack, how it had withered him to a husk of the man she knew. The most notable change wasn't physical. He seemed to stand taller, straighter, like a beast of burden freed from its reins. He seemed . . . less constrained by the chains that used to bind him, freer somehow but not completely free—maybe more in control of himself now than ever before.

Tiyago shook his head, mumbling about drinking too much of the blue and overworking in the fields, before exiting the room.

Yin waited until Tiyago's footsteps were mere echoes in the distance before shrugging off Lutyo's hold on her and preparing to fly away from him.

'Please don't fly away, little bird,' Lutyo said, holding her by the wrist.

She turned back to him and said, 'What do you want?'

'I . . .' He hesitated, hand still on her wrist, as if catching himself about to make a huge mistake ' . . . don't know.'

She narrowed her eyes at him and pulled her hand out of his grip. 'I don't believe you.'

'It's your magic. It calls to me,' he said, clamouring for words.

She folded her arms across her chest. Something about the way he said it felt like a lie or a truth masking a lie.

'It's why the redhead is after you. The magic called him to you like a . . .' He scanned the room and his eyes fell on the broken jars and vials. ' . . . like a *gayuma*.'

'You must be kidding. A love potion? Those things don't work.'

'Not without magic, and you and I have plenty of it.' His gaze lingered on her, his expression betraying his true disposition.

'You're still not telling the truth,' she said flatly.

He crouched to look into her eyes, searching. 'I wonder if this . . . heightened empathy is innate or if it's the magic—'

'Stay away from me, Lutyo,' she said, turning to leave.

'Wait. No,' he said, following her out the doorway. 'It is true. Your magic, it's like a . . . magnet.' He picked up his pace to block her path as they entered a grove of guava trees. 'I know you feel the same way about my magic.'

'I can't give you what you want.' She pushed past him and trudged along the rising slope up to her sanctuary, lighting her veins yellow to illuminate their path.

'You can learn from him.'

'Not now, Dian.'

He ran up to block her path again and held her there by the shoulders. 'Fine. You want the truth? It's this. I'm like you. A Dayo seedmage. We're a very rare breed.'

She still didn't believe he was telling the truth, but this confession she understood. Magic only came to the noble-born. Dayo were not supposed to be magical. Halflings who were born with it were killed instantly. The last few weeks after the attack had been some of the most confusing and disorienting days of Yin's life. And though she had Dian, she had felt like she'd had to face it all alone with only the vague hope that she wouldn't be alone later.

'Still not the truth I need to know, but better.' She looked at his hands on her shoulders. 'Please let go of me.'

He pulled back tentatively, and she continued the walk up.

'Where are we going? And why aren't you flying there?'

'Home. And I like walking,' she said without looking at him as he walked alongside her. She'd set up a home under a mango tree near the atis tree. Since Tiyago and the Reds had found the atis tree the day she bonded with Dian, it couldn't be her sanctuary anymore, but she couldn't shake off the need to be near some place familiar. After fusing with Dian, the tree's magic seemed to have gone. Its leaves fell off, the branches blackened, weeds grew over the herbs, the grass around it browned. It was as if by taking out the blade, she'd also taken out everything that made the tree special. Her hand went to the hilt of her blade hanging from a rope belt around her waist and stole a glance at Lutyo, whose black cloak billowed behind him like smoke. 'You seem to understand what my magic is, but I don't understand yours.'

'Decay,' he said nonchalantly. 'Nothing complicated. Living creatures disintegrate at my touch.' He pulled off a glove and plucked a leaf off the nearest tree. It turned orange then brown then black and then crumbled to dust in his hand.

'And the shadow and smoke?'

'A manifestation of the magic in my body. Yours is much more interesting. Magic that instantly makes people love me? I wouldn't mind having that.' He whistled. 'You got one of the good seedgods.'

'That doesn't sound as appealing to me as it does to you.'

'Why not? We're Dayo. Magic or not, we were born at the very bottom of the barrel. You don't even have to lift a finger with that magic. People will just give you what you want. People will love you regardless of your skin.'

'But how do you know if it's real?'

He shrugged. 'Does it matter if it's real?'

'Of course it does,' she said, trailing off. She thought about her mother and the man who raised her who was not her father. She should have seen the budding resentment and guilt between them all those years ago. Yin thought, all along, that love was a transaction—giving back the equivalent of what one received from the other. Her father expected much from her mother, who knew that she could never repay the debt she owed him for saving their lives. Too late did Yin learn that it wasn't a transaction between her adopted father and her mother at all but between her and the people who raised her. Her mother may not have love for the man, but her love for Yin was like a well dug deep beneath the earth and constantly refilled by rain. And the man loved her mother enough to keep that well full for Yin despite the resentment he felt for having to give up his life and live a lie. 'Without love, life would only be a series of transactions. Sooner or later, you're going to run out.'

He didn't answer immediately as they continued to walk through the forest, following the path she'd paved with her own feet over the months of gleaning in this forest. She watched him from her peripheral vision. He looked so thoughtful, so distracted, that not even the brambles catching on his cloak could pull him out of his thoughts. Yin led him to the base of the mango tree where she had set up her small home, its branches teeming with green, unripe fruit.

'We're gods,' he said finally. 'We're infinite. We'll never run out.'

'Isn't that sad?' she answered as she called the winds to rustle the branches above them to shake some fruit off.

The green mangoes clung to their tree, unwilling to let go of where they came from.

'Why?' he said, almost aghast.

'It makes our love worthless and the love given to us finite, scarce, rare.' She began to climb the tree to pluck the fruits with her own hands. 'The more we have of one thing, the less we value it.' He watched her quietly from the ground, as if waiting for her to explain more. 'No matter how much I love, no one else can ever match it equally. It makes love conditional. I'll never be happy.' She pulled off a bunch of mangoes and looked at him. 'Catch!' she said, throwing the fruits at him. It startled him, and he caught them in his ungloved hand, killing the fruits.

He gazed at her as if expecting punishment. Instead, she sighed and said, 'Sorry, I forgot. I'll get another one.'

'Aren't you lonely here?' he asked her later as they were eating the green mangoes, which Yin cut using her blade. They sat next to each other under the tree, watching the moons make their way across the Skyworld and usher in the Morningstar.

'I'm not alone.' She bit into a sour piece of mango. 'I have Dian.'

'You know what I mean.'

'I didn't have much even before the magic.' She turned to look at him as if to emphasize what she had said, but it came off as defensive, as if she was trying to convince herself. 'I'm trying to cling to the little things I have left.'

'It doesn't look like you have anything, little bird. Other than mangoes, of course, sour ones at that.' He picked up a peeled, unripe mango with his ungloved hand.

She watched the mango rot and melt in his hand, the scent of sour decay making her stomach churn. She tried not to cringe, but based on his expression, she must not have hid it well. She put down the piece of mango she was about to bite into. 'What about you? You have everything, but you're tethered to someone else. Wouldn't your master want to keep you close?'

'I'm rewarded with these little pockets of freedom when I do my job well.' He put on his glove and reached for Yin's blade.

She pulled it away before he could touch it. 'What are you doing?'

He raised his eyebrows, both surprised and amused by her knee-jerk reaction. 'I was just going to peel another mango for you,' he raised his other hand, holding a plump, green mango, 'since I ruined the one you just peeled.'

She narrowed her eyes at him, gaze darting from his face to the mango.

He burst out laughing. 'I was kidding. Relax, little bird. I wouldn't let my master get his hands on power like yours.' He flicked his wrist and from his sleeve came a small knife landing in the palm of his gloved hand. He began peeling and slicing. 'He'll ruin you.'

'Like he did you?' she said without thinking.

He smiled, but it did not reach his eyes. She'd struck a bitter chord.

'I didn't mea—'

'Don't,' he snapped, eyes still on the mango, but he wasn't peeling or slicing it anymore. 'You're far too honest, little bird, for me to believe that you didn't mean that.' He sighed, let go of the fruit, and slid his knife back into his sleeve. 'I should go,' he said, standing up and dusting his clothes. 'My master doesn't know I rewarded myself this night.'

Yin stood up, too, and grabbed his elbow. 'You snuck out? You can do that.'

'Only if he's not concentrating on my dagger.' He ran a hand through his black hair and scratched the back of his head, sheepishly saying, 'Besides I didn't kill enough people for my master to give me a reward. But he's too busy with the jokers at court to focus on his hold over me.' Her hand dropped from his arm, and he laughed at the expression on her face. 'Did anyone ever tell you you're a little jumpy?' He rolled his shoulders and cracked his neck. 'I'd leave this dump if I were you, little bird. Nothing is tethering you here.' He looked at her with a mischievous glint in his eyes like he was about to say something clever. 'Nothing real at least.'

Her jaw dropped as his body turned to smoke and shadows.

'Wait! I . . . have more questions,' she said.

'If you're still here when I return, I'll give you answers—if I have them—or maybe I'll give you lies. Let's see,' he said, grinning at her before the shadows engulfed his face and his dark cloud flew into the dawn sky.

He left her there alone, another man promising to come for her, another little thing to tether her to the ground.

Chapter 5

Yin

Lost and alone, Yin found herself adjusting to a quiet, patient life in her mountain better than she expected. She'd come to know the mountain like an old friend, and there was a satisfying calm in the way the dusk and dawn ushered light across the sky. It felt like that sky was intimately hers from the moment she woke up in the morning to the hour she closed her eyes at night. From where she stood on the mountain, feet planted firmly on the ground, she felt closer to the sky.

'It's not the same,' Lutyo said one night when he *rewarded* himself again. 'You can actually touch the sky, little bird.'

He was lying next to her on the grass in a clearing, his cloak bundled up into a makeshift pillow under their heads. He bit into a piece of dried squid, called *daing na pusit*, which he had brought from wherever he came from this time. This, after complaining that all she fed him when he visited were mangoes. She responded by shoving a handful of sour, sticky guava into his mouth, which he spat out in disgust. He had a taste for meat—things that fought back before they became food, he joked. He came to visit her more frequently. He always had a reason for coming, a question that needed to be asked, a thing that needed to be retrieved, a person who needed to be found. Always, he stayed even after he'd done what he came to do, and she'd come to expect his regular visits. If she was being honest with herself, maybe she wasn't getting used to being lost and alone, at least not all the time. Once before, an entire week had passed without him coming, and loneliness sank its claws deeper and deeper into her the longer she didn't see him. She had seriously considered leaving the island.

Of course she didn't leave. She was still waiting.

And she didn't think he actually wanted her to leave. She could tell that he liked having a reason to come to her mountain, even if he won't admit that the reason was her. They both understood that the only person who knew loneliness like they did was the other. Loneliness is a brand unique to every person that never quite heals, but it helps to have someone else see it and not shrink back in fear.

'But then you won't have a reason to reward yourself,' she answered, feeling cheeky.

A corner of his lip twitched upward, and then he shrugged. 'Just saying. It's a big world, little bird.'

She turned to him, planting her elbow on the grass and propping her head up on her palm. 'You speak like you've seen the world.'

He kept his body facing the sky, but his eyes went to her. 'I have seen some of it. I have gone as far as my master has allowed me.'

'How far have you gone?

'I'd say pretty far. Yumbani was nice. The Obsidian Sea looked like an extension of the night sky from the Yumban beaches. It felt like a vacation. I've seen a little bit of Korolina and Pobezhden but only from the sky. I haven't tried flying further up north or south. Didn't think Vatanatu and Tenyatu were worth the trip, knowing that they're likely just frozen wastelands. I didn't try to see *all* of Lasta. Their war with the Tukikuni has all but destroyed their country. I got to stay for a while in Lamigin up in Tukikuni.'

'What were you doing there?'

'Secret mission,' he said, pointedly not elaborating. 'If you're going to Tukikuni, try to avoid the Spider Empress. That one's got too many clouds up in her head, if you get my meaning. She treats death like it is a game that everyone loses and she always wins.'

She lay back down on the grass, gazing at the many moons in the sky. Lutyo usually left at midnight. 'Why do you talk about death so . . . flippantly?'

'I'm the God of Death, Yin. If I don't take it lightly, I'll constantly have thoughts of death and dying, and the irony is I can't die.' He paused, a pensive expression flashing across his face, gone before Yin could pinpoint what it meant. He swallowed the last of his squid and continued, 'Vessels can't harm themselves, not while they carry a seedgod. So I can't kill myself. Not unless you stick another seedgod's blade in me and take all the magic that's keeping me alive and immortal.'

She frowned and narrowed her eyes at the boy next to her, hands clasped on his stomach, one leg resting over the other knee. His eyes were closed, his lashes long enough to touch the apples of his pale cheeks. He'd let his slicked black hair fall into disarray so that it was a mop of black curls over his forehead, punctuated by thick brows below.

'You refer to yourself as a god?' She couldn't hide the laughter in her tone.

He grinned and opened one eye to look at her. 'Why wouldn't I? We're immortal so long as nobody damages our mortal bodies enough to kill us, and we have magic beyond anything the Kayuman could create. What about you? You're the Wind Goddess; people love magic like yours. They would worship you—they should, they do.'

She pursed her lips and rolled her eyes. 'Their worship implies that I have a duty to them.'

'This coming from the girl who would be terribly unhappy if life were only a series of transactions.'

She bit her lower lip and turned away from him to hide her face. He did that a lot, turning what she said against her. She knew she was blushing when he sat up, laughing, to get a better look at her face.

'Look at it this way, people worship weather gods, and they fear gods like me. Either way, both our magic plays a natural role in the cycle of life, even if we don't actively participate in that cycle.' He offered her a hand to help her sit up. 'But we're Dayo halflings. We don't belong to either the Kayuman or the Dayo, and they've both expressed that to our faces openly. Why should we care about what they think? We can spend our immortality and magic however we want, and they can't do nothing about it. The world continues even without us intervening.'

'So what do we do with our magic?' She wrapped her arms around her knees and pulled them close to her chest.

'I barely use mine, and I assume you use yours frequently,' she said, gesturing at his gloved hands.

'Something tells me that it should be the other way around.'

'Yeah, but your master forces you to use it,' she said.

'But is it actually duty if you're forced to do it?'

'Isn't that what duty is? Things you have to do no matter how much you don't want to do them.'

'Not if I choose not to do it willingly.'

'Sounds like a terrible way to spend your life.'

He laughed out loud. 'If only you had my blade, then maybe life wouldn't be so terrible.'

'Does it have to belong to anyone else other than you?'

'Wouldn't you have use for the Death God's magic?'

'Everyone who matters to me is already rotting.'

'Life springs even from rot. A corpse can die a dozen times and still have a little bit of life in it.'

She cringed then laughed. 'Why, *Ginoong* Lutyo, that was so profound. My simplistic world view simply cannot keep up with your wit.'

He guffawed. 'All I'm saying is death has its uses. Most important of them, I think, is ushering in rebirth,' he said.

'What about my magic? Yes, the winds summon storms but what about the other one?'

'You mean the love magic?' He couldn't help grinning at that. 'Like the seduction spells used by the village quack doctors?'

She rolled her eyes. 'Well, if you say it that way, it sounds silly.'

He fell silent, growing serious all of a sudden, eyes trained on her. 'Love isn't silly. If life is a series of transactions then love must be an infinite currency. There's nothing I wouldn't do for someone I love.'

They stared at each other silently—their expressions soft, stunned, inviting, unsure, like rain clouds on a summer day—the seconds stretching longer than they felt. Neither wanted to leave; both wanted to pull away.

Without her mother, her adopted father, Galenya, and even the father who had promised to come for her, Lutyo was the only person she had, the only one she could trust, the only thing that held a lonely life at bay—a solid anchor. She wondered if it was only the magic that kept him coming to her.

He stood up, and she followed suit, allowing him to take his cloak back and drape it over his shoulders, eyes pointedly facing away from her. 'I've been summoned. I should go. If you want anybody dead or decaying, just let me know, little bird,' he mused before rising as a dark cloud into the sky, leaving her lost and alone again.

Two things she decidedly thought she wasn't at all good at.

Chapter 6

Yin

Yin wasn't expecting anything special to happen that day, but a realization hit her like a gust of wind on an otherwise calm day. She had forgotten what it was like to be free. The way one would forget something important on the way out the door—a thick scarf, good shoes, a blade on a day she was supposed to glean through the mountain forest. She had abandoned proper society, lost herself in the thickets of the mountain, and lived off the land like a true creature of the wild.

There was a tyranny in being alone with her thoughts.

Her thoughts had a bad habit of running away from her. Something innocuous would stew until it became a horror, unrecognizable even to her. Her mind conjured visions of her father—her adopted father—hanging from the Kanlungan, a symbol of tyranny defeated by the Dayo he oppressed or so Tiyago would have everyone in their little village believe. She knew in her heart that her father—her adopted father—despite his flaws, his insecurities, his many missteps in life, hadn't deserved a death such as this. He had protected her, cared for her and her mother, kept her safe from the very people who had hired him to take them out. He was a good man . . . No, he did what good he could do by them. And now, he was gone. It was still unreal for Yin.

Yin still felt rage at the Dayo—Tiyago specifically. He had been kind to her in the beginning, made space for an outsider in this little town, made her feel that she could really belong. She had the same lingering questions about him. Had he been genuine then? Or had he just been buttering her up because he could use her later on? Had she been so desperate for a friend that she had trusted the first one that showed any interest in knowing her and being with her? It felt like a betrayal, a manipulation of her naivete, an abuse of her need for a home, a place where she belonged.

Her father—adopted father—hanging from the dead tree was answer enough. Yin had tried her best to deny the truth. She'd searched for her father's body, justified its absence with all sorts of far-fetched theories. But corpses do not magically disappear. Even the Shadow of Death leaves a trail of dust in his wake. No, her father's corpse had not been magicked away. It was hanging from the Kanlungan. Even being the father of a goddess had not been enough to evoke mercy among the Dayo, although one of the Dayo had once been a friend. Every time she saw the corpse and remembered this betrayal, an unquenchable anger built up inside her, waiting to be expressed, not just at him but at herself for being so naive as to trust such an unscrupulous man so easily.

Dian was still pestering her about leaving the island and fulfilling some nebulously grand seedgod duty that she hadn't signed up for, much less took seriously. And then there was the promise of being saved by the man who was her father.

She's forgotten which reason tethered her to this island.

Yin wondered if seedgods, the real ones or the ones better than her, like Lutyo, ever got confused about the truth. How did they keep their heads straight when there were so many voices speaking at once in their heads?

So, today, she made a decision: she was human, and humans deal with one problem at a time.

She did this as she was flying over the Kanlungan, looking down past its ashen grey branches and at the Kayuman bodies that hung from it by their necks. When the Kayuman hung Dayo from the Kanlungan's branches, it was the family's job to take down the body that the Morningstar had mummified. Now that only the Kayuman—mostly soldiers from across the ocean—hung from it, the bodies stayed. No Dayo would take them down.

After weeks of hanging from this tree, her father's body had mummified under the harsh morningstarlight. He would have been barely recognizable had it not been for the tattoos—black stripes up and down his arm and the tiger sigil on his chest. This was the same man who had lied about her true father, who had kept her hidden from their village like a dirty secret, who had asked her to forgive him with his dying breath. Someone from the Dayo village must have found his body in the forest and hung it here with the other Kayuman masters and slavers. Yin considered looking for the Dayo who did it to explain her father's case and take down the body herself, but every time she talked herself into doing it, she bailed. She wasn't ready to face her adopted father yet, wasn't ready to let go of the binds that kept her there, because if she did then where would she go? What would she do? Who was she without the veil under which her father had hidden her all these years?

But what did it matter now?

Though there had been no love lost between her mother and the man hanging from the tree, she couldn't deny that he had come to love her like she was his daughter, the way an ageing man came to love a pet, enough to feed it and keep it alive. This was the only love Yin had ever known.

The villagers had begun gathering in the plaza below, heads tilted upward to look at her, pointing at her like she was an odd apparition in the sky, her dress and dark hair billowing around her like the cloud of smoke floating next to her.

'See how they worship at your feet, little bird,' the cloud said, a face forming from the smoke, the tone bemused and dry at the same time.

'Not funny, Lutyo,' Yin said, glaring at the crowd distastefully until she realized why she was lingering. She was searching for a face, a fire under the morningstarlight. Looking for beauty was a habit that was hard to shake off apparently—no matter how much she and Tiyago disdained each other.

'Who says I was trying to be funny?' The smoke swirled around her, pushed back by the winds that carried her like a wall.

Yin turned to fly back to her mountain, Lutyo following her like a dark shadow in an overcast sky. Lost in thought, she forgot to cushion her descent, landing so hard on the ground that she fell on all fours.

Lutyo stepped out of the cloud, the smoke smoothing over into his black cloak. 'What's bothering you, little bird?'

'I still couldn't take him down . . .' she mumbled, barely audible, and then got up and walked to her camp under the mango tree.

'What?' Lutyo said, following her to her camp by the tree, swinging a black bag he had been carrying over his shoulder.

She gazed at him like she'd just been forced awake, then shook her head. 'It's nothing,' she said, trying and failing to be nonchalant.

He grabbed her by the forearm before she could take another step away from him. He gave her a look that told her he didn't believe her.

She softened her face for him and placed a reassuring hand on his hand on her arm. 'It's really nothing, Lutyo. I'm fine. Nothing to worry about.' She led the way to her camp and began building a fire. 'You hungry?' She checked the jar in her tent for rice, and finding it empty, looked up at the tree. 'There are mangoes . . .'

The whole time, Lutyo watched her with his arms folded across his chest, a curious, unamused look on his face. He looked like he was about to say something important but diverted the topic elsewhere, 'I brought actual meat today. From my master's kitchens,' he said, plopping the black bag on the ground next to the bonfire and sitting down next to her.

'Your master's kitchens?' she said absently, blowing on the small fire that the flintstones had sparked. She straightened up, her mind finally focusing. 'What'd you do for your master to reward you oh so generously?'

He raised that bag and drew out a slab of meat, beef or *kalabaw* by the looks of it, from the bag, the bottom of which was dripping with blood. 'You wouldn't want to know.'

Yin took a black clay frying pan—among the things she'd been able to salvage from Galenya's house—from inside her

tent and placed it over the fire. Galenya had been the only
Dayo in Masalanta who treated her like she wasn't the master
slaver's daughter. She had taught Yin about herbs and natural
healing, and in many ways, in all the ways that matter, Yin
looked to Galenya the way she would have once looked to
her mother.

When she turned to Lutyo, he had both hands on the slab
of meat, still dripping with blood, which he had raised up
to her face. Cringing, she took it from his gloved hands and
placed it on the pan.

They sat in silence as they waited for the meat to cook,
fat sizzling on the side, the red slowly turning to brown. She
could tell that something was bothering him, too, and that
he hadn't come to her to amuse himself. Though she didn't
know if he actually wanted her to ask him about it. He had
always been reluctant to talk about what he did or what his
master made him do.

She hugged her knees to her chest, resting her chin on
top. 'Tell me about the seedgods you've met, Lutyo.'

'Oh, there are so many, I wouldn't know where to start.'

'That Spider Empress then.'

'Other than the fact that she rears seedgods and eats
them on a whim? She's actually a fascinating creature.
She's one of the oldest godvessels to carry a seedgod, and
possibly the only one who has carried more than two and still
somehow resembled her human form from before she first
fused with a god.' He took off his gloves, leaned back, and
propped himself on his hands so he was sitting a little more
comfortably. He did that often around her, a level of comfort
and security she assumed he only got when he was with her.
The grass around his bare hands turned black. 'Funny you

should ask about her. She's turned her campaign to this country, you know.'

'What? Why?'

'It's probably my fault.'

'What were you doing in Tukikuni anyway?'

'My master sends me often to spy on the spider, which I do at least once a year. You know, check up on potential threats and allies, see if they've become more than a threat. Always smart to do that.'

She turned to him, surprised. This was the first time he'd talked so openly about what his master made him do specifically.

He sank to his elbows, eyes closed, his face turned up to the sky. 'I talked to one of her seedgods, a fire goddess. It was warmer around her even in the snow. Her children, the spider calls them. She'd have made me a spider child, too, if my dagger hadn't already been claimed.'

'You're being exceptionally flippant about this.'

He shrugged. 'That's all in the past. I'm here, so it turned out pretty well, don't you think?' The waning morningstarlight kissed his face as he smiled. 'Anyway, we Kayuman won't know how good we've got it till the frozen wasteland of Tukikuni goes south.' He let out a long, satisfying sigh. 'The sun in our country always feels a little warmer than the rest of the world.'

'Is that what you do for your master? You spy on enemies?'

He opened one eye to look at her. 'Among other things,' he said, closing his eye again. 'I'm very talented, you know.'

'I'm sure you are,' she said, rolling her eyes again in mock disdain and then laughing. She poked at the meat and turned it over. 'So what did you do to get this piece of meat?'

'If you meant you, Yin, I would be outraged. I see you as more than a piece of meat,' he said, effectively dodging her question. 'But I wouldn't mind getting a few slaps in if you get my meaning.'

Yin groaned. 'Since when did our jokes start becoming lewd, Lutyo?'

'Only when you pry into matters you'd likely be squeamish about.'

'Now that makes me think you're hiding something bad.' She copied his posture and let the waning light warm her skin. 'And I am not squeamish.'

'No, you're not. You like staring at corpses hanging from trees.'

She turned to him just in time to see the grin forming on his lips.

'You going to tell me what's bothering you? Or should I just assume that you have a morbid fascination with death?'

'Likely the latter. We are friends after all.'

He laughed out loud. 'I had that coming.'

They fell into a comfortable silence again, one charged with much more than a shared laugh. And she realized that she actually was comfortable around Lutyo, secretive and cryptic he might be. She had known him long enough to understand that he hid behind the flippancy, hoping no one would catch him in the lie. Hell, she knew him well enough to know that he was still lying about many things.

She took a gamble. She was lost and alone after all, and this man had found her somehow. 'That was my fa— adopted father—hanging from the tree.' She sat up straight, pulling her knees up to her chest again, poking at the sizzling meat absently.

He opened his eyes and turned to her, though he remained propped up on his elbows. 'He's why you're still here?' The way he said it lacked his usual cocky, glib tone.

'Maybe.'

'I murdered an entire family again—from grandmother to grandchildren,' he said, lying all the way back down on the grass. 'My master sent me to assassinate a political enemy. He'll likely send me to kill more in the future.'

'Do you have to do it?'

'I'm literally compelled to do it, little bird. I have no choice.'

'Nonsense. Everyone has a choice.'

'What if I take your blade now? See if you have a choice when I make you take your father down from the tree and burn him.' He was trying to sound cheeky again, but it came out more like a threat. 'Sorry.'

She joined him on the grass. 'I've always wondered what my life would be like if my family had never left the city. I've been on the run half my life, and this island was the first place I really settled in. I didn't really have a choice then, did I?'

He frowned, facing her, their eyes meeting. 'Do you know who you're running from?' Somehow, Yin got the impression that he had asked a different question from the one she thought he was asking.

'I don't know. My parents never told me who, but I assumed it was someone powerful.'

'Didn't you ever want to find your real father?'

'He's supposed to come find me here . . . after the raid.' She turned away, feeling sheepish about that admission. 'Now that I think about it, it doesn't make sense anymore to stay here after waiting for so long. For all I know, he could be dead.'

He sat up suddenly, eyeing her like he was reading a particularly difficult text. Then, his expression softened, as if he was looking at a flower blooming in morningstarlight.

She sat up next to him, confused. 'What?'

'I'll be right back,' he said before disappearing into a cloud of shadow and smoke.

He came back a few minutes later with the mummified corpse of her father on his shoulder. He dropped the body at her feet.

She gasped, hands covering her mouth, and scrambled to stand up. 'Are you insane—'

He cut her off, took off his gloves, and presented both bare hands, streaked with black veins, to her. 'Say the word, Yin, and I'll cut your tether.'

Her jaw dropped, her gaze shifting from Lutyo to her father's mummified corpse. Lutyo had no right to do this, to take her father off the tree. Family did that, not strangers, and certainly not gods of death. She searched for the rage that she should have been feeling inside but found nothing there except relief and festering hope. She looked at her father, his tattooed skin dry and clinging to the bone. This was the man who had raised her when her real father couldn't. He fed her, sheltered her, protected her, and gave her and her mother a home. He didn't have to. He was a stranger, and even if it was guilt, for whatever sin he'd committed against her, that pushed him to do so, he did it anyway. He gave up an old life for one with her in it. Her father must have loved her. Till the end, he protected her. Till the end, he was tethered to her life. He was not free.

She fell to her knees and touched her father's mummified face. 'Yes,' she said softly, weakly, an apology more than a request.

So, the tether was cut by Lutyo's own bare hands, the smell of burning meat rising around them, the body disintegrating to ash, the dust being carried off by the winds. Her father was free of her, and she of him.

Chapter 7

Kalem

Kalem felt like a stranger next to his father, who was still exhausted from last night's party. In the dim passageway leading to the metaphorical and literal amphitheatre of politics that was the Congress of Datus, Kalem's father hobbled, taking slow, measured steps forward. His father's ornate staff tipped with their house sigil—the turtle, a symbol of power—was being used more as a third leg than a walking stick. The house pattern was wrapped over his father's shoulder and around his torso, falling just below his knees over white slacks. On his head was an elaborate headdress of shells, beads, and precious stones set in a woven, patterned cap. Kalem wore a sash around his waist bearing their house colours—perpendicular line patterns in indigo, white, and silver—over white cotton slacks. His torso and arms were exposed, tattoos on full display, the Obsidian Blade hanging from a leather belt around his waist.

The Congress of Datus required the datus to be present to cast votes in person, forcing them to leave the provinces over which they held dominion. This happened often in times of war, such as the Obsidian War. The last time this had happened, Kalem had still been a toddler, barely able to appreciate the splendid architecture of the Katipunan Capitol, the venue of the Congress of Datus and the central government offices.

Katipunan Capitol started out as the fifth Maragtas king's vacation mansion built in a crater at the centre of the island, just across the Mayalakanon Strait before Castel became Kayumalon's centre of commerce, education, and governance. During the Pretender's War, when two brothers from opposing bloodlines fought for the throne, one brother, Makatunaw the Pretender, made Castel his seat of power.

The amphitheatre itself was oval-shaped, with ten tiered terraces that housed the offices of the datus cascading downward into the arena below. Staircases divided the tiered terraces, which were dotted with windows and doors. Each terrace was decorated and designed with the tapestries and patterns of the datu assigned to that tier. Bannermen, minor houses, and government workers would stream out the smaller doorways to fill the tiered terraces overlooking the arena below.

The King's tiered terrace was at the very front, bigger and more ostentatious than the rest, with a gold door at the very base from which the King would emerge to take his throne in the arena below. The other tiered terraces merely had open doorways over which the patterns of the reigning datu of that province hung.

Maylaya's doorway was directly opposite the King's golden door, allowing them full view of the King's and the datus' tiered terrace. To the left of the King's elevated throne was the Payapa seat, with no banners hanging over its doorway. To its right was the already filled in seat of Datu Satalon Sekoya, the Horselord Datu of Lupang Bakal, with his Tikbalang retinue behind him. On either side of Maylaya's tiered terrace were the three Dalaket strangelords to the left and the Asinari merfolk to the right. The Datus of the Maragtas Isles and Olimawi came after the Asinari.

The walk from outside the arena, through the passageway, and into the open doorway was meant to be taxing for even the healthiest members to symbolize the weight each leader's vote carried.

His father, the Obsidian Datu, refused help, though the pain painting his face showed how much he needed it.

Kalem had spent ten years of his life trying to understand seedsickness. And all he could do for his father now was walk next to him and pretend that nothing was wrong. Seedsickness blurred the boundaries between being a family curse and scientifically-proven disease in his ancestors' biographies and his academic predecessors' experiments and studies. It only affected specific members of the Maragtas bloodlines. Still, nothing he had learned in all those years could explain what he'd done to help his father—nothing except the seedgod who trailed him everywhere in wisps of indigo smoke and mist. Even Kalem didn't believe the lie he had told everyone about it: 'arcane seedmagic'. Only Panday understood, and the man was very loyal to him.

He did try to convince his father not to go to this thing, to send emissaries to cast his vote, but his father had insisted on being a part of this.

'This is important, son. This will shape your reign,' his father had said when Kalem had asked if this was really more important than his health right before they left their estate.

'Then maybe I should decide,' Kalem had answered, earning him a laugh and an amused sideways glance. Even in pain, his father kept his sense of humour.

'How would you decide then, Son?'

'I'd decide to send you home,' Kalem had said, making his father laugh louder even though he did not mean it to be a joke. '"A broken body heals itself." I would have voted as you would.'

Now, they walked through the tunnel, their aides Narra and Panday trailing behind them. The rumble of footsteps above sent dust motes down from the ceiling. Netted indigo glowlamps hung from elaborate sconces on one side of the wall, illuminating half their bodies

In front of them was the arched doorway leading into the arena. Through there, Kalem saw that many of the seats along the sides of the arena had already been filled by bannermen and minor lords from all over the country. None would miss such a rare event; a momentous, historic event; a scandal of epic proportions just waiting to happen. Through the doorway, he saw the nine other doorways from which would emerge the datus of the nine major provinces of the country and their retinue. Their seats were on the main floor, just a few steps away from their houses' respective doorways, with one main seat elevated and decorated with the patterns of their houses—they were middling thrones really, purposely built lower than that of the King's. The dark doorways and thrones dotted the semi-circular wall facing the pedestal upon which the King's throne was placed—empty now, even of servants and minor aides.

A sinking feeling grew at the pit of his stomach, but he brushed it off with an explanation that even he wasn't sure he believed: '*The King likes to be ostentatious. The King likes making a scene. The King is desperate to make a mark.*'

'What if the vote isn't unanimous, Father?' Kalem had asked in their embassy home before coming to the Katipunan Capitol.

'It is about more than the vote, Son,' his father had said, and Kalem knew what his father meant—now it was about more than waging war against an invader. It was a war against an enemy within, a disease that had bloomed and festered in his body, and now the body must heal itself. The south respected his father. The datus would follow the Obsidian Datu's lead. Four out of nine votes were firmly in his grasp. The three Dalaket kings, always at war against each other, would band together to rally behind the southern king who would fight the Tukikuni invaders with them. Even without the two remaining votes, his father was already the most powerful man in the country, even more powerful than the King himself. All this had been orchestrated while Kalem was playing scholar at Kolehiyo.

At the threshold between the tunnel and the arena outside, where dim indigo light skirted past the bright light of day, his father stopped, breathing hard through his mouth, steadying himself with the staff. Kalem was tempted to reach for his father, to drag him back where they came from, but he understood that this was something his father had to do. Just as his father, even if it broke his heart, understood that going to Kolehiyo was something Kalem had to do. Empathy ran deep in his family's bloodline.

'Son, I'm sorry that I failed you as a father,' his father said, facing his son, his tone breaking, but his will, implacable.

'You haven't—'

His father stopped him with a sharp shake of his head.
'No, Son. I have failed you. My pride has brought us here.
Now, the best I can do is give you a fighting chance.'

'I don't understand, Father.'

'Do you understand why I've brought you here now after
ten years of keeping you from this?'

Kalem looked away, his hand falling on his sword's hilt.
Of course he understood. His father was announcing to his
allies and enemies who his successor was, to transfer whatever
influence he had to his son. But Kalem wasn't delusional to
think that he could ever copy his father's ink. 'Are you sure
about me, Father? Uncle—'

'Your uncle will bring us all to ruin.' His father turned
away, as if heartbroken by the admission, and faced whatever
was awaiting them beyond the threshold, shedding off the
father and letting out the Obsidian Datu. 'You are the future
of our house, Kalem. The future of our people.'

Kalem's lips pressed into a thin line, his mind scrambling
for an answer that may stop his father from doing whatever
it was that he was about to do before he walked out the
doorway. Everything he could think of felt like a goodbye, a
punctuation marked before its time. He had wasted so much
time, and now all he wanted was for his father to just be his
father. 'I love you, Father,' he said, but it came out weak—too
soft, too sweet, too unguarded.

His father smiled and nodded at him, as if that
had encouraged rather than dissuaded him, before leading
the way out of the dark through the doorway and into the
arena. He looked so much stronger, more determined, more
adamant than the sick, dying man who had been eating

rice cakes at nightfall. The Obsidian Datu had always had a weakness for the saccharine.

* * *

Nine of the most powerful datus were supposed to gather in the Katipunan Capitol. How small they looked, standing in neat rows in front of a throne carved into a large tree. The arena of the coliseum was too small for a leadership that was about to go to war against a foreign country.

On regular days, only the datus' chosen ambassadors would come here to debate, vote, and pass legislation. They made up the House of Peers. The tiered seats along the walls of the arena were reserved for legislators and bannermen from the provinces of each Balangay who made up the House of Banners.

Major decisions that shaped their country were reserved for the Congress of Datus to debate on.

'War is a simple decision because it's usually the only choice available to us,' his father said as they waited for the datus to take their place with them.

A restless energy rolled like a tide over the coliseum, the murmurs of bannermen and peers and other lesser men washing over the space like ocean waves in a storm. An unnerving calm seemed to have fallen over his father, the air twisted with a resigned finality, the way the eye of a typhoon sits quiet and alone while the winds howl into its ears.

As they were taking their seats in the section of the arena dedicated for Maylaya, his father on the elevated throne for the Maylaya Datu and Kalem on a lower seat next to the throne, Kalem said, 'If war is so simple, why is it taking everyone so long just to get here?'

'Condemned men rarely walk with harried steps on the way to the execution,' his father said simply.

Kalem found that hard to believe and for some reason thought of the animals he'd killed during his study. *Prey usually falls into the trap, not the hunter,* he wanted to say for the sake of winning this argument with his father but thought it cruel and uncalled for.

Another steady, restless silence fell between father and son, and Kalem had to turn away from his father, just to stop the hair on the back of his neck from rising in fear, like something was amiss here.

'I assume there are others like me, like you, Damu,' Kalem said to the turtle swimming in his line of sight.

'It is a safe assumption.'

'Is it a correct assumption?' Kalem's gaze went straight through the turtle and at the man in black, his skin covered, standing at the main doorway reserved for the monarchy. *Never trust a man who hides his skin,* a saying passed down from the first tattooed king to the last. Honesty and truth was paramount on a day like this. No one would cover their tattoos and risk being called a liar. Not on a day like this. Not especially on a day like this.

'Assumptions are usually partly correct.'

He kept his eyes on the mysterious man in black who walked the perimeter of the wall around the four datus and their respective staff across them. Kalem's hand went to his sword's hilt. *'Unless they're wrong. I didn't think gods could be glib.'*

'I didn't think humans could be so oblivious, but here we are.'

Frowning, he tore his eyes away from the crowd on the bleachers, in which he had lost the man in black, and focused instead on the turtle swimming happily in the space before him, its indigo mists forming and reforming into its shape. The Earth God said it so callously that the answer felt like a thing that had been sitting right in front of his face—so close that it was blurred, so far that it was out of plain sight.

The winds battered at the patterns flying behind each contingent. Grey and white clouds floated past the Morningstar, masking light and casting shadows all around. The scent of salt and brine wafted from the docks. And the sound of the ocean lapping against the shore mixed with the murmur of the stadium, which looked empty in some spots and too full in others. Amid it all, it was silent, the kind of silent that felt like a rubber band pulled too tight.

'I'm not the only one here, am I?' Kalem said, though he didn't need the turtle to answer to know that he was right. He could feel it, like a magnet could feel one like it in its general vicinity. *'I'm not the only godvessel.'*

Narra came up to his father's side, leaned down, and whispered into his ear before rushing back to the tunnel to speak with a messenger. Panday stepped closer to his ward. Kalem could already smell the seedmagic wafting from his skin—something was going on. Panday was preparing for a fight.

Kalem looked to his father, his lips parted, about to ask what was happening when Narra returned, running to his ward, hoof heavy on the dirt floor. He nodded to the Datu who understood and turned to Panday.

'Take Kalem to the docks. Keep him safe. Deliver him home. Trust no one,' his father said, before limping off with

Narra toward the King's closed golden doors where the other southern datus were waiting for him.

Panday wordlessly grabbed Kalem by his shoulder to drag him back to where they had entered from, but he shrugged Panday's hold off and ran after his father.

'What's happening, Father?' Kalem asked when he caught up to his father, Panday hot on his heels.

His father glared at him and then at Panday, but didn't speak, anger raging in the furnace of his eyes, waiting, hesitating to be let out. Narra spoke for his Datu, 'The King is not coming. The Kalasag Corps have surrounded the Katipunan Capitol. We are under attack.'

'Panday!' the Datu called, startling Kalem. He had only heard of his father's rage, never seen it. His father continued forward without looking back at his son even once.

'You can't escape together, Kalem.' Panday grabbed Kalem by the shoulder again and dragged him away. Kalem watched his father limp toward the King's doorway, feeling helpless and so utterly useless. Again. He gritted his teeth and pulled away from Panday and ran to follow his father, weaving past other datus and lords—Dalaket, Tikbalang, Asuwan, and Asinari—towering over him and crowding the King's threshold.

The man in black dropped from the upper tiers, blocking their way, his hood over his eyes, a black mask covering his nose and mouth.

His father stopped, drawing his own blade with one hand, the other still on the staff. Narra placed himself between the man and his ward, axe in both hands.

Kalem felt the desperation of a man unwilling to say goodbye. Through it all, Panday never left his side, joining the Maylayan warriors and drawing blades ready to defend his liege. Soldiers in black and crimson uniforms spilled into the arena from every doorway and the bleachers above, where bannermen were fighting the imperial guards. The man in black stood still, sword raised in one hand. His other hand was open, palm up, from which cascaded streams of black mist, like the shadow of night creeping over the Morningstar-lit sky. The air pulsed with an energy so dark, so heavy, that Kalem felt a cold shiver run down in his spine.

'He's like me . . .' he said, stunned, to the Earth God, more a statement than a question. A hand pulled Kalem back from a swinging sword, making him almost fall to the ground.

'Kalem, we have to go,' Panday said, defending him from an onslaught of blades, snapping Kalem back to the present. His grip around the hilt of his own blade tightened as he watched his father, from the side of his eye, barely holding back the never-ending stream of soldiers blocking his path. Narra stood by him, his axe a maelstrom of metal amid the carnage. The other datus were drawing their best weapons—claws, fangs, vine ropes, living wood stakes—against their attackers.

'No!' Panday yelled, followed by a stream of curses in their dialect, defending Kalem left and right.

Another stream of black mist, more powerful now, more solid against the earth underneath their feet, spread forth from the man in black, the shadows swirling around his body. The people closest to him dropped to their knees, their veins, once reserved for magic, black underneath the tattooed brown skin. The shadows didn't discriminate between allies and enemies. His father fell with the rest of them.

'Father!' Kalem yelled, but Panday pulled him back just as the remaining Crimson Guards of the Kalasag Corps ran from the mist of death. Kalem struggled in Panday's hold, fighting to reach his father who was convulsing again on the ground, like he had the night before, while the rest—including Narra—lay still, black veins leaving permanent stains on their skin like cracked fault lines in the ground. The shadows continued to roll over the arena, growing thicker and more opaque the further out they reached.

'I can still save him! Let go!' Kalem yelled, pushing away Panday, who was running with him, dragging him this way and that, shoving him toward the nearest exit farthest from the Shadow. He'd never noticed just how much smaller he was compared to Panday, how weaker, how fragile. 'Please, Panday! My father needs me!'

Panday gave him a blank stare and shook his head, increasing his pace so that their stride turned into a run. 'It's too late. You have to live.'

Kalem looked over his shoulder, at the rippling shadows that shrouded his writhing father, at the man in black veiled in black magic. Kalem's veins lit up, sending indigo mist outward, like a pebble in a pond, smaller circles rippling outward, the turtle swam with the tide, the magic pulsing from him as much as it pulsed from Kalem, and a part of him hoped that where the two opposing ripples met, his own would prevail.

It was as if time had stopped between them, light and dark magic meeting at the threshold of space and time, and two godvessels stared at each other in the void. Panic, anger, fear, grief, and an unwavering hunger was exchanged between them. The push and pull of magic driving up nerves. It was about survival now. Which power would ultimately win over this new, unspoken, insidious, holy rivalry beginning between them?

In the end, like equals like, and two gods of equal power could only negate each other, sending both mages hurtling away from one other like opposing poles of a magnet, time restarting again.

Panday pulled Kalem up and dragged him away to safety, but Kalem could not resist looking over his shoulder at the Shadow, could not resist the pull of magic that he thought so rare only he could have access to it, could not ignore the danger of knowing a being such as himself, so imbued with the magic of a god who could only be death.

In his head, his failure echoed like a confession said under the veil of a temple's bell.

He failed. Because, of course, he would fail. He was helpless and useless and so very finite.

So, he ran, like the coward he had been that day he left for Kolehiyo and broke his father's heart, that day he stood by and watched his mother die in pain, that day he left Kolehiyo having accomplished nothing.

None of it mattered as much as the stab of pain in his heart at the idea that his father died knowing his son had abandoned him again.

Interlude 1

Dakila

Never count someone as dead unless there's a body. Maybe not even then.

Dakila had seen some strange cases in his time at Kalasag, and if there was anything he'd learned, it was this: Not only were seedmages hard to kill, they were also efficient at murder. The religious would chalk that to mages being the gods' favoured children, but even Dakila was too pragmatic to accept divine intervention as a plausible explanation for the worst of crimes being committed by mages.

People hurt people. Gods, being eternal beings, had nothing to do with the will of man.

Still, the bodies lined up in neat rows in the Magiting Garrison compound managed to momentarily unsettle his beliefs. Their veins were stained black. No common seedmagic could cause this much death without some form of divine intervention.

The most powerful men and women in the country, reduced to dried, black husks of what they had once been. Had to be seedgods—he was even related to many of them.

Dakila walked between the rows of bodies. The Asinari Datu, Sedhaj Malik, was curled up in a ball of dried black-green scales and fins, like a fish left too long under the Morningstar, his limbs and claws twisted in odd shapes, his paunch and black, beady eyes hollowed, his blue patterned sash and bahag stained with blood. Even the Asuwan Datu, Stark Natera, already a grey-skinned creature of death, did not survive the attack, his veins black and thin, like spider webs. Two Dalaket datus, their plant-based bodies, black and ash grey, were burnt stumps on the ground nearby.

His blood ran as cold as the ocean before dawn when he saw a familiar face among them. His uncle, Patas Laya, the one man who could undermine the King. Rumours of his uncle's seedsickness had been around for a while at court. Dakila did not know if the rumours were true, but what he knew was that even they were not enough to diminish the power of this man—the Obsidian Datu, the victor in the war against the Yumban marauders. Yet, here he was now, shrivelled and dead, the shadow of the glorious man he had once been. Next to him was the big bulk of his Tikbalang aide, Narra, black veins showing on the patches of flesh where he'd shed his black mane. He stared at the man, feeling shock freezing him over, an unsettling disorientation taking hold of him.

Maralita caught up with him and started saying, 'Surviving guards say that a man in a black cloak summoned a cloud of poisonous smoke—' He was cut off by the sight of Datu Patas Laya on the ground. 'Holy Skyworld, is that—'

'My uncle,' Dakila said, clasping his hands behind his back, his nails digging into his knuckles. 'The most powerful people in the country are dead. The pressing question now is who survived.'

'We don't have a definite list yet, but I took the liberty of checking the casualties against the attendance list of the Congress this morning and the gathering last night to see who's supposed to be here but is not. It's not a very long list,' Maralita said, handing him a page torn out of his leatherbound notebook. The man was meticulous about his notes when he was investigating a case. It provided a glimpse into how his mind worked. Maralita was thorough, but he reserved making conclusions till he thought he had enough evidence to build his case. He had an odd way of looking at the world—a byproduct of where he came from, he always said as if to remind Dakila that he did not belong to the noble side of Dakila's life—the life of a prince, the life of the King's second son.

'My brother's not on the list,' Dakila said before he realized that he'd said it like a fact instead of a question. 'Kalem Laya, too.'

If Maralita noticed the tone, he didn't show it. 'The King isn't on that list, too, but unlike Masters Maylakan and Laya, we know where the King is.' He stopped there, an abrupt pause more than an invitation for discourse. 'I know what you're going to say, Dakila, but it can't be him. It can't be the King. Why would he do this? What would he get from the wholesale murder of an entire House—which hasn't happened in over a decade, until now with House Payapa, not since the fall of House Talim. Now this. It has to be someone else.' His own tone was incredulous.

'Are you so blinded by your loyalty that you deny the evidence in front of you? No one was spared in this massacre. Not allies. Not rivals. Everyone here was a target.'

'That doesn't exactly narrow down our suspects, does it?' Maralita said half-heartedly, his own resolve breaking as the bodies stared back at them.

'It doesn't leave room for doubt either,' Dakila said. 'Only one person benefits from the fall of the Congress of Datus.'

A beat. A hesitant, aggressive pause from Maralita, as if every fibre of his being was pushing back against this argument. Why was it so hard to convince a man to let go of his loyalties when the very reason he should not keep them was right in front of his eyes? Was Maralita's faith in the crown worth the integrity he was losing to keep it? What would it take for Maralita to let go?

Maralita remained silent, but his face was a canvas of questions and doubts and hesitation and . . . perhaps a potential change of heart. Dakila could only hope for so much from one he loved. 'My father is a petty, vindictive man,' Dakila said, but even as he said it, he heard Dangal's voice echoing in his mind. He resisted touching the man. 'My father has always seen Datu Patas Laya as a threat, even before the Obsidian War.'

'What happens now?' Maralita asked, his tone flat.

Dakila handed the list back to Maralita and walked away from the bodies, making his way to the main building, pointedly avoiding the side wall near the back exit. Maralita caught up to his pace, the question left hanging on his face.

'The King will try to appoint his cronies to key seats. He'll want to weaken the south by overturning Maylaya. If Kalem Laya doesn't turn up soon, it's likely that his uncle will announce his death, take the title for himself, and swear loyalty to the King. The move will splinter the south.'

'And your brother?'

Dakila continued walking, making an effort not to look at Maralita and resisting the urge to purse his lips or to display any gesture that might indicate the lie. Maralita frowned as he watched Dakila's face, serious, stoic, almost absent of expression, as if hiding something that shouldn't be there.

Dakila, of course, knew where his brother was and why he wasn't in the coliseum during the attack. Of all the trouble his brother could get into, he had chosen to marry a Dayo and birth a Dayo halfling with said woman and was now out looking for her, at a time when he was needed here. The idiot.

'Can't you do something?' Maralita finally said, seeing that Dakila was not answering. This was not Maralita, the earnest sergeant, he was talking to now. He shed that facade for Dakila and allowed himself to be vulnerable, a sense of betrayal marring his beautiful face.

'If I could, I would have already done it.' And he did. He gave his brother the chance to get away before the nightmare the Day of the Bleeding Banners had been.

He had faith that his brother would do the right thing. 'Let's go. We're not needed here.'

'Where are you going?' Maralita said, stopping at the top of the stairs, just a couple of steps above him.

'To see the woman last seen with my brother,' he lied, turning sharply, heart racing, and forced himself to keep a deadpan look on his face, afraid that Maralita knew him too well and would see through the lie.

Maralita narrowed his eyes at Dakila, who was headed away from prisoners cells. 'And you don't think she's in the prisoners' cells?'

Dakila frowned. 'She's only a suspect in a murder, and she's Dayo.'

Maralita studied Dakila's face, his own face contorted in deep thought. He didn't say anything for a while, didn't move another step, as if any sudden move would scare away whatever it was he was looking for on Dakila's face. 'She's not in the prisoner's cell.'

It was as if Dakila's heart had stopped and he was just waiting for the sword to fall. He cleared his throat. 'Well, where is she? The witnesses' hall?'

'No,' Maralita said matter-of-factly, and Dakila held his breath 'A seedmage snuck in here last night and helped her escape. But given the events of this morning, we haven't been able to spare the men to search for her—or the seedmage.' Maralita cast him a concerned look. 'Are you all right? You look . . . unwell. You weren't at the party last night.'

Dakila was stunned. Had Maralita really not see through the lie? Was he actually in the clear? But the look of concern on Maralita's face said it all. Maralita loved him too much to suspect him. It blinded him to Dakila's faults. Did Dakila dare to hope for so much from a man who loved his country and king almost as much as he loved him.

'I was there. I stayed out of sight for the most part of the party.' Dakila cleared his throat. 'She couldn't have gotten off the island.' A fact he knew for sure was a lie. He had sent her to hide in Maragtas Isles south of Castel. 'The city governor closed all ports for public transports save for imperial ships and the datus' ships right after.' He pushed past Maralita and climbed up the steps again to speak with the quartermaster.

'You're not on the list, either, Dakila,' Maralita said from behind him. 'Where were you last night during the gathering?'

He turned slowly to face Maralita again, chin upturned slightly so he was looking down at the man. He hadn't attended the Congress because he'd freed the Dayo woman who had helped his brother escape. He had stayed out longer because he had to wait until the vein stains subsided. This didn't seem to perturb Maralita. In fact, it seemed like the man took it as a challenge, matching the sharp rigidity of Dakila's gaze. Dakila hoped that his expression didn't betray what he knew and that it asked Maralita in as many words: 'Do you dare doubt me?' Of course, Maralita could catch Dakila in a lie. Of course, Maralita could tell when Dakila was keeping secrets. He'd let down his walls for this beautiful boy. He'd let him in, let him see Dakila for what he was without the masquerade.

'I have nothing to gain from this wanton murder of my relatives, Maralita.'

'I believe you,' he answered almost just as defensively. Though Dakila could feel a sudden change in the man's posture. The softness he'd come to associate with the man he loved wasn't there. It was a subtle shift, the first stone of an impending brick wall. 'But that doesn't mean you still don't have secrets.'

'You doubt me still.'

'I'm loyal to the King and my country,' Maralita said, his jaw clenching.

'But you love me,' Dakila said, echoing his lover's own words back to him.

'I have a duty to my country. Please don't make me choose.'

'Duty is nothing without love,' Dakila said almost pleadingly, knowing that they'd finally arrived at a juncture, one that Dakila had seen coming the moment he had met this beautiful boy. His father's voice answered for him in his mind: *Love is weakness, boy.*

Maralita met Dakila's eyes, the softness returning to his face momentarily before being replaced by the hardened exterior of Maralita the soldier. A weakness burnt in him—the kind that was sparked in the pit of the stomach and spread like wildfire through the veins. He'd let his walls down for this man. He'd let him in, allowed him to see every facet of him—the good, the bad, the weak. Only one other person could make him feel this way, like a boy desperately cowering away, with a heavy hand on his shoulder, while watching the woman who they say was his mother convulse in pain and insanity. Only one other man could make him feel this weak and vulnerable, and King Duma blamed Dakila for the Queen's sins. Dakila loathed the King at this moment as he stared into his lover's eyes.

Dakila lit his veins violet for flexibility and then quickly switch to red for agility as he jumped out of the building and away from the only man who knew many of his weaknesses and still loved him for who he was.

ACT TWO

Chapter 8

Yin

Reading the sky was a habit reserved for ageing spinsters among the Dayo. They say the way the seven moons appear in the sky foretell events to come. What better way to spend the rest of one's lonely life than look up at the sky and watch for signs of when the loneliness would end?

Yin did not read the sky as much as watch for black clouds on the horizon, a bad omen most would say. She, however, had come to see black clouds as a temporary reprieve, though from what, she was afraid to admit.

So, naturally she was astonished when her black cloud fell out of the sky, shapeshifting mid-air into a man in black, his dark cloak billowing behind him.

Yin leapt and summoned the winds to push her upward, taking the man in her arms and landing back to the ground, more gently than he would have crashed. She cradled his head on her lap and found his pale face caked with dried blood—she suspected that it wasn't his. She attempted to comb the hair off his face.

A gloved hand grabbed her wrist. 'Careful. Or you'll lose a hand, little bird.'

She held his gloved hand on his chest instead. 'What happened, Lutyo?'

'I did many very bad things. I had to fight another vessel like me.' He forced a laugh, still trying to be flippant, but, by now, she could see through this wall, this shield he put up to keep his pain to himself.

'Was it your choice to do it?' she asked simply, head bowed so she was looking straight into his black eyes.

He turned away from her in shame. He took his time responding, as if enumerating all his regrets in his head. 'I don't know anymore.'

'Was it justified?'

'I don't know.' He shook his head. 'It doesn't matter. I can't change anything while someone else controls my powers.'

'He could still summon you then.'

'Maybe.' He turned back to face her, eyes piercing in the moonlight. A decision had been made there, a certainty that had long stood on weak foundations. 'Run away with me. We could see the rest of the world together.'

Yin's jaw dropped, the words turned to ashes in her mouth before they could leave her lips. She'd certainly fantasized about running away, about seeing more of the world outside her safe, immutable island. Day in and day out, the seven skygods raced across Skyworld, the mango trees bore fruit, the seed plantations went through the cycle of planting and harvesting in a season and repeated it all over again in the next, and all this while, she hid in her mountain waiting, always waiting. The island stayed the same. Life stayed the same. She stayed the same.

Lutyo sat up and faced her, seeing the indecision there, the doubt, the tethers still tying her to this place. 'What's still holding you back, Yin?'

'I—' she began to say, the words turning to ashes. She stared at him, the fierce certainty on his face, the will that was all his own, the defiance towards the chains that tied him down. He was not completely free, and if he ran away now, she could risk losing him too. Her eyes explored his face—the pale cheeks, stained slightly by the black veins; deep, black, longing eyes; sharp nose; dark hair, dishevelled and wild; and lips that were parted slightly in anticipation.

She instinctively leaned into him. He flinched but didn't draw back. 'Don't,' he said, though he didn't resist, didn't pull away from her. She pressed her lips on his, tasting blood and rot and the subtle tones of life beginning to bloom from the decay. And him. She tasted him, and he answered reluctantly at first, but the eagerness, the hunger came in like a storm, building and building and building into a crescendo of howling winds and chaos. His gloved hands wove through her hair, and she wrapped her arms around his neck, pressing him to her body as she fell back and pulled him on top of her.

He straddled her, carrying out an expedition with his hands and lips over her, finding parts of her that even she didn't know were there. His lips trailed maddening lines on her skin; his hands fell on bare and clothed skin, feeling increasingly unsatisfied with every brief collision. His touch was lightning and her moans the thunder.

She pushed him back and rolled him under her, straddling his body, and piece by piece took off the clothes that still separated her from him. He watched her, pain and hunger on his face, as she untied the halter strings that held her dress up and let it fall around her in a pile at her waist. He reached forward, hands covered, and she trembled in his grip.

With shaking hands, she began to take his gloves off—

'Stop. I'll only hurt you,' he said, but couldn't finish the rest of what he wanted to say.

She kissed his lips and then pulled back to show her face, veins glowing slightly with magic—black magic. 'See my face? I'm okay,' she said, taking the gloves off and working her way down the buttons of his clothes, lips pressing against unconcealed skin.

Cloak off, gloves off, shirt off, he held her shoulders to pull her down so he could mark skin that he had not touched with his bare hands. Startled, she inhaled sharply, and he took that momentary distraction to roll on top of her, drawing a line on her skin with his thumb, revealing black veins that faded as he moved past them. He hungrily watched her face, eyes drooping, lips parted, hands buried in the tangled mess of her hair on the grass. She propped herself up on her elbows to hold him close to her again, wanting, needing more of his skin melting into hers. 'Lutyo.'

He pulled away suddenly, and her eyes shot open to see what had taken him away from her. Two gods, two birds made of mist, a maya and a raven, hovered over them, voyeur and participant at the same time.

His face was a question, a reluctant, lingering fear, a dwindling doubt, but hers was the answer, the consent, the assertion, the aggression, the courage. She intertwined her hands in his and pulled him to her to kiss him.

The magic flowed between them, surging through veins, golden and black mingling and mixing in the pool of their passions, their shared breaths, their shared darkness and light. She said his name over and over, the way worshippers beseech a god for mercy, and closing her eyes, fingers clawing at his shoulders, she gave herself willingly at his altar, to his body, to him—the God of Death and Rebirth.

He took and took and took, until a sharp pang of pain shot through her. Gasping, she stared up in horror at him watching as he watched her react to him. The pain grew, an ember at first that became a bonfire and now a wildfire that was consuming her. Panic rose up her throat and alarms rang in her head as she watched the yellow flow back to him, the black giving nothing in return.

The raven and the maya spiralled over them, mixing in a pool of magic. But it wasn't the magic that was causing her distress. It wasn't the parts of her that were immortal. It was the human part his magic was killing that had pulled her back to reality.

She let go of him, palms on his chest, trying to push him away. She felt the magic drain out of her, the way typhoons take from the ocean before making landfall. 'Lutyo . . . Stop . . . Lutyo . . .' A sharp, painful intake of breath. 'Lutyo, you're hurting me.'

Lutyo's eyes opened sharply and pushed himself away from her, scrambling back to put distance between them, his glowing black veins fading, her yellow flowing back to her, the connection broken abruptly.

'No. No. No.' He pressed the heels of his palms against his eyes. 'I can't even have *this*?'

Yin crawled to him, reaching a comforting hand out. 'Lutyo . . .'

He looked up at her, eyes tear-streaked, in which pain had returned, fear had returned. 'I could have killed you.'

'You didn't,' she said, reaching out, but out of instinct, she stayed her hand just inches away from his bare skin. He saw this hesitation, the fear, the longing, looking like he'd lost something, the one thing he had that was his, the one source of joy in his life. She felt tears stinging the corners of her eyes, too. Grief, dismay, regret, befalling her in maddening waves of pain all at once.

'I can only destroy.' He couldn't even look at her. 'I need to go,' he said, body turning into a cloud of shadows and flying up into the night sky.

'Lutyo!' she called, desperate not to lose this new tether that kept her on the ground, waiting for his dark cloud to graze her sky.

Chapter 9

Kalem

Kalem's life suddenly felt too fragile, too abstract, as if made of too many pieces barely held together, like sandcastles. It was unravelling faster than he'd anticipated, faster still since the Day of Bleeding Banners.

Numb, Kalem was still recoiling from the shock, curled up on the floor with his head between his knees. He unconsciously bit the inside of his cheek while running the events of that day over in his head and tasted blood almost constantly in his mouth.

When it was darkest in his mind, the Shadow's black-veined face flashed before his eyes, looking at him with such sinister curiosity from the darkness that Kalem would wake up gasping for breath, as if the very tendrils of deathly smoke emerging from the Shadow's 'playful' fingers were wrapped around his neck. He felt deep, dark fear, like dipping his toes in a pond only to fall away into the depths of the ocean and drown. He was drowning in it all, in fear, in anger, in loathing, in the lingering doubt about himself, and in his own power.

Not even Kalem knew the extent of his power, but to see one such as himself wielding magic that could wantonly slaughter just showed him that he was way out of his league.

Despite Datu Patas' command, Panday had not taken Kalem directly to the docks and had traded their finer clothes for plain tunics and trousers. It was the right choice. The docks swarmed with Crimson Guards, seizing private ships of nobles and inspecting merchant and transport ships for stowaways. They said they were looking for the assassin. They said they were looking for Berdugo rebels. They said they were looking for an errant noble who thought himself bigger than his position.

It really was a hunt for witnesses and survivors. Not all the patterns of the ten great houses were found in the aftermath of the attack. Only seven of the ten blood-stained patterns flew like flags over the Katipunan, remnants of the datus who had worn them. The only significant people who were yet to be found were the Asinari Najima Malik, the Tikbalang Satalon Sekoya, and the Dalaket Elv Hares of Ilogani. The flag was supposed to be a sign of respect, but Kalem now knew better. It was a warning to all who would dare threaten the King.

The balangays now scrambled to replace their lost datus, many errant nobles seeing the chaos as opportunities to claim power. This included Kalem's uncle, Batas Laya, who had all but announced that he was the rightful datu and reiterated previous claims that Kalem was a Dayo halfling.

'I found a boat that leaves tonight for Masalanta,' Panday said, entering their hideout in Tatsulok, a spartan room on the seediest street in the seediest district in the entire island.

Panday had several of these safe houses all over the island, some close to the Kolehiyo. A precaution, he explained. But Kalem realized that Panday had been preparing for an event like the slaughter for a long time.

Kalem looked up from the corner where he was sitting, making him look small in the already small room. He didn't say anything, only watched Panday go through the motions of packing their things and preparing to move hideouts again for the night.

'The Reds have relaxed their search. The sooner we get off the island, the safer we'll be.'

Safer from what? Kalem wanted to ask but didn't. His father said, 'Trust no one,' but it seemed like Kalem's entire life hinged on everyone else's choices. The Kolehiyo, the datuship, now this, his life in the palm of his friend's hand. Panday was loyal, but Panday had stopped Kalem from saving his father when he had the power to do so.

'I know the captain. He can take us as far as Masalanta where another boat can take us to Asinar. It'll be easier for us to return to Maylaya from there.'

Kalem buried his face between his knees, his mind running with so many thoughts he felt blank. This was the part of his life that he had ignored while at school, pretending he was something else, someone else.

'Men like us aren't afforded the luxury of pursuing our dreams, not with the weight of duty bearing down our shoulders,' his father had said, followed by an apology as if Kalem choosing to pretend that he wasn't a part of this life was his fault.

Kalem wasn't sure if he had been apologizing for not being able to let Kalem pursue his dreams.

Master Makabago had explained it better. His father had been trying to give him more reasons to do his duty than it just being a birthright. Love, same thing that happened to him when he was born. *What is duty if it's not born out of love?*

Life didn't stop while he played scholar; it didn't make concessions for him while he avoided the looming weight of duty. Everything that happened was a by-product of decisions, manoeuvres, and strategies that had been set into motion long before he was born. His father winning the Obsidian War. His father uniting the south. His father rallying the Dalaket in defence of this country. Planned or unplanned, strategy or luck, it had all led to that horrible day. Kalem wondered if leaving for Kolehiyo had been his conscious decision, their enemies' strategic manoeuvre, or just a terrible, stupid mistake. Where did his decisions fit into the tapestry of his father's plans? He had always been the unpredictable variable, the wild card. Ultimately, he had become his father's weakness.

And now, he was his father's last card.

'You should know that your father wasn't planning a coup,' Panday said, sensing Kalem's mood and seeing the questions colouring his face. 'He loved this country. He would never do such a thing,' he added, the idea of it hitting harder than it should.

Kalem scowled. *He would never do such a thing,* Panday had said, as if he knew Kalem's father better than his own son. And Panday knew, too, that a coup was one of the things that crowded and clouded Patas Laya's mind.

'Then why did we willingly go to Congress like livestock for slaughter?'

'Your father wouldn't consider violence to solve our country's problems. We can't say the same for the King and his cronies.'

'What was my father's plan? Are the Tukikuni actually coming?'

'Oh, make no mistake, that invasion is real. So is the Day of Bleeding Banners, the Siege of Masalanta, the destruction and slaughter of House Payapa, the King's diminishing health, the Berdugo rebellion, the frost in the north, the famine in the south, Dayo slave rebellion and its resulting labour shortage, the seed trade wars between balangays—all of those are real.'

Shame tugged at the muscles in Kalem's chest, his shoulders slumping as if from a new weight pulling him down. All these were things he was supposed to know—should know. Panday stopped, pausing to look at him square in the face as if seeing something new or perhaps something he had never noticed until it mattered.

Kalem knew that look, or at least he understood it. It was the way his uncle looked at him in the garden the night he couldn't sleep in his own bed, the way Master Makabago addressed him in Kolehiyo the day he left, the way his father's eyes fell on him that day he went back home. Those faces were disappointed by his naivete, his ignorance of the machinations of the world, his failure to live up to their expectations of what he should be instead of what he actually was. He was underwhelming. He was not enough. He was finite.

He turned away from Panday, unsure how he could answer that question on his face. 'Sorry,' he said, though he was unsure what he was apologizing for: his ignorance, his obliviousness, or fate for promising the world a datu's heir and instead delivering him. Just him.

Panday cleared his throat, sensing, too late, Kalem's discomfort, and continuing to pack clothes into two woven bags. 'It's natural for a country to go through crises, Kalem. How we deal with it is what matters.'

Still, Kalem didn't look up, didn't let the shame eat him up from the inside though it lurked there like a hunger—waiting, eager to be fed. 'You don't have to pander to me. I'm nothing.'

A beat. A long, tense silence. The heavy thud of bags falling on the floor. Heavy footfalls on the creaky floorboards. A hand grabbing at the collar of his shirt and easily lifting him up from his miserable corner, legs dangling beneath him helplessly 'You're nothing? What does that make me? What does that make everyone else who doesn't have what you have, you idiot? Stop bitching. This is about more than you.' Panday slammed Kalem onto the bed.

Kalem glared at Panday and lunged at him, who simply pushed him back onto the bed, pushed him over and over again, until he tired and saw the madness of trying to physically subdue someone bigger, stronger, and much more adept at fighting than he was. Kalem stared at the ceiling, panting hard, chest rising and falling, skin hot, mind racing, and so very tired.

'Why bother with me then? Why don't you find someone else who'd do it? Or better yet, why don't you do it? You seem to know better what I'm expected to know!' Struck by what had come out of his mouth, he covered his eyes with his forearm, willing the hitch in his throat, the sting in his eyes to go away.

He heard Panday sigh and felt the bed dip with the new weight on it. A comforting palm touched Kalem's forehead. 'Kalem,' Panday began, the tone of voice shifting from resigned to placid so fast, Kalem couldn't gauge his friend's mood—wasn't sure if he should brace himself to be thrown like a sack of rice across the room—'You're not nearly hot enough to bitch like this.'

Kalem propped himself up on one elbow, glowering at Panday, and then slumped back on the bed when Panday smiled a sad smile—the scarred face of a friend who understood loss and saw the telltale signs of it in a person's face.

'My father is gone. It's my fault,' Kalem finally said, the last thread finally uncoiling, his voice cracking, stumbling over the words. 'I left him there to die.' The admission washed over him like cold water after staying out under the sun too long. At the base of it all, he blamed himself: for staying away as long as he had; for pretending that the only thing that mattered were the things he could do like study and research and hide under books; for hiding under the guise of pursuing knowledge and learning. What was knowledge without action? What was study without application? In the end, it couldn't do anything to save his father.

It was his fault. His fault. All his fault.

Pandy scoffed. 'You think too highly of yourself, Ginoong Laya.' He then got up to pick up the bags he had dropped to the floor, behaving so casually that Kalem wasn't sure if he was joking.

Kalem sat all the way up and followed his friend who set their bags on the table. 'Didn't you just say that this was about more than me? I blame myself!'

'Yeah, for everything.' Panday pulled the drawstrings of one bag so hard that it bounced on the table, pushing the other bag towards the edge. 'I knew I should have dragged you out of that musty school before you got too comfortable, but your father said to let you stay longer.' He looped the strings, tying it, sealing the contents within.

Kalem caught the other bag before it tumbled over the edge of the table. 'What are you talking about?'

'You're the smartest person I know, Kalem, but you can be such a big idiot sometimes.' Panday took the bag from him and took out two triangles of warm, white *puto* wrapped in banana leaves. 'The world doesn't revolve around you but that doesn't mean you don't have a part to play in it.' He placed one triangle in Kalem's hand then picked up the sword that was laying in the corner.

Kalem watched him sling one bag over his shoulder. 'How do you do this? How do you not mourn after a death?'

Panday touched the pink burn scar that marred half his handsome face. 'I've seen death, Kalem. Life goes on after it. If it doesn't, we might as well be as good as dead ourselves,' he said sadly, his usual genial tone faltering as a memory gave him pause, hand still on the scar. 'But that doesn't mean I don't mourn. Your father knew he was dying. He didn't waste away sulking until the crazies got to him. He had time. He had power. He had position. And he wielded all those like weapons.' He presented the hilt of the Obsidian Sword to Kalem.

Kalem didn't immediately accept, his gaze intent on the blade and the magic that it emitted. 'What if I die from seedsickness before I can?'

'You can't fool me, Kalem.' Panday forced the blade into Kalem's hand. 'Whatever you did with that thing, it gave you power. Enough that it calmed your father. Enough that it slowed down the shadows so we could escape the arena. Enough that the seedsickness won't kill you.' He placed a hand on Kalem's shoulder and squeezed. 'I'm sorry about your father. He was a good man. A good king.'

Kalem met Panday's eyes, and a dull ache throbbed his chest. He bit the inside of his cheek, drawing blood, the pain reminding him to hold back, reminding him of his father at court, reminding him where he was and what he was supposed to do. He wrapped the blade in a ratty cloth, hiding away his father's memory. He would mourn him later. All his life, he would mourn him and all the time he'd lost. Now, he had to live. He would not waste the life he had.

Panday patted his shoulder once. 'Now, unless you plan to pay me more to listen to you bitch all day, let me do my job.' He pushed the other bag toward Kalem who pulled it over his own shoulder.

'I'm not paying you.'

'Which is something we need to talk about when we get home.' Panday led the way out the door and Kalem followed. 'I'm getting a promotion after all. Must be better pay, being the datu's aide.'

Chapter 10

Kalem

His father had laid out a clear, simple plan of escape, but Panday was a creature of instinct, something Kalem obviously lacked. And while it seemed prudent to follow his father's commands—*Take Kalem to the docks. Stop at nothing. Deliver him home. Trust no one.* Panday had broken all of them in some way, taking them all as suggestions instead of actual instructions. They had many close calls as they switched hideouts across the island, going to the Sirena Coast of Castel, south of the island city. Kalem would have been caught already had it not been for Panday's quick thinking.

Still, Kalem had a bad feeling about getting on the small, dilapidated fishing boat bobbing up and down in the bay around Castel.

Sirena Coast was the unofficial Asinari district of Castel. It was full of stone and clay shops and carts manned by the merfolk, selling fish, pearls, corals, and all manner of underwater merchandise. The merfolk didn't stay on land long and had set up their homes far from the harbour, where the city's trash spilled out. Except for a few Asinari guards in blue patterns, this part of the Castel coast was usually deserted at night. Panday whipped the sand at his heels as he trudged toward a triangular tent next to a man huddling under a cloak and cooking fish speared through with a stick over a bonfire.

'Lihim?' Panday called when they were within earshot.

The man didn't look up from his fish, turning it over to reveal the blackened side. 'Who's asking?'

Kalem stood at attention upon hearing his voice, commanding and clear like a statesman, but with a tinge of gruffness that reminded him of Panday. He instinctively bit the inside of his cheek.

'Panday Talim.'

The man lowered the hood of his cloak, revealing a clear, handsome face; long, dark hair lay loose over his forehead and shoulders; his beard and moustache covered his chin, cheek, and upper lip; and his big, black eyes seemed all too familiar. The scent of seed alcohol and recreational seedshooters hung thick in the air around him. He wore a dark tunic with long sleeves, black trousers, and fingerless gloves. *Never trust a man who hides his skin.* Alarm bells rang in Kalem's ear. His father's instruction, 'Trust no one,' kicked in, and he leaned into Panday. 'Are you sure we can trust him, Panday?'

Lihim answered, 'Has anyone told him he's too jumpy for his own good?'

Panday waved a dismissive hand at Kalem and sat across Lihim. 'He's not used to being a renegade.'

The man snorted and handed a fish to Panday. 'Sit down, boy. Can't leave yet. The Asinari haven't settled into their homes.'

Kalem sat down next to Panday out of an inherent reflex to obey after years of being defiant for the sake of being defiant. It was easy to be defiant, after all, when the stakes weren't so high. Panday handed him the fish.

'Business as usual for them scaled skins, ain't it? They're taking the siege of Masalanta too lightly?' Panday said, accepting another fish from the man, 'Considering Masalanta is smack dab in the middle of their waters.'

'The Asinari try not to bother with the affairs of the Kayuman, much less a seed-rich island claimed by three datus, even if it's close to their capital,' Lihim said, raising a fish up to his lips. The light from the bonfire illuminated the man's face from below, leaving parts of his face in the shadows. Kalem rubbed his eyes with the heel of his palm, unsure if he was seeing the man right. His beard seemed darker in this light.

'Not the mermaid queen, I bet,' Panday said, biting into his own fish. 'And not after what happened to her husband.'

'What a loss, but the merqueen Najima Malik is a pragmatic woman,' Lihim said. 'She's not prone to exacting revenge when no one is sure who orchestrated it.'

'I bet she knows,' Panday said, casting a knowing look at the man. 'I know you do. Not very many datus have a mage assassin at their beck and call.'

Lihim exchanged a long look with Panday, one that unnerved Kalem. He felt like he was purposely being left out of the conversation.

'Look,' Kalem said, announcing his presence, still very much there with them. 'I've been out of court for a while and I have been kept in the dark about it. Who is this assassin? Why won't Najima retaliate?'

'The assassin murdered my house, Kalem,' Panday said flatly, avoiding Kalem's eyes by taking a swig out of his bottle.

'It was an act of revenge against my mother,' Lihim explained when Panday refused to say any more. 'And his brother for their . . . indiscretion.'

'Oh . . .' Kalem said, but before he could say anything else—an apology, platitudes, poor excuses—to hide his ignorance, Panday stopped him by saying, 'Don't say anything, Kalem.'

Kalem didn't, knowing that Panday wasn't the kind who took kindly to empty words. He was a man of action, and if there was anything that Kalem could do to make him feel better, it was this: keep them alive and safe until he got home, until he took his place as Datu of Maylaya, until he used the power that came with the title so that nothing like the murder of the Talims or Payapas could happen again, until he fulfilled the duty thrust upon him by fate.

'Even if Najima knows, she wouldn't dare. Too many people are after Masalanta, and if anyone of them tries to make a move, it'll be the spark needed to ignite the civil war that's been waiting to happen for a long time,' Lihim said, mercifully breaking the tension. 'Masalanta is no man's land for now.'

'Aren't we going to Masalanta?' Panday said, which made Kalem do a double take at the two of them.

'Why are we going to Masalanta? I thought we were running from the King's Reds?' Kalem asked Panday.

Lihim cast an accusatory look at him that made him shrink back in fear, but this angle reminded him of his own time in Kayumalon court as a boy, seeing his cousins in the King's home in Maylakanon. Kalem tilted his head to look at Lihim from a different angle, see the familiar corners of his jaws and the shape of his eyes, as if he was looking at one of the portraits hanging from his father's estate. Kalem narrowed his eyes and saw the tiger-stripe tattoos under the man's too-black beard, saw the black shade of his irises, the strong set of his jaw, the distinct shape of his eyes. Then, his eyes widened, and he gasped in realization.

'Does he always stare at people like that?' Lihim asked, pointing his chin at Kalem.

'His mind wanders easily. You know how it is with the seed—' Panday said but was interrupted by Kalem.

'You were supposed to be at the Congress. My father needed you to be there—my father advocated for you, and you didn't come!'

Panday nudged Kalem in the ribs and glared as if this wasn't the right time to talk about this. Kalem glanced between both men, both staring at him not in the way a stranger would stare at carnival freak, but in a way that said both men were in on some big secret that Kalem was not privy to.

Panday covered his mouth before Kalem could talk.

'Don't say the name, Kalem,' he hissed, adding in the old tongue, *May tenga ang lupa. May pakpak ang balita.* 'Secrets were never kept secret if they were spoken about.

'You know, your father used to brag all the time about how smart you are,' Lihim—Dangal said, smiling as he finished off the last of his food.

A gnawing anger crept up the back of Kalem's neck, and he had half a mind to leave, and would have, if Panday hadn't been holding him down to his seat on the sand. Panday sensed the question that Kalem was grappling with in his mind, and he nodded reassuringly—as if that would be enough to assuage Kalem's anger at the man whose father killed his.

'My father trusted you,' Kalem said, sounding defeated.

'Your family is not the only one my father betrayed,' Dangal said and then stood, snuffing out the bonfire and packing his tent. 'We'll talk on my boat.'

* * *

Panday and Dangal had such a cordial relationship with each other that they seem like old friends, but then Panday did have an inherent talent for making people like him, at least in the first meeting. It was only after the second, third, and successive meetings that they noticed the perpetual grief that coloured his dark grey eyes and the slow, careful regard he had for the little things about a person he met, as if he was keeping souvenirs of them in his mind. Kalem had never thought his cousin, Dangal Maylakanon, the prince, would take a liking to a man like Panday, but then he didn't really know enough about his cousin to make wild judgments like that.

As they rowed the boat away from the harbour, Kalem lit up green to shroud their vessel in optical mist, copying the way the light fell around them and basically rendering them invisible to those within the perimeter of the mist. Dangal steered the ship away from the spotlight of the lighthouse down the coast nearer to the docks. They fell into a quiet, steady rhythm as they rowed and the waves lapped against the boat's hull . The island city receded into the horizon behind them and the vast Kayumalon ocean expanded to infinity before them. The faint sour guava scent from the green magic was a reminder of summertime in their hometowns, when even the sourest fruits were sweet.

At daybreak, as the ocean breeze picked up, they took a break. Lightheaded, Kalem dropped the green shield and slumped where he sat, his veins stained green. Panday took out three triangles of white puto and a flask of water, handing one sweet cake each to Kalem and Dangal. Dangal scarfed down the puto, took out a waterskin of blue wine, and drank from it to push down the cake, before passing it Kalem. 'To calm the nerves,' he explained, but Kalem could tell from his permanently faintly stained veins that he drank it to stave off withdrawal from seed addiction.

Kalem took a bite of the puto and wondered out loud if this was all Panday had brought for the entire trip.

'I brought a bag of *tuyo*, too.' Panday dug into his bag and took out a pouch filled with dried seafood of varying shapes and sizes. '*Tawilis, bisugo, danggit*, and *dilis*—all kinds of wrinkled, salty, dried seafood. There are shrimp *okoy* fritters here, too. Take your pick, your majesty. Just not the dried squid—*pusit*. I'm saving that for later.'

Kalem sneered at his friend and took a strip of pusit from the pouch just to spite him. 'What's happening later?'

Panday tucked the pouch back into his bag. 'For when I feel like getting drunk and making you do all the rowing yourself. Can't you use your new magic to get us to Masalanta faster?'

'Huh. I actually don't know. I hadn't thought of it.' Kalem raised the pusit up to his lips and bit off a piece.

'You've spent the better part of the decade searching for it, and now that you've got it, you don't use it,' Panday bit into his puto.

'What new magic?' Dangal asked, one hand on the boat's tiller.

'Seedmagic, but not the common variety. I haven't had time to study it yet,' Kalem said.

'Probably never will,' Dangal answered. 'Your new job will take up *all* of your time.'

Kalem frowned, the pusit suddenly tasting like ashes in his mouth. Maybe some part of him hoped to still pursue his research on the side. Even older kings had time for the things they loved. And how dare his cousin make comments like that? He was expected to take over as king in the aftermath of the Congress of Datus. Kalem wasn't the one shirking responsibility.

'Why are *you* running away, Dangal? The country has been looking for you,' Kalem said, making a point of using his cousin's real name.

A wry smile crossed his face. 'I'm looking for my daughter.'

Kalem's eyes grew wide, and his jaw dropped, food hovering halfway to his mouth. Dangal laughed a dry, humourless laugh, one that didn't follow a joke but irony.

'I had a wife years ago,' Dangal said nonchalantly as if he was telling a simple story over wine and *pulutan*. 'She was Dayo. I married a Dayo woman, and we had a daughter. They were in hiding when my father found out and sent a soldier to kill them—only the soldier didn't. They just disappeared, cutting off all contact from me and my father. It took me so long to find them again, and now, after so many years of futile searching, I know where my daughter is.'

'Why? It's been years, Dangal,' Kalem asked, shaking his head. 'She probably doesn't even know about you.'

'When you get to my age, you hold on to every good thing in your life no matter how small. It's much easier to lose things the closer we are to the end.'

Kalem's father flashed across his mind, the last time they had *merienda* together in his favourite dessert shop uptown that night the seedsickness had taken hold of him. The day he had said he wanted to stay in Kolehiyo to pursue his passion. He had missed so much while chasing his goals and he wondered if what he'd lost was so much more than what he knew.

'My father believed in you. He wanted you to become king,' Kalem said with gritted teeth.

Dangal met his glare with an apologetic gaze. Kalem had seen that same look in his father's face before he walked into the arena. It was probably the same look he'd given his father when he left for Kolehiyo. It was something he had to do.

Kalem slumped back down next to Panday, face in his hands, eyes stinging with tears, his mouth tasting like blood. 'My father died for you,' he said silently.

Panday finally spoke up. 'Your father didn't die for him. He lived for you, Kalem.'

* * *

Kalem had never known true exhaustion until this trip. The subtle aches, the screaming strains, and the long periods of unnerving quiet that permeated between one harried breath and the next. It was enough to keep his mind distracted and busy and blank.

He was tempted to use one of the few seed shooters to compensate for the energy he was spending on this trip. Panday had been thrifty about it, going so far as to calculate exactly how much they needed to get to Maylaya and how often they should consume them so their bodies won't waste the magic they couldn't metabolize fast enough. Kalem actually snuck one out of Panday's bag before it was time to drink again, but Panday stared at him blankly, nodding and quietly judging him for turning to magic for every little ache. Kalem dropped the vial, still uncorked, and it rolled under a tangle of ropes on the far side of the boat. He didn't even have the energy to pick it up. He kept rowing.

By the third day of rowing for hours under the sun while lighting green when Crimson Coast Guards passed them, Kalem was so tired, he would fall asleep rowing, only to be prodded awake by Panday trying to take the oar from him. Sometimes, he'd happily let the man take over.

Masalanta was half a day's worth of travel through the Himpapawid Trail and a day and a half through the Karagatan Trail. And that was if they took the seed engine ships—Dalaket ships powered by seedmagic. Their little boat could never compare. This was the most strenuous exercise he'd done in his life—and he did combat training every day in Kolehiyo. He thought he'd last at least as long as Panday, but he was learning that training within the safe confines of Kolehiyo was nothing compared to the real strains of surviving life the way Panday had.

'We're about a day away from the island. We'll need to take turns lighting up green till we get there,' Dangal said, so comfortable and relaxed that Kalem was directing all his resentment towards the man.

Next to him, Panday looked bigger, more solid. Kalem looked down at his own body and wondered how much he'd changed from the lean, lanky scholar in his first year in Kolehiyo to this combat mage many years later.

While rowing, there is a point when the entire act becomes automatic, mechanical, like losing feeling of the body after the third hour of running non-stop. Kalem felt like he was outside his body and his mind wandered toward the books he had left behind, the experiments he'd botched, and the magic he'd tried to understand back in Castel. When the Earth God wasn't swimming wherever it felt like it wanted to go, Damu followed Kalem as ribbons of light formed and reformed his shape, totally in his element in this wide open space over the sea. Every so often, the turtle asked him questions, some difficult, some dumb, some he couldn't answer at all.

'Kalem, if I'm seedmagic and I have a mind of my own, what kind of magic are you using to make the green bioluminescent magic?'

'That is a complicated question. It's the theory I'd been trying to prove back in Kolehiyo. I hypothesized seedmagic is only the simplest manifestation of a higher form of magic—common seedmagic, germachemy, is but a branch splintering from one source. I think your magic stems from a noble, purer branch of magic that's more directly linked to the source magic, the Vita. I called that sister branch theochemy and the super source, Vitalurgy. I suppose pure, untainted Vita is what gives you sentience. Common compounds are the magic in the seedshooters and wine and drugs. Think of them as approximations of what you are,' he answered, taking on

the tone of a Kolehiyo master delivering basic lessons to wide-eyed students.

'Kalem, are you tired?'

'Yes, Damu. Yes, I am,' he answered with the veiled impatience of a master drilling facts into a particularly dim student. *But it's not because of the rowing. Probably not because of the magic I've been spending without seedshooters. Seems to me that I don't need shooters to wield now that I have you. No. I am tired because I have not the time to process everything that has happened.'*

'Kalem, if I can cross over into the mortal realm, can you cross over into Skyworld?'

'I don't know, Damu,' he answered after a long stunned pause, feeling like a dim-witted student himself. He hadn't even thought of that, but how could he? The realms of Skyworld were thought to be mythological. But the turtle was waiting for an answer, so as a salve for his wounded pride as a master, he said, *'I suppose it's a thing people find out when we die.'*

Half a day away from their destination, the turtle was quiet and pensive, and it seemed Kalem had caught him by surprise by asking, *'Damu, how did your magic fight back that shadow god?'*

'I don't think it's considered "fighting" if we were equally opposing each other. At least, it felt like it was opposing mine.'

'You can defeat it then?'

'To defeat another like me, I have to be more than I am, twice the god. Hmmm . . .'

'Land ho!' Dangal called from the helm, eyes on the island ahead of them, pulling Kalem's attention away from the turtle.

Panday leaned forward, squinting at the horizon. 'Kalem, light up green.'

Kalem sent clouds of green mist around them, squinted at the island, too, and saw what Panday was seeing.

Battleships, still and silent and broody under the hot Morningstar. The ships looked abandoned, debris and bodies floating in the rising and falling ocean water.

'Reds?' Kalem asked.

'I don't know. They're not flying patterns,' Panday answered, still rowing forward, but a lot slower.

'Crimson Guard,' Dangal confirmed, a grim look on his face. 'Those ships belong to a special unit of the Kalasag, the King's private fleet.'

'Berdugo rebels took down five fully armed Crimson Guard ships? With no armada of their own?' Panday said, incredulous.

'Is it so hard to believe that rebels could grow in power?' Kalem asked and only realized how stupid and naive the question was when it was out of his lips. The Crimson Guard ships were the only ships moored near the island. 'It *is* bold of them to take the island knowing that three—no four—datus may try to claim it.'

'They have a protector,' Dangal said, teeth gritting. 'But no seedmage could cause this much . . . massacre.'

'I know of one,' Panday said, looking to Kalem for confirmation.

'It couldn't be the same Shadow who brought the Bleeding Banners, but it could also be one like him,' Kalem answered, earning him a look from Dangal that seemed to ask, *how could you know?*

'I don't think we should dock here,' Panday said.

Dangal clenched his jaw. 'We're docking anyway. You don't like it, you can swim to Maylaya.'

Panday and Kalem exchanged looks, but it was Kalem who made the decision for them this time. 'We'll go with you. If the Berdugo rebels and their protector see the King as their enemy then we must be their allies.'

Panday spoke up. 'Did the King really try to take over the biggest seedmagic plantation in the country?'

'It's shared land,' Kalem said. 'It's *disputed* Kayuman land since the Pretender's Civil War. Taking it would give House Maylakan control over the biggest producer of magic in the country and make them an absolute superpower of Kayumalon.'

'But *they* didn't take it,' Dangal said with a tone of finality, speaking as if he was not the heir of that very same house and steered the ship through the dead and debris. 'We'll dock at the far side of the island.' The winds blew, heavy with the scent of mangoes and magic, making Kalem's skin prickle and the hair on his arm stand on end like static. 'Let's go get my daughter.'

Chapter 11

Yin

Watching the sky for dark clouds had become a vigil that Yin feared would never end.

Days had passed since Lutyo had left her alone, feeling so vulnerable after she opened herself to him completely—mind, magic, body, and soul.

That connection they'd made, built over time and reinforced by shared pain, it culminated in that one moment, that one beautiful, delicious, frightening moment. For all the powers of her seedgod, none had made feel more divine than Lutyo's skin on hers; it was as if the Skyworld had opened its gates for her. She wanted him, and he wanted her, and then he wanted *all* of her.

The magic she'd grown accustomed to draining out of her made her shudder. It was like having all of her veins cut open and the blood flow out in endless crashing waves.

She had quietly understood that she was dying.

She hugged her knees to her chest and propped her chin on her knees. Even scared, she didn't dare look away from the clear dawn sky.

Dian hovered along the edges of her vision, her glowing mist blending with the waning light of dawn being chased away by the Morningstar; the scent of ripe mangoes and decay was thick in the air. The seedgoddess seemed smaller, diminished, and as fearful as her. Dian perched on Yin's shoulder, her magic making the air tremble around them.

The magic. It was the magic. Surely, he wouldn't have killed her willingly. Surely, he felt the same for her as she felt for him. Surely, he wanted her and not just her magic.

What happened to us, Dian?' she asked the bird.

'We almost died.' There was cruelty in the simplicity of it.

'How? I thought . . . Our kind dies by the blade of one like us. Lutyo didn't have his blade.'

'But his magic tried to kill the mortal part of you. I'm only here so long as your body is alive here.'

'You're not a god, are you? Not a full one at least. Your kind, you're all pieces of a whole, aren't you? And the connection, that's how you find each other. You're supposed to create one full god.'

The bird didn't answer, but Yin felt it wasn't to keep a secret. It could be that she simply didn't know.

Still, fury bloomed in Yin's heart and sparked a fire that burned so deeply, so harshly in her. Vitriol laced her words. *'Are the gods even real? How could they make one measly life so miserable and still take more from me than I could give? They must be cruel gods indeed.'*

'I never said I was a god.'

'Or maybe there are no gods. Only fools who can't stand their own lives so they need to pass the duty of living to someone else.'

Silence fell between them, god and mortal alike cast in the harsh light of day, the truth bared open, like a small, gutted prey. Yin gritted her teeth, ignoring the pang of hunger in her stomach, the weight in her chest, and the cold morning dew hanging on her skin. Magic beyond anything she could ever imagine. And, still, she was mortal, mundane, hungry. She would have laughed at the absurdity of that if she weren't so hungry.

'For what it's worth, I don't think the Shadow knew that he could do that.'

She turned sharply to the bird, who fluttered back, and glared at her, waiting for an answer.

'All I'm saying is that I don't think he ever intended to hurt you. He seemed to care about you.'

She clenched her jaw, gritted her teeth, drummed her fingers on her leg, manifestations of all the negative thoughts and feelings that had been plaguing her these past few days. Lutyo had left her here, lost and alone. And she wasn't good at being lost and alone. Before she knew it was happening, his constant visits had become a lifeline, a promise that she wouldn't have to be lost and alone, but it served as a reminder that she would be when he left.

He'd extended her an invitation to see the world with him, but he made no promise that he wouldn't ever leave her.

She was a fool to think she could entrust her life to someone else, first her adopted father, next her absent father, and now this. Mortal men making promises that they couldn't keep. This was her fault. By not deciding what to do with her own life, she'd sealed her fate.

She stood, the piercing hunger reminding her of just how firmly her feet were planted on the ground, and breathed the new day in deeply. Her veins lit yellow, her body charged with divine magic, the winds lifted her up and up, to the realm of gods, fully intent on chasing the dark clouds away and taking back the skies.

Chapter 12

Kalem

The Morningstar had climbed to its peak when the trio pulled their boat to shore. The sand scorched their feet inside their sandals, a stark contrast against the cold ocean water lapping at their legs as they ran along the beach to pull the boat out of water.

Breathing hard, Kalem sat on the sand, propping himself back on his arms and letting the hot sun touch every part of his exposed, tattooed skin, his hair wet with sweat and ocean water. He kept the green up. Damu twisted anxiously around him, his shape deformed by Kalem's sharp breaths. A cold shiver ran down Kalem's spine, and he scratched the back of his neck, feeling an uncomfortable prickle there. *Bungang araw*, it was called—star rash from staying under the sun for too long.

Panday stood over him and dumped their bags next to Kalem, a hand shielding his eyes from the sun as he examined the thick line of trees beyond the sandy beach.

'Looks deserted . . .' Panday trailed off, leaving out the rest of what he meant to say.

Dangal strode up next to him, a bag over one shoulder and a longsword in the other hand. His cloak fell like a dark shadow over the other shoulder. 'Do you feel that?'

'What?' Kalem asked, squinting at the shadowy figure of his companion against the backdrop of the sky.

'The air is still,' Panday said, passing seedshooters to each of them.

Kalem got to his feet, finally recognizing the signs, the anxious feeling coming to a boil inside him in the prickling on the back of his neck, the shivers down his spine, and the magnetic surge of magic through his veins. He emptied the shooter into his mouth. *There's another god here.*

Damu floated next to his head. *I feel her, too—*

An arrow flew past Kalem's head, barely grazing his ear. Panday pushed Kalem behind him, sword already drawn, veins lit orange. Dangal, too, drew his sword and lit his veins orange, steeling his skin in time for a second volley of arrows.

'Run for cover!' Dangal said, veins already red, running away from the arrows and toward the white and grey arch stone formation along the coast. Bags already over his shoulder, Panday dragged Kalem after Dangal.

'What are you doing? Light red!' Panday said as Kalem stumbled on the sandy floor.

Kalem's veins lit red, infusing magic into his muscles, allowing him to run faster and more efficiently on sand and then on rock. The rain of arrows stopped chasing them when they reached the arches.

Kalem got there last, barely stopping before slamming into the full mass of Panday, sending him sprawling on the ground behind him. When Kalem recovered, he found them surrounded by pale-skinned Dayos wielding bows and arrows, slingshots, and spears.

Panday and Dangal kept their swords up while Kalem unsheathed the Obsidian Blade.

'We told you Reds to stay off our island!' yelled the bulky man with fire-red hair and a fresh line of scar tissue running across his face.

'We're not Reds!' Dangal answered.

'We heard that before!' Spear in hand, the red-haired man led his group forward, launching their weapons forward, a clash of metal on metal.

Panday lit up orange, shielding Kalem from the spears while Dangal expertly held back blades and swung in all directions.

'Kalem, run!' Panday said, orange-lit right shoulder taking an arrow, which ricocheted away from them. He joined Dangal in the fray, parrying, dodging, and cutting down enemies with skill, a warrior in his prime. Dangal had the grace of a duellist, thinking five steps ahead when an enemy could only think of the next. But no amount of skill could overpower numbers, and they were indeed outnumbered, five to one.

Seeing that Panday was taking extra care to protect Kalem, the red-haired Dayo went for him, lunging forward, spear in hand, targeting his heart and then his neck. Flustered and panicked, Kalem barely held his own, backing away with every attack, his blade barely parrying the spear.

Kalem's back hit a rock wall, and he ducked down just as a spear landed where his head had been. He lit red, body moving fast as he dodged sideways along the length of the spear, cutting it in half with the black blade, but the move made him lose his footing on the sand. He barely caught himself with one hand because of the red magic and tossed his blade away out of reach. The shortened spear point hovered over him as the spearman pulled it back, preparing to stab. The shorter handle meant more time for Kalem to react with his red-lit body, allowing him to roll over to one side and then the other, nimbly evading the assault by the skin of his teeth. He caught the quick glint of his black blade in the sand just as the spearman prepared for another stab. Kalem threw sand in the man's eye, clumsily letting some of it fall on his face.

They pulled back from each other, each trying to clear out his eyes, while Kalem frantically felt for the blade in his hand. A foot fell on his hand just as it closed around the hilt, and he was pulled back up to kneel before the red-haired spearman, the tip of the spear against his neck.

'Stop or he dies!' the red-haired man screamed to the mess of blood and bodies and blades.

'Kalem, you idiot, I told you to run!' Panday screamed, attempting to run to him, but was subdued by three Dayos at once.

Dangal dropped his sword in the sand and knelt. 'We mean you no harm!'

'Lies! No Kayuman would spare a Dayo!' the red-haired man yelled, the spear point drawing a drop of blood from Kalem's neck.

'You attacked us first!' Kalem said, leaning back hard into the man, struggling to shrug off his hold. The spearman shoved him forward, giving Panday the opening to go to

Kalem. Seeing the big bulk of Panday coming for him, the spearman slashed a deep, straight gash across Kalem's neck.

Panday paused, stunned, but didn't stay still long enough before the rage set in and he came barrelling at the spearman, veins lit red.

Blood spilled on the front of Kalem's clothes. His hand shook as he touched the cut on his neck, clean and swift and straight. He felt blood gurgling in his throat. The world slowed, fell silent, muffled under sand and panic. His vision tunnelled and blurred as the Earth God swirled before his eyes. His father's face flashed in his mind. He lived for Kalem. Now, he was dying for nothing—the grief, the regret, the dismay at being so stupid, aches far more powerful than the bleeding gash across his neck.

'You are the earth,' the Earth God said, though it reached Kalem's ears as incoherent sounds. *'You are the earth. You are the earth.'*

'I am the earth . . .' Kalem repeated over and over, his lips moving soundlessly as if chanting a prayer or a spell under his breath. He fell to all fours, hands on the rock and sand floor, the magic surging up his veins as his body surged downward, blood gushing out. He was the earth. The earth was him. He was the earth. Even as his hands went cold and numb, he felt himself spread out over the island, every root a part of his veins, every branch his fingers reaching up to the sky. The mountains, the valleys, the rough paths and paved roads. He felt all of it, a part of him. *'A broken body heals itself.'* The magic came to him in small increments, speeding up, warming his body, and repairing him. He rolled over, back arching as the magic sewed the cuts and injuries all over his body, repaired

the muscles he'd exerted on the way here, and the lightheaded daze the blood loss had left in its wake.

He drew in a breath that came out as a gasp and sat up slowly to an audience that was staring at him in shock. A dead man rising.

The winds picked up around him as Panday ran to get him, but he stopped abruptly, falling to his knees and clutching at his chest and neck like air was being taken out of his lungs. The others around him too fell to their knees, fighting for breath.

Panday watched him with frantic eyes as if in a futile fight with an invisible enemy. Kalem went to him instead, but he slipped on his first step, not on sand but on a wayward gust of wind that pushed the back of his knees and carried him upward in a hurricane, away from the rocks and deep into the jungle before the wind was taken out of him, and he lost consciousness in the process.

Chapter 13

Yin

Whatever had possessed her to lift the Kayuman away from the beach stained with his blood, it wasn't magic. Pride. Power. Control. Loneliness. Maybe unsatiated hunger. She didn't know which one, but she was sure it wasn't magic.

She had watched him run from Tiyago on the beach, sand flying up around him with every step; watched him draw a black blade, black through and through like her own blade, against Tiyago's feeble spear; and then watched him bleed and die on the beach. *The black blade was just a black blade after all*, she thought, before moving to fly to her intended destination, only to realize that she'd intended to chase after Lutyo even if it meant searching the world for him. It was just as well that she didn't fly away so soon, otherwise she would have missed the miracle, the dead man rising as the earth shook beneath their feet.

And now he was here, in her sanctuary within her mountain. She felt like a fool for falling into the same habit, the same trap of trusting a man because he appeared kind.

Here she was, sitting on her haunches, watching him sleep, and contemplating touching his skin.

The magic that healed his wound felt familiar and warm, like a hearth on the night before a storm. The Kayuman called to her like a beacon of light from across the ocean. Where Lutyo was dusk and the Morningstar setting, this man was dawn and darkness fading.

Her eyes fell on the gash on his neck, cutting across the black hexagonal ink patterns wrapped around it like an elaborate neck piece. Blood soaked through his grey tunic that stuck to his skin, revealing the hills and fissures of his body. Dark curls fell over his tattooed face, gentle in sleep.

Dian flitted over his face, looking almost as curious and fascinated as Yin.

'Will he hurt me?' Yin asked, hand halfway to the Kayuman's neck, still remembering the feel of Lutyo's skin on hers.

'Not while he's asleep, I assume,' Dian answered, earning her a wry look from Yin, who drew her hand back.

'You know what I mean.'

'He's like us, I think, but different.'

She nodded. *'His magic doesn't feel the same as Lutyo's. With Lutyo, our magic circled each other, always at odds with each other. This one feels akin to mine, like a twin, identical mostly.'* She waited for the Wind Goddess to answer, to confirm or validate that she wasn't just imagining it; that not every seedgod would come after her to take her magic from her. When she didn't answer, she tried a more direct approach. *'If I touch him, will the decay come for me like when I touched Lutyo?'*

'His magic doesn't feel like it's from the same vein as the Shadow's. You saw him, he healed himself, he summoned the earth. His magic seems like it's of growth, like yours. If anything, he might add to your own.'

'If that happened to me—' She pointed at the pinkish scar along the Kayuman's neck. *'Will our magic heal me before I die?'*

'I think if someone attempts to hurt or kill your mortal body, it cannot heal itself the same way as this one did. I assume this magic is only specific to him.'

There was an eagerness in the way the bird spoke to her and observed the sleeping Kayuman. It was like talking to a child finding a toy long thought lost. She couldn't help thinking that the bird was masking speculation by exuding a pretence of proficiency in the subject. All to convince her to touch the Kayuman, although the goddess couldn't answer her questions earlier. How could Yin trust her to know what she was saying now?

'What do you have to lose?'

She narrowed her eyes suspiciously at the bird then raised an eyebrow. *'You're not serious, are you?'*

'Well, it's not like you have anything else going on.'
'I was about to leave the island.'

'To go chase after the Shadow, who can hurt us. This is a preferable alternative. Go on. There's only one way to find out, you know.'

She hated agreeing, but Dian was right. The question was why she wanted to know. She could just fly away right now like she'd intended to do. What was she thinking saving this man just because he'd exhibited magic similar to hers? She had Lutyo—who'd hurt her and left her alone, she reminded herself.

Lutyo had left her alone after he let her hope that she wouldn't be. He was the only person she knew who could understand what had happened to her, understand the magic that flowed through her veins.

Now, here was another person like her, another who might also understand.

Before she realized what she was doing, she pressed her palm against his forearm, over the sleeve that covered his entire arm up to the wrist. Every part of him—save for his face, neck, and hands—was covered up, like he was hiding his skin, ashamed of its rich, brown colour. If she looked hard enough, she could see the tattoos through the fabric. He had many of them, more than her father ever had. Her father once told her that the tattoos were symbols of status among the Kayuman. This man must be very high up the hierarchy then, to have these many. In fact, she'd never seen these many tattoos on a Kayuman, not since the cloaked man who would bring her nice things and make her mother smile and cry.

'This man is Kayuman nobility,' she said to the bird, not really expecting her to understand the implications of that. Could this man perhaps know her father?

Her eyes fell on his neck again, on the pinkish gash that cut a clean line through his tattoos, and she found herself reaching for it as if to check if she had only imagined the long bleeding gash on his neck. Her fingertips brushed the surface slightly, and she instinctively pulled back when the touch sent ripples of static through her skin. She looked at her fingers, wiggling and clenching them over her palm. She exchanged looks with the bird.

'Did you feel something?'

'Only a slight ripple, but I'm not sure. Try placing both hands around his neck.'

She glared at the bird. *'And if he wakes up with my hands around his neck?'*

'If he's a danger to you, all you have to do is squeeze.'
'Didn't you just say our magic is of growth?'

'I imagine you'll grow in knowledge after you find out what happens when you touch him.'

'This is a side of you that I haven't seen before.'

'Well, you're stuck with me till someone takes me from you.' The bird flitted about her face, flapping her wings frantically and urging Yin forward. **'Stop delaying.'**

Yin pursed her lips and tentatively placed one palm on the Kayuman's neck. She felt the blood flowing through his veins and the beating of this heart under his skin. He felt warm and comforting. Up close, he smelled like freshly cut grass and morning dew—new, clean, and fresh.

And then she felt it, the magic like her own, the magic of nature and life and growth, flowing in frenetic paces under his skin and streaming out of him like heat rising from the ground on a hot summer's day. She gasped when his veins lit indigo under her palm and spread out over her skin and up her wrist gently. She should pull away. She knew she should pull away, but she felt his magic flow into her, filling her, healing parts of her that she didn't know were aching.

The hunger was a jolt of lightning flaring from within. Where she expected the hunger to feed on his magic, it instead danced with the indigo, flowed like rainwater in the ocean. Without thinking, she pressed her other palm against his neck, gingerly wrapping her fingers around it, drawing more and more of him into her.

Yin knew what it was like to want something she couldn't have, to want it so much that it hurt. For most of her life, it seemed all she knew was wanting and never getting— wanting the beautiful redhead boy from afar, wanting a permanent home to settle down in, wanting more of the Shadow, knowing it would hurt her, wanting to fly, only to stay tethered to the ground.

But this, this was a different kind of wanting. It was insatiable and comforting in its endlessness.

So, she took more, her hands wrapping around his neck tighter.

His chest rose sharply as he struggled for breath, and his eyes shot open, startling Yin and making her fall back, weak and invigorated, satiated and hungry, whole and broken, lost and found at the same time.

It wasn't magic that compelled her to touch him. But whatever it was, she'd almost choked him to death to get it.

Chapter 14

Kalem

Kalem woke up gasping for air.

As the world came into focus, the events before he had fallen unconscious came tumbling into his mind like a landslide. It was close to dusk already, and he wondered how much time had passed since he was swept away from the beach. In a fit of panic, he felt for the gash on his throat and found nothing there but smooth skin where the cut should've been.

He was sitting under a mango tree, its branches alive with fireflies. He groaned as he adjusted out of his slouching position, feeling phantom pains where his muscles should have been aching, where injuries should have been screaming. The scent of ripe mango was thick in the air, making his mouth water and his stomach grumble. A light gust of wind, heavy with scent of fruits blew past him, rustling the tree branches and unsettling the fireflies.

His eyes darted open, startling the girl on top of him, and making her fall back. He stared at her, wide-eyed and confused, a Dayo girl with bright, light brown eyes that looked golden in the light, now hovering upside down over him.

'You're awake,' she said, shifting in the air so she was right-side up. 'You should be dead.'

'I . . . I thought I was, too,' he said, his hand shifting to his neck.

'The cut is completely healed, but the tattoo on your neck is ruined,' she said, obviously keeping her distance from him, but scrutinizing him like ants under a magnifying glass. He dared not tear his gaze away from the floating girl. 'Why have you come to this island, Kayuman?'

'I'm just trying to go home,' Kalem said, the realization jumpstarting his system. He'd left Panday and Dangal on the beach with a bunch of murderous Dayo rebels! 'Where are my companions?' He stood up, but a gust of wind forced him to lie on his stomach on the floor, his cheek and palms pressed against the dirt, like a wall had been laid over him.

Yin ignored the question as she landed softly on the dirt floor in front him, the winds dissipating around her as she crouched. 'You have magic, too,' Yin said.

With that, he summoned the earth, and the mango tree's roots shot out of the ground and twisted around the girl's ankle, raising her upside-down mid-air. The winds reacted to her, but the tree's hold was tight. She commanded the winds holding him down to raise him wrong-side up before her.

'Let go!' they screamed at each other.

'You first!' they screamed again at the same time.

'Fine! On three, let go!' Kalem yelled, the blood rushing down his head. 'One, two, three!'

None of them budged. The girl yelled, 'You said "on three"!'

'But *you* didn't let go!' he snarled, practically growling.

'You didn't, too! Again! I'll count. One, two, three!'

The magic disappeared, and she landed on him just as he turned over, legs straddling either side of his waist. She procured a blade that was already pulled back, ready to stab him.

He raised his arms to shield his face from her. 'I swear, I'm not here to hurt you! I'm just passing through on the way to Maylaya!'

'Why would you pass through here? You're Kayuman. You have the Himpapawid Trail!'

'I'm on the run from the Reds!' he said, hands shielding his face. 'Please, put the knife down. You know I can heal myself.'

'Not after this knife is done with you,' she said, lowering the point close to his eyes, over the gap between his fingers, trying and failing to protect his face. It gave him a better look of the blade. It was black, like his own sword, with inscriptions along the blade and a crystal pommel filled with glowing, swirling yellow mist.

'Is that your seedgod's blade?' Kalem said, raising his head a bit to get a better look. 'Fascinating. It's smaller. Can you heal yourself, too?'

She frowned, eyes falling on the black blade in her hand, long, straight black hair falling off pale shoulders with veins lit slightly yellow. She was practically glowing, brighter than the fireflies drifting from branch to branch on the canopy above, brighter than the moons in the sky. A sweet nectarine scent came off her, making his mouth water and his insides churn.

'I can't, but—' She stopped upon seeing the expression on Kalem's face and she growled, standing up and tucking her blade back into the sheath hanging from an abaca rope belt around her waist.

'But what?' Kalem said, sitting up and leaning back into the tree's trunk.

'But I have an . . . effect on people,' she said reluctantly.

'What do you mean?' He sat comfortably, watching her pace back and forth, clearly avoiding his eyes.

'Like how you were just staring at me with that stupid look on your face!'

'I see . . .' Kalem said, squinting at her glowing form, trying to understand her, trying to isolate separate physical variables that he'd observed from her. She smelled like nectarine, sweet and enticing. She glowed, and not just the glow that came from her lit veins. There was a sheen to her pale skin that felt natural and looked soft and warm and supple. Her big, golden pupils were dilated, too, like she was constantly impassioned. Her cheeks were flushed, pinkish over her clear, pale skin.

He examined his own reactions to her. He was staring at her, that much she had said. His heart was racing, his palms felt cold, and his face felt warm. He was sweating profusely, too.

'Yellow? Pheromones?'

'What?' she said, stopping her pacing abruptly and turning sharply to him. 'Did you just insult me?'

'No, I meant, your magic, it's pheromone magic. You said you had an effect on people. If I'm right, then you have inherent yellow magic, the same one we get from seedshooters,' he said.

'Oh . . . How do you know that?'

'I studied germachemy—seedmagic in Castel. There are seven noble compounds with seven common compound counterparts—' Her face scrunched up, eyes squinting, concentrating. It reminded Kalem of his days back in Kolehiyo, soaking up knowledge, getting lost in his studies. He pressed his lips into a thin line. Kolehiyo suddenly felt like a lifetime ago. 'There are two types of seedmagic. The one you have inside you—us, it's probably pure magic. Theochemy. It means it hasn't been touched by other chemicals and is naturally originating from the primary source, Vita. It means you are able to tap into the *purest* magic. Magic from seed shooters is the second type. Germachemy. Think of it as borrowed magic.'

She raised her blade up. 'I got my magic from this. Where does common seedmagic come from?'

'From plants that grow on lands that are rich in noble compounds,' he said, letting a smile lift his face. 'This very island used to be one of the richest seed farmlands in the country before the Berdugo rebels took over the place.'

'Berdugo rebels? You mean Tiyago and the other Dayo villagers?'

'They attacked when we landed on the beach.' He pointed at the scar around his neck. 'Their redhead Dayo leader did this.'

'That's Tiyago, all right, but the Dayo rebel group here was way too small to matter before I drove the Reds away. Tiyago was one of the Dayo sent to Castel to learn new technical skills.' She frowned at him, reading his face, his confusion. 'You think Masalanta is a rebel base, don't you?'

'The entire country thinks that.'

'More Dayo have come to live here from all over the country, looking for safe haven from their Kayuman masters, but Masalanta has no army, no weapons, no soldiers.' She tilted her head to the side, and he stared at the way her hair danced with the motion. 'Plantation Dayo are seed farmers, no more skilled with a sword than a pig with a saddle, before I came and used my powers to send away the Reds.' She stared at him, trying to read him, testing how good a liar he was. Narrowing her eyes, she asked in a tone that was more accusatory than questioning, 'You're a nobleman, aren't you?'

'How do you know that?'

'You have that air of privilege about you that I want to knock off,' she said, straightening the hem of her skirt over her lap.

His jaw dropped, but he found himself smiling. 'I don't know about privilege, but I do have that look. Something about my face that makes people want to punch me.'

She bit her lower lip, trying to stifle a laugh. 'Maybe it's that look you get when you're going on about gods know what?'

'Probably just the hunger emptying my brain when there really isn't much in there to begin with.'

'I can fix that, Lord Ginoo,' she said, laughing, and with a simple flick of her hand, the winds shook the tree, dropping a clump of mangoes. The fireflies scattered around them as the winds cradled the mangoes, landing softly between them on the dirt. 'It's mango season so the fruits are sweetest this time of year.' She picked one up, poked and peeled the yellow skin with her nail, the sweet juice dripping down her hand. She bit into the succulent fruit, her lips making squishing sounds upon contact with it, her tongue sliding over her lip. 'What? Don't you like mangoes?'

'No, no, I love mangoes!' he said, picking one up and trying to copy the way she had peeled one, poking at the hole where the stem had been.

'You don't know how to peel a mango, do you?' She moved closer to him so that their arms were touching, took the mango in his hand, and peeled it for him. He watched her in wonder—the easy way she warmed up to strangers, the comfortable indifference in every touch they shared as if they were old friends, the frenetic silence of someone who saw more than their eyes could. 'There. It's just like peeling a banana, but messier and sweeter,' she said as if she'd just helped him break through a maddening experiment. She placed the mango in his hand.

He bit into it, and the sweetness spread through his mouth, making even the hair on the back of his neck ripple with goosepimples.

'Good, right?' she said.

It was the sweetest, most delicious mango he's ever had, sweeter even than Himagas' mango rice cakes that his father loved so much.

'What? You have more complaints?'

'No, it's nothing,' he said, hungrily biting into the mango again and again down to its seed, avoiding prying eyes that saw too much.

'Anyone ever tell you you're whiny, Lord Ginoo?' She finished off her mango and went for another one. 'It's not like we're not alone here.'

Kalem bit into the mango again. 'Where are we anyway?'

'The mountain overlooking my village,' she said, slapping his hand as he reached for another one. 'And you're changing the subject.'

He sighed and rolled his eyes. But then he poured everything out easily, willingly for her. 'Fine. It's just that my father would have loved these. He had a sweet tooth like you couldn't imagine,' he said, taking a mango when she let him have another one. 'It used to drive me crazy whenever he skipped proper meals for sweets. Mango rice cake was the last thing we ate together.'

'Where is he?'

He shook his head, suddenly losing his appetite. He put the fruit back down.

She stared at him with those big, golden eyes, the scent of her yellow mixing with the fruit so that he couldn't tell them apart. 'My father had the same problem. My mother used to call him out for eating way too many mangoes in one sitting, "Hiwaga, too much of that, you'd die with sugar sweetness gnawing at your legs." So my father would say, "Caritas, I have nowhere else to run to anyway".' Her face glowed while she talked, and Kalem convinced himself that it was probably the magic that was making her look like that. *Just the magic. Just magic.*

'What are you doing up here? Wouldn't your family be looking for you?'

'I lost my mother to seedsickness years back, and my father—adopted father—died in the siege,' she said, like water sliding off her shoulder, leaving traces on her glowing skin, not a like a weight pulling her down, at least not anymore.

'I'm sorry.'

'Why? Were you one of the Reds that attacked our island?'

'Seedgods, no! I'm more likely to fall on my sword than stab someone else with it—which, I know, makes me sound like an incompetent fool, but I'm not. I know how to wield a sword at the very least.'

She tucked a strand of stray hair behind her ears. 'I didn't think you had it in you.'

'Why do you say that?' Feigned shock and offense showed on his face.

'You have that look,' she said, smiling and throwing him a sideways glance.

'You've got to be more specific than that.' Kalem turned his body so he was facing her. 'Tell me what you see when you look at me.'

She pursed her lips and furrowed her brows, eyes examining him like an animal in the wild. 'Passion, so much that it spills over you and you have to pause to try to catch it all in the palm of your hand. And yet, it pours into everyone and everything else around you, and it makes you wonder—and fear—if you'll run out.' Her head was tilted upwards, her face caught between deep thought and being mesmerized by the glowing moons and stars in the sky. She looked back at him again with a self-satisfied smile on her face, and seeing the way he looked at her, she said, 'What? Am I wrong?'

Surprised, he shook his head, his face warm, the words jumbled in his head. *Just the magic. Just magic.*

'Now, tell me what you see when you look at me,' she said as if afraid to get an answer.

He stared into her eyes, glowing golden in the light of the seven moons racing across the sky. Her hair glittered with the thousand yellow-orange pinpricks of light from the fireflies. Her skin, clear and pale and pinkish, with the yellow stained veins, reminded him of subtle glowlamps that illuminated the rows of books in the Alaala Archives. She was staring at him with a hopeful, almost buoyant look that bordered on fierce just enough to make his heart race.

Just the magic. Just magic, Kalem. Magic.

'I . . . I see . . .' He wanted to be careful with the words. He wasn't sure if it was the magic or the hunger or even sugar rush from the mangoes that made him lightheaded, lending the atmosphere a heady, airy glow. He drew a breath, still just staring at her, her words ringing in his ears. *Just magic.* '. . . you.'

At first, she looked stunned, almost immobile. But after, her face did not betray how she felt, only the nervous rush to stand up. His heart sank, thinking he'd offended her, ruined this perfect moment, and that she'd leave him up here, lost and helplessly alone.

'You know I never got your name,' Kalem broke the silence, clearing his throat and standing next to her as if to follow her or to stop her from leaving him.

'That's cause it's not yours to take,' she said, but she was grinning. 'It's Yin. My name is Yin.'

'Yin,' he repeated as if tasting the name on his lips, expecting it to taste like the first mangoes of the season. 'Yin.' It did, and he grinned back. 'I'm Kalem.'

'Well, Kalem, I'm still hungry,' she said, the air winding around her and lifting her up. 'Do you want to come with me for something more than mangoes?'

Just the magic. Just magic. It's . . . magic.

Sighing, Kalem nodded and said, breathlessly as the winds cradled him again, 'I am hungry for more.'

Chapter 15

Kalem

Everyone has secrets, but the girl with the Wind Goddess guarded her secrets like a fine dress that fit every contour, every valley, every crest of her body, hiding the person underneath.

She willed the winds to carry them both as if it was her arms that cradled him in mid-air, floating across the night sky with the moon gods staring down at them in contempt.

The winds threw him around at first, like debris in a typhoon, and his stomach twisted into tight knots, sending the mango back up his throat. He flailed about in the winds like dead fish on dry land, helplessly fighting an invisible enemy that was flipping him in every direction it pleased. He clenched every muscle of his body, holding tight to steady himself, his earth magic holding him down, an anchor at sea. He stayed still mid-air, the winds hitting him hard like boulders, but he remained upright. The tree doesn't bend from a typhoon. The mountain doesn't bow to the winds. His resilience earned him a few moments of steady footing, enough to watch Yin floating before him like a dancer held up by strings, her arms raised to the side, toes pointing downwards, hair swirling like black silk in the air. He let go of his hold and the winds thrashed him about again, sending him careening over the top of coconut trees. He held on tightly to one of the tress, wrapping his arms and legs around its trunk like a tarsier.

She drifted to him gently, blithely, her laugh like the rustling of trees at night.

'I'm starting to think that you don't like me, Yin.'

'I like you, Kalem . . .' she said, pausing abruptly as if surprised by her own confession. They looked away from each other as if there would be anything more interesting than a girl floating mid-air and a grown man clinging to a coconut tree. Clouds drifted past moons, shifting the light, painting the entire island in an iridescent palette of colours unlike anything he had ever seen in the city. The air glittered with the yellow seed pollen floating around. He instinctively turned to her to watch the moonslight dance on her skin, veins stained yellow and glowing. He swallowed the lump in his throat, feeling thirsty and hungry all of a sudden and then not at all. *Just magic, Kalem.* She smiled at him, and he held his breath.

' . . . so far,' she added to break the tension and then laughed. 'It was funny watching you thrash in the air like a fish out of water.' He buried his face between coconuts, partly ashamed, partly annoyed, though he was pretty sure he wasn't annoyed at her.

'Kalem?' she called.

'Just leave me up here,' he answered, face still hidden. 'I'll find my way back.'

A sharp slap on his arm, like a whip, jerked him back, and he stared at her, surprised and now actually annoyed at her.

'Dance with it,' she said, though the winds howled, it carried her voice to him as if she was whispering the words directly into his ears.

'What?'

'You need to dance with the winds, Kalem, in order to ride it. If you meet it with the force of a mountain, it will try to bend you. Dance with it like rice stalks in the fields.' She held out a hand to him, an invitation to dance with her. 'Do you trust me?'

He scowled at her and then at her offered hand. 'Mountains don't bow to the winds.'

'But winds wear mountains down to gravel over time,' she said, frowning now, but when she began to pull her hand back, Kalem took it with the desperation of someone lost at sea would grab onto a lifeline.

'I trust you,' he said. 'Don't go,' he pleaded, his hand trembling over her own.

She nodded, squeezing his hand back. 'You need to let go though.'

Reluctantly, Kalem let go of the tree, and his stomach lurched as he fell for a second before she caught him. She took his other hand and coaxed him into her hurricane, helping him stay upright, keeping him steady.

'Don't fight it. The winds are singing. Follow its song,' she said, gently guiding him into the rhythm of the winds and he found himself swaying with her mid-air as if actually dancing.

She pulled him closer to her, placing one hand and then another on his shoulder, still guiding him but also letting him dance with the winds on his own. He felt his body responding to her touch, to the winds embracing him, to air that kept them apart.

'That's it . . .' she said, smug and joyful, a teacher watching a student learn his craft after working so hard for so long. His eyes wandered to hers, and he drowned in the glowing, golden pools. His heart raced, his mind was blank, and only the need to pull her closer to him kept him tethered to consciousness. With shaking hands, he held her by her waist and pulled her close. She gasped, shuddering at his touch, and he knew then that he'd made a terrible, stupid mistake.

They let go abruptly, losing control of the winds carrying them, which sent them hurtling to the ground. Yin recovered from the surprise just in time to call streams of wind to cushion their fall. She landed gracefully on her feet, while he fell clumsily to the ground like a cow caught in a storm.

She made an effort not to look at him, but she helped him stand up, asking if he was all right.

He had a million things he wanted to say but none of them were brave enough be spoken first. So, instead, he simply nodded, afraid to make another mistake again.

'The village is near here. We can walk there,' she said, suddenly so distant, leading the way to a trail near the remnants of a stone house, burned down to its foundations, on the outskirts of the forest. She stopped by it, picked through the rubble, and finding nothing, unwrapped the scarf around her neck and handed it to him. 'Cover your ink and stay out of sight. The Dayo will kill you if they see you.'

A cold shock ran through him, and he cursed himself for wasting so much time. 'Are my friends dead?'

Yin shook her head and said grimly, 'Dayo hang prisoners at midnight.' She avoided eye contact with him afterwards, and a sharp pang of pain stabbed at his chest, knowing he'd just ruined something good, though what it was, he did not know. Still, her face carried a kind of dismay and distance that pulled him back to the ground and kept his feet firmly planted there. He was the mountain. She was the wind.

'I need to save my friends,' he said.

She didn't disagree. 'They'll be tied up in the village square, under the Kanlungan tree. We can go around the back of the tree, but all eyes will be on them. Tiyago's especially.' He noticed her slight tremble at the mention of that name.

'Tiyago is the red-haired man with the scar across his face? The Berdugo leader?'

'Yes,' she said through gritted teeth, a quiet anger settling on her face. 'I won't use my magic on the Dayo.'

And two seedgods wielding magic on an island so close to the capital would surely draw the Reds' attention, if not the Shadow God's himself. 'We can't use *our* magic, but we can use magic.'

She frowned at him, confused. 'That doesn't make sense.'

'It's magic,' he said, grinning and feeling like a gloating, lovesick fool.

* * *

Yin flew them back to Dangal's boat abandoned on the beach. Kalem crouched on its side and dug around the ropes for the seed shooter he'd left there. It wasn't long till midnight.

She stared at the vial, fascinated by the glowing iridescent liquid swirling like storm clouds inside and was tempted to take it for herself.

'You called that common magic,' she muttered, a statement said like a question. He didn't seem to hear. 'But there's just one,' she added. Another question. But he was so engrossed in his thoughts that she suspected he barely understood a word of what she'd said. She let it go, convincing herself that she wouldn't know what to do with it anyway.

He looked up, a blank expression in his face, except for his eyes—his eyes were wellsprings of a thousand thoughts and memories and calculations. His mind, it seemed, was constantly running a race, to a thousand different places at once, while she was rooted to the ground here, right now, in front of him. Then, a new expression dawned on his face, one of knowing, realizing, completely taking in her presence there. She had to turn away, suddenly feeling too exposed in her own skin. But his mind was already so far away. She couldn't keep up, and she wasn't sure if she wanted to try. He was the first to break the moment.

'I'll light up green to create a distraction. You cut my friends loose,' he said, downing the contents, his face contorting into a strange look that Yin had seen on her adopted father's face when he was trying to guess the weight of a sack of rice with just a look.

Doubt marred her pale face. 'I have a bad feeling about this.'

His veins lit red, and he held out a hand to her. 'Do you trust me?'

Her lips parted, ready to say no, but she took his red-veined hand and, possibly against her better judgment, said. 'I do.'

He grinned and, quick as lightning on red-powered limbs, he picked her in his arms and ran back to the village before he could finish saying, 'Hold on tight.'

* * *

They stopped at the edge of the village. Yin climbed off him almost violently and stood dry-heaving on the ground. Kalem switched from red- to green-lit veins, shrouding them in an illusion that rendered them invisible to anyone within the perimeter of the magic.

'You could have warned me first,' she said, straightening up, but it didn't seem to bother her too much. Already, she was distracted by the green mist and his glowing, green veins. 'Can I do that, too?'

Kalem smiled. 'Presumably, yes. If you're able to host a seedgod then you can wield similar magic with seedshooters, of course.' He added the last bit without thinking, his mind already in a hundred different places. He stared at her pale skin with the veins underneath so clearly visible, like yellow tattoos. Only the Kayuman could wield seedmagic in Kayumalon, as far as germachemical studies had shown. Now that he thought about it, how could she carry a seedgod? The answer came before he could stop himself from blurting out, 'You're half-Kayuman? We share the same bloodline.'

'You know, Kalem, for a smart man, you're terribly oblivious,' she said, already making her way toward the tree. He followed her meekly, through winding streets between quaint stone houses with pots of herbs, flowers, and vegetable gardens on the side. Dogs, cats, chickens, pigs, and cows turned to them when passed by, smelling the seedmagic thick on them like a cloak. Some brayed, barked, or meowed, but most ignored them like flies hovering over their bodies.

'Stick to the shadows,' he said, gently prodding her to the side, and he felt her slightly flinch. What happened to the girl he had met earlier? The one who smiled so easily, who let their skins touch without thinking? 'The green only works if the target picks up the scent.'

Yin was more guarded, more unwilling to let him in, and he wondered more and more if he'd done anything to make her recoil from him.

Music from kulintangs, kudyapi, and dabakan echoed in the night, layered with the murmur of people talking, laughing, and playing games. The great big tree at the centre of the plaza loomed over them. It must have been a fire tree once, like the one growing over the Alaala Archives, but this one was burned black, grey, and ash white, its branches stretching like claws across the night sky. The closer they were to the plaza, the more people they passed by on the way, the more anxious Yin seemed, as if the veil of invisibility would fall anytime and any one of the Dayo would grab her.

Kalem reached forward to place a comforting hand on her shoulder then decided against it, knowing she'd be startled again by his touch—too guarded, too wary of people coming near her—and squeak, revealing their position. So they kept ploughing on.

After a few minutes of tense silence and avoiding direct eye-contact, Yin stopped just a few paces from the tree, hiding behind a cart parked on the side of the ruins of a tall white stone house. People were dancing in front of the tree and tables with heaping piles of food were set up all around in crooked rows. A lechon was roasting over a bonfire on the side, and there was a long queue for the barrels of *lambanong* yellow and blue wine on the other. The red-haired man, the Berdugo leader, sat on cushions set on a dais. A serving girl stood on the side with bottles of varying colours of wine, waiting on him. Kalem tapped Yin lightly on the shoulders and pointed at the bottles of seedwine.

'Those are weaker versions of the shooter. You'll get drunk, but you'll get faint traces of the magic, too,' he said, a teacher to a student, remembering the hunger on her face when she'd watched him down the lone seed shooter.

She nodded, eyes on the wine bottles. 'The yellow wine is wind magic?'

He shook his head. 'Wind magic is pure magic. The chemicals only approximate secondary, physical reactions of the host—healing for indigo, agility for red, pheromones for yellow, green for eyesight, orange for muscle mass, blue for hormones, and violet for flexibility.'

'You said you were a scholar. I can't imagine why you stopped.'

He clenched his jaw and pursed his lips. 'My father needed me.'

She touched his forearm comfortingly, an instinct or perhaps a need deeply embedded in her rising up to the surface. And suddenly, the walls were down again, the girl in the woods who smiled all too easily was back. Somehow, he saw in her eyes that she understood his pain and that they were in the same boat. 'We do what we have to do for the people we love.'

Their eyes met again. A beat. A moment. A second that stretched on and on but didn't feel long enough. *Just the magic, Kalem. Just magic.*

The spell broke when the redheaded man's voice boomed in the distance, more a battle cry to please the crowd than the *hermano mayor* of a party that would go on well into the night. She shuddered where she was crouching, her hands gripping the sides of the cart like a claw.

'Comrades! I bear the scars, the burns, the lashings that the Kayuman have dealt, but mine are nothing compared to many of you who have been abused far more by the mudskins, nothing compared to the death they brought at the siege. For our labour, they gave us scraps. They treated us like livestock. They took our women, our children, and when we died, they threw feasts and used magic to force the last of us into making more slaves. And they killed us and lay waste to our islands needlessly in their petty rivalries. I bear the scars of their abuse.' His hand went to the pink slanted line drawn from the right cheek, over the nose, and to the lobe on his left ear.

The people cheered, screaming, 'Godsdamn the mudskins!' 'Down with the monarchy!' and 'Hail the Berdugo!'

Yin stayed still, stiff, absently watching the man on the stage.

A frenetic hush fell over the crowd when Tiyago swept his gaze across his audience. 'Still, the mudskins lay the blame on us. They called us hungry for blood. They named us Berdugo as if it wasn't our blood spilled on this very ground. But they forget: This is our island. This is our home. This is the fruit of our labour.' He picked up a bottle of the red. 'The Kayuman must pay. The Kayuman will pay and their bodies will hang from the claws of Kanlungan as they hung the brethren we lost in their siege.' He broke the bottle against the tree, showering its black, charred trunk with red magic that glowed upon contact, alive again, back from the dead black stump it had become when the Reds attacked. The red magic surged through the tree, lighting up its veins and spreading to every root, every branch, every twig until red flowers bloomed from its claw-like branches, sprinkling the plaza in the red petals. Two unburned nooses hung from two branches across each other, swaying as the branches dipped a little under the new weight.

'Your illusion, will it work?' Yin asked, eyes not leaving Tiyago as he continued to speak, egged on by the crowd.

'Yes, similar to invisibility. The illusion can be projected on something else,' he said. 'But I need to get close enough to the crowd for the magic to work.'

'Are you sure about this? How will you get away?'

'Magic,' he said simply, starting to see why this was a stupid plan, as simple as it may be.

Tiyago continued, his voice low and dripping with rage and authority, 'Tonight, the Berdugo spill Kayuman blood. Bring out the prisoners!' Tiyago yelled. The crowd cheered and opened a pathway for two prisoners tied up in chains, heads covered in black rice sacks, both struggling to get out of their captors' hold.

Kalem's words clearly didn't allay Yin's anxiety, but she nodded anyway, her veins beginning to light up yellow. 'All right. I'll go to the other side of Kanlungan. Once the prisoners are on the dais, make the illusion. I'll take your friends to your boat. Get there *fast*.'

The two men were pushed up on the platform. The nooses were placed over their heads and around their necks.

The ropes were pulled upwards just enough so that Panday and Dangal were standing on their toes, barely keeping their footing.

Kalem wrapped the scarf over his face, covering as much of his exposed skin as he could. Still lit green, he slipped through the crowd, looking for a safe hiding spot from where to shift the green's magic to project illusions outside of himself. Green could only be used in one of two ways, one at a time.

He found a spot behind the barrels of wine and sent waves of the green mists outwards, which formed and reformed into human shapes—Kayuman Reds, the ones he remembered from the Day of the Bleeding Banners, including the Shadow God, marching from the edge of the crowd and weaving through it toward Tiyago.

A man with blond hair looked back and screamed, 'Mudskins!'

The audience became a frenzied mob. People scrambled, some picking up weapons, others running away from the plaza, the rest stood petrified at the sight of Kayuman Reds, their uniforms already bloodied, their veins black from the Shadow God's magic, marching towards them.

Tiyago was given a sword—Kalem's black blade—and he jumped off the dais, ready to kill the Reds.

A gust of wind gushed over the place, momentarily distorting the green mist and the illusions with it. Kalem saw Yin on the branches of the Kanlungan, hidden behind the fire flowers, landing softly on the branch that held Panday's noose. Her weight pushed the branch down so that Panday's feet were planted firmly on the dais.

Kalem immediately recalled the illusion, but not fast enough to hide him from Tiyago's gaze. He barely evaded the slash of his sword held by Tiyago. Kalem felt a pull toward the man, an urge or rather a dissuasion, which prevented him from hurting the man back. Instead, the sword hit the illusion of himself that stood where Kalem had previously stood. Tiyago's men followed suit, slashing at illusions and hitting nothing but mist, their blades dragging the green glitter magic as they whistled past. Kalem kept the illusions coming so no matter how much Tiyago and his men attacked, none of the illusions would fall.

Tiyago drew back, eyes narrowing at the intangible Kayuman Reds suspiciously.

'Stop!' he screamed and turned just in time to see Yin sawing through the knots of Panday's noose with a blade. He threw the sword at her, barely missing her head, lodging the blade deep into the wood, which turned to ash grey again around the black metal. She turned to her attacker and saw Tiyago glaring at her. A wave of fury and fear washed over her face, and she fled upwards into the tree branches, hiding from view.

'Clear the plaza! Find the seedmage!' Tiyago barked at his men, taking a spear from the person closest to him. He turned back to the tree, eyeing the branches Yin had fled into. 'Yin! I know you're there. You can't run away from your duty to your people forever!'

The winds blew. It pushed against the people. It carried a note of anger and resentment, a sharp pang of emotion fuelled by a dark memory, swinging the bodies of Kayuman nobles and soldiers alike.

Panicked, Kalem ran with the stampeding crowd away from the plaza, the scarf falling from his head and revealing his skin.

'Mudskin!' a Dayo close to him yelled. 'Green veins!'

Kalem ducked into a narrow street between blocks of stone houses. Yin flew to him, grabbed his hand, and flew back upwards just as a group of Dayo soldiers grabbed him. He barely escaped the grasp of one that had held onto his ankle, who let go before they were too high for him to land safely back on the ground. She flew toward the trees and the mountain.

'Yin! Panday! Dangal! We have to get them!'

Yin stopped mid-air and summoned a gust of wind to raise him up to her eye level. She grabbed his shoulders, shaking him. Kalem was barely staying upright. 'We can't take all of them at once! People could die!'

Before Kalem could answer, a line of black mist wrapped around Yin's waist and pulled her downward. She lost control of the winds and dropped Kalem in the process.

Kalem lit orange just seconds before he hit the ground, the floor cracking underneath his magically-reinforced weight. Groaning, he lifted himself up and saw shadows creeping around Yin's body, the Shadow God standing before her, reforming from his smoke body into that of a man in a cloak, watching her agony like it was a chore.

Holding on to his sides—orange may have steeled his body but it didn't make the impact of the fall any less painful—Kalem ran to Yin. The Shadow God didn't see him charging towards him, and he tackled the man in the cloak to the ground. The Shadow God's hood fell off his head, revealing a pale face webbed with black veins. He tackled Yin in the process, making her fall to the ground, too stunned to react and defend herself. Orange empty, Kalem scrambled to his feet, switched back to red, and grabbed her hand, running toward the plaza and disappearing into the crowd waiting to kill them. It could not be helped. It was a choice between the angry Dayo rebels with makeshift weapons and the shadow with the magic of a god—the godvessel who slaughtered an arena of people, who wiped out the leaders of this country, who murdered his father in cold blood.

The shadow assassin was here, but he came for Yin not him, and he followed them as a dark cloud toward the plaza. Knowing who Yin was, knowing what the shadow assassin had done, knowing who could benefit the most from the Bleeding Banners, it all finally clicked into place. His fury blazed. His fury brought a tempest of fear and grief and hunger back tenfold in his heart, his mind, his soul. The Shadow was his equal, he knew now for sure, and that meant the Shadow was an equal adversary who could be defeated, subdued, relegated back into the shadows where he belonged. Though he feared the implications of a god with death magic that matched his, he found courage in knowing that there was still humanity in both of them. They were still mortals. They were still human.

The murder of House Talim. The slaughter of the Payapas. The Bleeding Banners. All of it talked of a shadow assassin.

At first, it didn't seem plausible. The murder of House Talim had been decades ago but knowing what he knew now of seedgods, it wasn't farfetched to conclude that the Shadow had a seedgod too—and he served the King. The King had a shadow seedgod at his disposal. He remembered Dangal and Panday talking about this on their boat. He remembered the cloaked man parading about around the King during the Datus' Ball. A Dayo halfling from the Maragtas bloodlines.

This meant that it would only be a matter of time before the King knew that Kalem had survived, before the King knew that the son of his political rival had lived to fight another day.

Kalem looked over his shoulder, watching for the Shadow God, checking if he was already pursuing them. Nothing. The thought didn't assuage his worries all the way to the tree where Panday and Dangal were.

The nooses holding Panday and Dangal were pulling them upward, not high enough to snap their necks but just low enough that they were barely standing on their tiptoes, their bodies thrashing and struggling to get free. Yin had recovered from the attack and threw gusts of wind at both men to carry their weight as the ropes pulled them up higher. Kalem lit pure indigo, Damu's indigo, and willed the Kanlungan to break its branches and free his friends. It followed him and snapped its own branches off, dropping both Panday and Dangal, the older man had already stopped struggling. The fire petals turned to white and then drifted into the night as grey ash.

Kalem and Yin stepped into the plaza, eyes only on Panday and Dangal's bodies on the dais, and were surrounded immediately by Tiyago and his men. Panday was getting up on all fours. Dangal was unmoving.

Yin stayed at Kalem's back, but he knew from her tense stance that her impulse was to go to Panday and Dangal on the dais, and she was stopping only because Tiyago was glaring at them. Kalem watched out for the Shadow too, knowing he was still around. He could feel that familiar, insidious energy emanating all around them like rain water falling inevitably into larger receptacles of water.

'How could you choose those mudskins over your own people, Yin?' Tiyago growled with gritted teeth, dividing Kalem's attention between the Shadow's lurking dark energy and the Dayo rebel leader in front of them.

'I was never one of you!' Yin screamed, stepping up in front of Kalem, who was distracted by the miniscule scent of smoke tainting the air. He knew—knew in his magic stained veins—that this was the dark magic that had haunted all his nightmares, the sinister face in the dark that was the antithesis of his own healing energy.

Yin was still on Tiyago, her rage making the winds tempestuous, vengeful, unforgiving. At this point, the winds that Yin had summoned grew stronger, their songs getting louder, an echoing howling that drowned out every voice.

But Kalem focused only the Shadow, shouting, 'What do you want from us?'

'This doesn't concern you, Kayuman,' the Shadow answered him, tone cold as ice and sharp as steel, seemingly invisible to the naked eye, but Kalem could feel his presence so near, the hair on his arms stood on end.

'You killed my father!' Kalem answered, voice breaking. The Shadow didn't answer, only Tiyago's voice filled the air. The Shadow was still there. He was still here. Kalem could feel it in the air, he could sense it in his veins, he could see it in the specks of smoke in the air.

Tiyago attempted to approach them, saying to Yin, 'And you think the Kayuman would take kindly to you now after you murdered a fleet of Reds?'

'You think I'd trust you after you hung my father's dead body from the tree?' she snapped back just as the air around the plaza took on a dark haze, smoke motes building and building and building all around.

'You are Dayo down to your roots, Yin. You belong with us,' Tiyago said, his grip on the sword tightening.

The winds stilled for a second, matching the confusion and doubt on Yin's face, and then it picked up around them, rising to a storm, a hurricane, swirling around them and carrying with it debris from the party and building smoke.

'I am my own,' she said with a tone of finality. The hurricane whipped her hair, and she stepped forward between Kalem and Tiyago, her rage lending a sharp, almost cutting, murderous edge to the air she summoned. 'Mine alone.'

The winds dragged random people into their whirlwind, circling the entire plaza and the tree. Kalem stood close to Yin—where the winds were subdued by her presence, tamed to her will alone—arms covering his face. His veins lit indigo and the Kanlungan's roots broke through the dirt and wrapped around Kalem's and Yin's ankles. He kept watch over the smoke, expecting the shadow assassin to swoop in and eliminate everyone in its path. He commanded the roots closer to the tree to hold Panday and Dangal in a nest of bark and dirt on the ground.

'Yin! Stop! You'll kill them all,' Kalem said, placing a placating hand on her shoulder, trying to wake her from the throes of magic. He looked up to find the shadow mists mingling with the winds in long tendrils of black and grey, weaving over and under debris, people, and animals caught in the whirlwind, trying to get to Yin. Tiyago was crawling to safety, grabbing at dead roots protruding from the ground to stay grounded until he reached the hollow of the dead tree, in which he stayed hidden, safe from the magic of warring godvessels.

Kalem turned Yin to face him. 'Yin, stop!' She stared at him, blinked, and then blinked again as if waking up from a restless dream.

The Shadow God thrust through the walls of winds and reformed into the shape of a man in the black cloak. His hood fell off, revealing his black-veined face. 'Yin, what are you doing?' the Shadow God said disbelievingly, approaching them.

'Lutyo? Help me—' Yin said, trembling.

He cut her off. 'I can't. I'm not here for you.'

She seemed to become unhinged because of this man, and the catastrophe she had caused, he had made into his own.

The Shadow scowled at Yin, drawing a sword, his veins lighting up black. His black, beady eyes darted to Kalem's blade piercing the tree. It called to Kalem, humming with magic and power and fear, just as the turtle anxiously floated around him, seemingly unaffected by the winds.

'You killed my father!' Kalem said again, louder this time, angrier, hungrier for revenge as if the words themselves were blades that would cut and make the Shadow bleed, eliciting a reaction from Yin, whose gaze went to Lutyo and then back to Kalem.

Kalem's mind went to that last night in his father's estate, to the garden, when he had first learned of this magic. The turtle had said, to defeat one god, it's not enough to oppose it. You overwhelm it with others like him.

'Is that true?' Yin asked, uncertain, looking like she didn't want to know the answer to the question.

Kalem nodded. 'He slaughtered entire families. He could only be here to kill Dangal's Dayo daughter. He's here to kill you.'

Yin stared at the Shadow, dumbfounded, confused, disbelieving. Something passed across her face that Kalem couldn't quite pinpoint, but it gave him the sense that she knew the Shadow all too well. He took Yin's hand in his, held it fast, held it tight. She didn't flinch away from his hold but looked at him, waiting, unsure.

'Summon your magic, and I'll summon mine,' Kalem said, but that was all she needed to understand. Two gods against one. She hesitated, a new tension slowing her whirling winds surrounding them, but it didn't last too long, for she relented and followed Kalem's lead. Two gods against one. Two gods against one.

The earth shook beneath their feet, and the turtle grew gigantic as its indigo mists fed on more of Kalem's magic. Yin's winds renewed their force, raising the whirlwind higher, feeding it more and more magic. They were apart at first, Kalem and Yin, two separate creatures summoning magic too much for any one mortal.

Yin squeezed Kalem's hand. He intertwined his fingers with hers—and with it their magic. The walls were down. The doubt disintegrated. And it was just the two of them— mountain and wind—dancing to each other's songs. There he saw her god, the golden bird hiding behind her eyes, magnificent, awesome, astonishing all at the same time, its yellow mist ebbing and flowing into the Earth God until their edges blurred and they were one god at the same time.

The Shadow tried to pry them apart, but he was too late, too weak, too alone to stop them, and that was all Lutyo could do before the turtle and bird pushed back the shadow magic, pushed it so far that the cloaked man had to flee.

Kalem felt a wave of joy that enveloped Yin as they watched the Shadow run, but she felt more rattled to be sharing Kalem's feelings. Kalem and Yin faced each other, hands still intertwined. They felt every corner of their bodies, their lives, their existence combine and fight for space—two gods fighting over what to do. Their bodies groaned under the combined weight of two gods, as if one cart was forced to carry the weight of two. One needed to die to complete the process, they understood that much, one sacrificing power to the other, one god succumbing to the whims of another. And though the magic was exquisite and delicious and so very intoxicating, they reluctantly let go of each other—body and magic both, the space between them suddenly feeling like a valley, a trench, a world apart. The winds fell, the earth stilled. They were mortals again.

Gasping, they settled into separate existences, feeling like lesser mortals. Kalem tore his eyes away from her, afraid he would try to restore their link again and lose himself completely to her. He swept his gaze over the plaza and spotted Panday sitting up in his nest of roots and wood, watching the display with horror. Dangal lay still on his dais.

The Berdugo lay scattered everywhere, some unconscious, some moaning in pain from injuries that he and Yin had inflicted when they lost control, and some too stupefied to do anything further. Tiyago was unconscious underneath a pile of men that Kalem wasn't sure were alive.

Yin went to Dangal to check for signs of life while Kalem rushed to free Panday from his nest.

'It's like the Bleeding Banners again,' Panday said, sweeping his eyes over the bodies strewn on the ground around them.

Guilt, desperation, anger surged through him. The comparison between what he'd done here and what the Shadow had done at Congress offended him and made him so very angry. Kalem bit the inside of his cheek and ran for the crates of seedwine and found some indigo left in a broken bottle. He drank it all, not caring if shards went through his mouth. Blood filled his mouth, but the wounds were immediately magically healed.

He returned to the centre of the plaza and without thinking, disregarding who he was about to heal, ignoring the exhaustion in his body, his healer's instincts kicked in. He lit indigo, pure indigo. It pulsed out of him in ripples of magic growing bigger and bigger, dying and injured bodies absorbing a little bit at a time. He drained the indigo seedwine he had consumed and then tapped into whatever was left of the seed shooter from before. When all those were gone, he tapped into his own magic, already depleted and in need of replenishment with rest and more magic. When there was nothing of him left to spend, he fell to his knees and let the dark void where the magic was kept take him.

Chapter 16

Yin

Yin was running away again. She watched her island shrink back into the horizon behind their boat, both fascinated and dismayed by her sudden departure. She couldn't help feeling like she'd left too soon, that she'd left pieces of her behind that she hadn't meant to leave.

Kalem slept on the floor of the boat next to her, his veins a deep shade of indigo. The man named Dangal stood at the helm at the back of the boat, and up front was the scar-faced man rowing and pulling them further and further away from the island. Dian flitted about excitedly, the air around her practically buzzing with her energy.

Yin hugged her knees to her chest, making herself look as small as she felt, dwarfed by the expanse of the ocean that seemed to meld with the sky in the distance. She'd left her island. The fact of it finally dawned on her like the incoming night-time air.

She'd done it before she even knew she was, following the scarred man carrying Kalem on his back and the man who was her father, her real father. Her mind and body had been separate from each other, each trying to survive after she'd lost control.

She resisted the urge to stare at Dangal. It still felt unreal to her that that man was her father, a man who was essentially a stranger to her. All her life, it had only been her, her mother, and her adopted father. She hadn't known any other family, and now this. Now, she was suddenly the daughter of a man who seemed . . . important.

And she had almost killed him along with countless people because she had lost control.

She didn't even know she had power like that, waiting to be tapped into, waiting for the first crack in the dam. Of all things, it was her fury that had broken her, rage over being blamed for her father's death, rage over being told that her love should make her overlook the abuse she had faced rage over being left lost and alone by the one man she'd let into her walls. She knew now that it was anger that had kept her on that island. Some part of her, a part she kept in the darkest depths of her soul, told her that the Dayo of Masalanta deserved what they got for using her. That the reason she had stayed was because she couldn't bear leaving the people who had wronged her unpunished, and not because she had been waiting for men to save her like she had made herself believe.

It was a shocking, humbling feeling, accepting that she was a bad person. Bad compared to the healer who had used every drop of magic in his system to heal those she had almost killed.

The irony was, she rescued the men who were supposed to rescue her. Her gaze subtly shifted from Dangal to Kalem, who was sleeping like the dead on the floor with Panday, who was up front rowing, watching over him, a hound about to pounce.

'I'd want to stay on that island paradise, too, if I were you, princess,' Panday said. 'Your father ain't doing you no favours taking you away from all that.'

She raised her eyes to look at him, his arms straining with the rise and fall of the oars against the water.

She scoffed. 'You don't know what's good for me.'

He sneered. Panday cut a fine figure in his grey tunic and black trousers. Like Kalem, he hid his tattoos, but Yin was sure he didn't hide his ink for the same reasons. Panday felt solid and malleable at the same time, like dirt shifting from cracked stone to wet loam depending on what the day called for, what a person needed to see in him. He was in a constantly affable mood, marred only by the perpetually squinting right eye where a burn scar deformed his face. While his face showed Yin a man who was quick to smile, a deeper look into his eyes, scarred and unscarred, revealed a threat and warning alike. He would kill for the people he loved, and to him, she was a threat.

'Why do you hide your tattoos?' Yin asked, hoping to establish some measure of trust. 'Don't you Kayuman have a saying about that?'

He nodded. '*Nagbabalatkayo ang nagtatago ng balat,*' he said, the thick southern accent dissipating to give way to the rhythm and tone of the elder's tongue. 'Never trust a man who hides his skin.' He grinned, narrowing his eyes at Yin. 'Why? Want proof that you can trust us?' he said slyly, his thick southern accent back.

'Your tattoos mean nothing to me. I am not Kayuman,' she said absently and knew it was true. Neither was she Kayuman nor was she Dayo. She was something else altogether.

'Careful, princess, you'll break your dear father's heart if he hears you saying that,' Panday said, tipping his chin toward the man who was watching them from where he stood at the helm. Dangal raised an eyebrow at him and then paused when he saw Yin stealing glances at him.

She looked away from Dangal. She resisted looking at the man again as if that would deny the truth of who he was.

'You still don't believe that he's your father,' Panday said, more an observation than a question.

'I don't know that man,' Yin said. 'I've only known one father, and he sacrificed everything to keep me safe.'

She glanced at Panday, checking to see how he would react to that outburst or maybe to see if she'd finally said something that could awaken the protective fury hidden in his eyes. Instead, he tilted his head while studying her face, pursing his lips as if trying to solve a puzzle. Then, he laughed out loud, the sound extending outward over the water's surface. Dangal scowled at Panday. Kalem stirred in his sleep.

'Do you find my life funny?' Yin asked, more confused than offended by the offhand way he'd mocked her outburst, looking out again over the horizon at a black spot in the sky.

'No, not you, but you're part of the joke,' he answered between fits of laughter. 'The Skygods sure do have a cruel sense of humour.'

'What?' she practically screeched, the confusion now turning into annoyance.

'You know, explaining a joke ruins it,' Panday said.

Yin folded her arms over her chest and frowned at him. 'It's not a joke if I don't understand it.'

He rolled his eyes and finally offered her an explanation. 'Your father is arguably one of the most famous men in the country. And you, his daughter, don't even know who he is.'

'That's not a joke. That's irony.'

'Irony *is* a cruel joke, but it's a joke nonetheless.'

'It wasn't funny.' She met his gaze, focusing on the squinted eye before forcing herself to look at him whole. 'Well?'

'Well what?'

'Aren't you going to tell me who he is?'

'Nope. Better you find out straight from the horse's mouth . . .' Panday said, trailing off and stopping the boat suddenly, tipping his head upwards as if to smell the air and then glancing at Dangal, who nodded back in answer. 'Princess, I need you to stay close to Kalem,' Panday said, digging in his pouch for two vials of the thick, glowing, iridescent white liquid and downing the contents of one. He handed her the other, saying, 'Make him drink this. Hopefully, it will wake him up.'

'What's happening?' Yin said, pocketing the vial, picking up Kalem's arm and draping it over her shoulder.

'Black clouds like storm clouds in the sky, but the air doesn't smell like rain,' Panday said, going back to the oars and redoubling his efforts this time, his entire body lifting off the bench with every row. 'Princess, back of the boat! Now!'

Yin dragged Kalem's still sleeping form away from the prow and gingerly leaned him against the side of the boat. She pulled out the vial, tipped his chin up, and poured the contents into his mouth. He choked but swallowed it all.

She looked up to see what had alarmed Panday and Dangal. A dark cloud surrounded the front of the boat.

Panday's veins lit green, the scent of sour guavas and magic thick in the air, green, glittering mist emanating from him and then disappearing where the light hit it. She turned her gaze up at the sky and gasped. A big dark cloud continued forming over the boat, casting the vessel in its shadow, fingers of the smoke trailing and curling toward their boat, which was barely evading it even with Panday straining at the oars.

Dangal's green-lit veins faded, which left stains under his skin. He yelled at Panday, 'Forget the illusion, Pan—' He was cut off as the first fingers of the shadow cloud touched the deck, spreading out over the surface in waves of smoke wafting with the subtle scent of life beginning to bloom from the decay.

Yin called his name, 'Lutyo!' just as the Shadow began to take his form. He stared at her blankly, his eyes pure black orbs in their sockets, as if trying to place her in his memories. His arms were raised slightly at his sides, smoke billowing from his hands and the cloak floating behind him, part cloud, part corporeal fabric.

'Lutyo,' she said, gentler this time, tears stinging the corners of her eyes.

He tilted his head at the sound of his name passing her lips. A spark of recognition lit up his eyes just as quickly as it left. His arms lowered momentarily, the shadows and decay faltered slightly.

'Mayin!' Dangal screamed, placing himself between her and Lutyo on the *sampan*. Panday abandoned the oars, his veins lighting up red this time, kris swords with ridged blades in each hand. He stood on one side of the boat to defend it. Dangal took the other side, veins lit red, and slashed his own blade downward at Lutyo, rocking the boat in the process, ocean water slapping the sides.

Lutyo snapped at attention, morphing his body back to smoke and shadow, swirling and curling with the swinging blades.

'Stop!' Yin screamed, standing up to join the fray, Dangal's blade slashing through Lutyo's body, the metal dragging out smoke, disintegrating as it did. Panday followed up with an upward and downward swing of his blades next to Dangal, one foot on the side of the boat, rocking it with every movement, only for one of his blades to slip through the black mist. He let go of the hilt just as the smoke disintegrated his blade from within, his own fingers barely missing the dark cloud of death. He unsheathed another blade.

Dangal pushed Yin back behind him, ordering her to stay away from the heat of the battle.

Panday continued to slice at the Shadow, hoping to reach flesh and bone within and finding nothing but smoke that broke into tendrils and fingers and odd clouds of smoke over the deck. His glowing red veins illuminated the smoke, like red lightning in a storm cloud. He was a tempest of iron and steel, but his blades were no match against the Shadow, who destroyed every blade he wielded until he's used all of them up.

Dangal grabbed Yin by both shoulders. 'I will not lose you again, Mayin,' he said, pushing her back, sending her sprawling down next to Kalem. She stopped herself mid-fall when she saw the Shadow extending his fingers of smoke pointed at Dangal, who staggered back, barely avoiding the smoke touching his skin.

'Stop, Lutyo!' she screamed just in time, summoning the winds to follow the shadow cloud as it drifted upward and pushing her father away from Lutyo.

The winds shot her upward, fast like the crack of a whip, and she crashed into the shadow cloud that broke apart upon coming in contact with her.

She swooped through the smoke, sending gusts of wind to cushion Dangal's fall on the boat. She didn't see if her father landed safely, as the dark cloud enveloped her completely. Dian flitted at the edge of her vision with all the nervous energy of an animal trapped in a cage. The shadows wrapped around her like a cloak, light piercing through gaps, only to be shut out again, only to shroud Yin back into the shadows.

'Lutyo?' she called, feeling the black magic trying to take hers straight from her glowing, yellow veins.

'My orders were to kill his son and his bastard,' Lutyo murmured over and over, his voice echoing within his cloud, his voice layered with someone else's, something more sinister.

Yin swam through the Shadow, her winds barely fending off the decay trying to take her in its grip, her glowing yellow veins illuminating only as far as her own hand could reach. Her fingers brushed at the edge of a tangible cloak, and she pulled herself to it, dragging her body forward and crashing hard into Lutyo, who caught her by her shoulders. His blank face stared at her.

Hands glowing from the magic in her veins, Yin placed both palms on his cheeks, ice cold and stiff and veins stained black. 'Lutyo, it's me,' she said, tears falling down her cheeks now. 'Snap out of it,' a plea that fell on deaf ears.

A sharp force jerked at her skin, stirring the magic where her hands had touched his cheek, black at odds with yellow, sending a burning sensations through her, stoking a fire that burned her from inside-out. She whimpered as the fire grew, the black waging war in her body, one that she knew somehow that neither could win, not when he couldn't reestablish the connection with her. Still, there was pain.

'Lutyo, fight it,' she said between sobs and cries of pain. 'Fight *him*. Please . . .'

Lutyo blinked, eyes drifting between obsidian orbs and human eyes, his black, glowing veins blinking in the dark. Yin took that as an opening, an opportunity to end their war, and pushed the yellow through him, the scent of nectarine mangoes pushing back the decay. 'Fight, Lutyo!' she screamed, and with it, she shoved every bit of the yellow she could pull from within her into his body, wrapping her arms around him and pressing him against her body. 'Fight!' she screamed, the winds rising around her, catching bits of the dark cloud that hadn't returned to its body in its whirlwind. 'Lutyo!'

She felt Lutyo's hands on her back, his face burying into the crook of her neck, a sob coming from deep within. The winds stopped and the shadows took over again, the push and pull of two equal gods stuck in an endless cycle. Lutyo's hands clawed at her back, his face bit into her neck, his sob a grunt and growl. Yin struggled to push him away from her, but he held on, the Lutyo she knew absent, the Shadow that took his place menacing and hungry.

And she thought, she could keep pushing back, maintain the stalemate, keep each other alive but continue to harm each other in every imaginable way equal gods could. She looked into Lutyo's eyes, full obsidian orbs again. This wasn't the Lutyo she knew. He wasn't the man she deeply cared for. She would have given him everything if he asked so long as he never left her alone again, so long as he kept finding her when she lost herself. She cared deeply for him, maybe even loved him, and she knew that Lutyo, *her* Lutyo, felt just the same for her.

So, to save him, to stop herself from hurting him further, she let go, she let the black take her veins, she let him fill her with his magic the way water would fill the body. So much of him that she drowned. She loved him enough to let go of him. The yellow faded, the black roared. At the edges of her vision, the black raven overpowered the golden maya, but through the haze she saw a third light. Indigo. A turtle.

She fell out of the sky and went hurtling downward, diving so deeply and powerfully into the ocean that her body slammed against the hard seafloor, blood spreading outward, mixing with the dark depths of the ocean flowing around her like the comforting arms of a lover.

'Yin, stay with me. Don't let go,' a voice called to her, clung to her as she sank.

Her eyes drooped, heavy from the invisible aches, but she fought to stay awake, fought to move her limbs to swim upwards before the last of her breath was taken out of her own lungs. Her skin still carried the subtle hints of glowing yellow, the light blinking in the dark, illuminating the place she had landed.

She gasped out the last of the air in her at the sight: a skeletal tree, much like the Kanlungan, its trunk hollow, its branches like bony fingers reaching up to the ocean surface. Around it were domed stone and glossy metal houses unlike anything she'd ever seen before. It was a village, but it was empty, abandoned. Not even the merfolk went there, much less lived there, and she saw many of them just hovering around the perimeter of the village, watching her with wary eyes.

As her eyes closed, the world shrunk back around her, too tired to realize that she was floating deeper, too stunned, too scared to even try to run away.

Chapter 17

Kalem

Kalem prayed to his god in the void, though he did not know what it was that he was praying for, if it was to wake up and live another day, to wake up in a past life, or not to wake up at all. The gods, he'd come to learn, were just as prone to forgetfulness as he was.

'I almost lost myself,' the Earth God said, swimming with Kalem in the void, his indigo mist a smattering of stars across the darkness.

'What happened?' Kalem asked.

'I don't know, but I felt like rain falling on the ocean.' He hesitated to continue, the way a man would stop in the middle of the road after realizing that he had gone the wrong way.

Suddenly, the events that had led Kalem to this void came flooding back like a river overflowing. Panday's horrified face. Dangal's unmoving body. Berdugo Dayo bodies piled on the ground. The shadow raven, the turtle, and the maya. The push and pull of wind and earth. And then her, watching him fearful and confused.

'*Are we dead?*' Kalem said, turning inward to see that he had no body here, only the suggestion of it in the void. '*Am I dead? Is this the Skyworld?*'

'**This is not Skyworld, that much I know.**'

And though he was afraid to go back, Kalem asked, '*How do I go back?*'

'**You just need to wake up.**'

* * *

He gasped for air. He was lying on the floor of a boat rocking violently, rolling him this way and that. He pushed a palm against the floor and rolled over, groaning in pain and exhaustion, until, finally, he could steady himself on all fours, even as he continued to gasp for breath. Instinctively reached within himself for the magic to heal the aches he did not realize he had until now. His veins glowed indigo, the Earth God swam at the edges of his vision.

The boat swerved hard to the side, sending him sprawling back down hard on the floor. He sat up, holding onto his head, trying not to focus on his narrowing, darkening vision. He snapped to attention at the sound of Dangal yelling 'Mayin!' and he scrambled to his feet, swaying with the rocking boat as he got up on all fours just in time to see Dangal crashing into the water and Yin getting sucked into the dark cloud—the shadow assassin—hovering over their boat. Panday ran to the side, body hanging over the railing, trying to pull Dangal back onboard. Kalem joined him and pulled Dangal fully from the ocean.

'Mayin!' Dangal said, coughing out seawater on the deck and grabbing at Kalem's arm, the veins still glowing indigo.

Panday shook his head, switching glances from him to Dangal to the dark cloud above where Yin's body, glowing from her yellow veins, flitted in and out of vision as the Shadow enveloped her.

Kalem's veins lit red, and as he prepared to jump, Panday grabbed his arm.

'Don't be an idiot, Kalem!' Panday said.

'She saved us!' he said as if that was enough of an explanation and jumped on magically-charged legs, the boat sinking a few inches in the ocean, and switched to violet to whip his stretched-out arms upward, just enough to touch the cloud, and then switched to orange to reduce his mass, the force of the recoil shooting him, with the force of a slingshot, into the cloud.

The Shadow sucked him in immediately, and he floated idly within the dark mass, which curled around him, feeding into his fading orange veins, feeding into his magic. He felt it, going through his magic reserves, the perpetual magic of death and healing fighting an endless battle within him. He cut off the magic, and the black recoiled from him.

There were uncontrollable winds within the mass, and they threw his body around the way a cyclone toyed with debris. He recognized these winds, this desperation for freedom within the darkness, and it renewed him the way the Morningstar renewed itself with every coming dawn. Kalem kept himself upright, remembering Yin's voice telling him to dance with the winds, to ride them, to trust her, and so he did. He closed his eyes and listened to the rhythm of the winds, memorizing, imbibing so that he may know the steps to this new dance. The mountain listening to the winds.

He heard her voice then. *'Lutyo, it's me. Snap out of it. Lutyo, fight it. Fight him. Please . . .'*

It was layered in another voice, both otherworldly and mundane, like two voices in one at odds with each other. *'My orders were to kill his son and his bastard. Kill the son. Kill his bastard.'*

'You're the Shadow that killed my father,' Kalem said, feeling the same energy of death that he'd clashed with that fateful, dreadful day.

'I've killed thousands.'

'And you will kill more.'

A sharp piercing scream echoed within, and Kalem moved faster, this way and that, groping in the dark for something, anything, her.

'Yin!' he called out.

'This does not concern you, turtle,' the otherworldly voice said, the sensation of its words prickling his back, sending chills under his skin. The same voice spoke with it, against it, *'Take her. Take Yin. Save her from me.'*

For a moment the shadows pulled back and revealed Yin, her body glowing golden from her veins and holding tight onto the shape of a man, shifting from shadow to flesh where yellow fed it.

Kalem shot forward, lighting indigo, not common indigo, but indigo of noble magic, the magic of his god. The turtle shot ahead of him toward the raven and the maya, breaking the stalemate.

He grabbed Yin by the waist and wove his magic with her, pushing back the Shadow, prying off his hold over her, two gods against one.

Surprised by the sudden surge assaulting the shadow, Yin pulled back her magic and let go, sending them both hurtling out of the mass and splashing into the ocean and warding the Shadow long enough for it to escape from their combined magic.

'Yin, stay with me. Don't let go,' Kalem said to her, his voice muffled by the water. A sharp force pulled him back, forcing him to let go of her. 'No!' he screamed, bubbles of air spraying out of his mouth and nose.

The force pulled him upwards to the surface and threw him onto the deck of the boat, where he saw Panday and Dangal on their knees in front of two Asinari soldiers with grey and green scales pointing spears at their backs.

'Mayin?' Dangal demanded.

Kalem scrambled back up to his feet, ready to dive right back into the water just when a tall Asinari with indigo scales and silver seaweed hair rose from the water, carrying Yin's unconscious body in her arms.

'It seems it's not me who confuses magic with theology, Datu Laya,' Najima said as her tail morphed into legs on the deck, her long, silver-patterned halter and bahag dress replaced with black. 'I didn't know we have gods in our midst.'

Interlude 2

Dakila

All of Dakila's life, he had been trying to prove himself to his father, that he wasn't weak, that he was worthy of his praise, that he was worthy of love. In the decade since he'd left Maylakanon, he'd managed to convince himself that he didn't need his father's approval anymore. He was a decorated soldier, no longer the boy that flinched under his hand. He'd earned his titles and rank one accomplished mission at a time. But, surprisingly, it was during these moments of victories that he had craved his father's approval most, albeit begrudgingly. It was only when he failed did he bitterly shun his father's expectations.

And so, standing here outside the King's Castel estate, he asked himself what he was trying to prove, what he was seeking the petty, vindictive man's approval for this time.

He'd avoided seeing his father in any capacity outside of his work. He didn't want to be called weak again, didn't want to hear his father and ruler call him a failure, a hoax, a stain on his otherwise sterling legacy. The queen's bastard. He never let Dakila forget, though the rest of the country had.

Maylakanon Estate was a miniature version of his childhood home and his house's seat of power, Maylakanon, though that didn't mean that the estate was small in itself. It was the tallest and biggest structure on the largest plot of land owned by a single man in Castel. The palace stood on a hill surrounded by obelisks tipped with bronze statues of past kings over cascading stone platforms. There were three main houses, the queen's chambers to the east, the King's to the west, and the main house, which had the throne room and gathering hall in the centre. Their red tiled roofs were tipped with gold towers cascading down to the overhanging pagodas stretching like golden arms to the side, casting shadows over stone walls carved with bas relief of the Maragtas kings' history—their house's family history.

Dakila walked back down the path leading to a grand stairway, feeling a sudden spike of terror at having to face his father again without the mask of a soldier, just as a son born to the wrong father. He stopped at the sight of the imperious walls to the south. It was a grey and brown ridged stone wall that enclosed the entire property, separating it from the Datus' Village, the Congressional offices, and the rest of the city. To the north were the docks for the King's private fleet. One Dalaket ship was always ready to cross Lakan's Crossing, the strait between Castel and the mainland Maylakanon, and fly directly to the King's palace.

A flash of memory sparked in his mind. His mother crying and screaming about murder. His father looming over her, a hand raised and ready to strike again. Dakila's heart pounding, his cheeks stained with tears, his trousers wet with piss. He was afraid and he felt so small standing before his father, but it was the first time he'd stood up to his father, the way Dangal stood up to him. He would not forget.

He let his feet carry him forward, past the main house and obelisks of kings and datus and toward the King's chambers to the west. He stopped at the foot of the stairs leading up to the double doors of the King's chambers. A Dayo man in a black cloak stood there, idly leaning on the doorframe, tossing up and down in his gloved hand a ripe mango and watching it go up and down the air.

'I'd turn back if I were you,' the cloaked man said without looking down at him from the top of the stairs and began his descent.

'You're Death's Shadow,' Dakila's hand went immediately to the hilt of his sword. 'The Bleeding Banners, House Talim, House Payapa, those were all your doing.'

Dakila saw the shadow of a grimace on his face, the same way a man wrongfully convicted would grimace at being sentenced to death for a crime he did not commit.

He gently placed the mango on a protruding rock on the bas relief wall and slowly descended the steps. 'My commands were to execute any threat to my father and his power.' He took his gloves off and cast them aside.

'Your father?' Dakila started at the revelation. 'You're one of his bastards?'

'I am the *only* bastard left,' the Shadow said. 'And you are his adulterous queen's bastard.'

'After what you'd done, the massacres you've committed, between the two of us, you're the bigger threat.' Dakila stepped back just as the cloaked man stepped off the stairs. 'You'll never find Dangal.' He sensed death permeating from the Shadow's skin and the perpetual scent of blood that hung about him like his cloak. The cloaked man looked younger than him, but he could sense that he was way older through the weariness in his eyes.

The Shadow scoffed. They circled each other, prowling slowly, two tigers in an arena waiting for an opportunity to pounce. The veins on the Shadow's hands glowed black and he launched at Dakila, hands reaching out, and clawed at him, seeking to tear his skin off. Dakila barely evaded the man's attack, drew his blade to him ward off, as his legs seemed to turn to shadows of clouds under him in a blink of an eye. 'I found her months ago. I know where the Dayo princess is.'

A gasp escaped Dakila, and startled, he raised his sword before him, waiting for that stretched out second that it took the Shadow to approach him, waiting for an opening to strike, fast and true. The Shadow hung before him, and he launched the blade forward, straight through the heart, but instead of piercing flesh, he pierced smoke, the overspent force throwing him off balance. The tips of his fingers that touched the Shadow sizzled with pain and he let go of the blade just in time before the pain shot up his arm. The blade disintegrated. He looked up at the Shadow's face or at least at the spot where the smoke had formed the shape of a face, grinning menacingly.

'You think iron would kill me?' he said, sending fingers of smoke toward Dakila, threatening to come closer at the Shadow's will. Dakila stayed still, sweat beading his brow. 'In a different life, maybe it would have been Dangal who'd take the Death God's blade.' The corner of his lips lifted up in a sinister one-sided smile. 'Or maybe even you, and I'd get to be raised as a trueborn prince.' The shadow assassin's body reformed into the shape of a man, the smoke disengaging from flesh and bone to reveal the cloaked man within. 'Do you know what it does to you? The wanton murder of innocents against your will?' He said the last part so softly that it seemed to have pulled him away from reality and into the inner reaches of his memories. 'To be treated like a weapon and not a person? It chips away at your soul little by little until nothing is left.'

'I've never understood why Father favoured you over me. I bear the magic of a seedgod. I am a weapon, the King's sword, and you offer him nothing but vengeance on a dead woman.' Fingers of smoke drifted toward Dakila, who watched it warily, but stood unmoving from his spot, as it was enough of a bluff to stave off the Shadow. 'You're not even his trueborn son, and he raised you with the privileges of a trueborn prince. While I languish as his slave.' The tip of the smoke stopped in front of Dakila's face, taunting him, daring him to make any drastic movements. 'It should be you in my place.' The smoke surged forward, and Dakila reacted just in time to narrowly avoid touching it. 'It should have been you carrying out his darkest deeds.' He stepped back and back and back as the tendrils of smoke continued its assault. 'It should have been you who isn't free.'

The blade of a rope dart shot scraped the side of the Shadow's neck, still human, still made of flesh.

Dakila drew away from the Shadow's reach as he stumbled backwards, his body transforming back from smoke and shadow to flesh and bone. Surprise showed on the Shadow's face as he instinctively pressed a bare hand to his neck but felt nothing there but his own grazed skin, a drop of blood drawing a line down his pale, black-veined neck.

The knife was pulled back to its owner. Maralita stood there, blade raised and ready to shoot forward again, eyes piercing and dangerous. 'Maralita?' Dakila asked.

He threw the blade forward, forcing Dakila to close his eyes, unsure how to respond to his lover trying to kill him, but when no blade pierced his skin, his eyes shot open just as the Shadow said, 'This won't kill me, but nice try.' The Shadow turned to the side, a black-veined hand pressing against the side of his neck, the other hand holding the rope tied to the blade. The rope disintegrated under his hand in a scatter of ash and dust in the winds, and the blade fell at his feet. He stood still and raised both arms to the side as if in worship of the gods, his cloak billowing around him and transforming into shadow mists, spreading out.

Maralita took Dakila by the arm and dragged him away from the spreading shadows, the cloaked man's shape in smoke merely standing there. Soldiers that had begun to gather around them hesitated to approach. A putrid, rotten smell wafted from the smoke, stretching outward, fingers of black mist attempting to take hold of the closest living flesh. This was the Shadow that had killed the most powerful people in the country. What good would their mundane weapons do against the God of Death? What good would Dakila's common seedmagic do against a god on a mission?

But the Shadow was still human, Dakila knew. The drop of blood from his neck was still red, it was still flesh that the blade cut open before it disappeared into its smoke form, it was still anguish, so very human and so very flawed, that marred the man's pale face.

Dakila pulled away from Maralita's grip and faced the Shadow. The Shadow and him, they were the same, two sons used and abused in ways that broke them close to destruction, all to please a man who saw them as tools of his vengeance rather than as the sons he had raised.

'You don't have to do this!' Dakila pleaded, voice too loud as if his volume would matter in convincing the Shadow of his truth. The Shadow stilled for a second. 'We're the same, you and I. We're not slaves.'

'You mistake me for you,' the Shadow hissed. 'I'm his trueborn son, but I'm a slave. You're his wife's bastard, but you were raised a prince.'

'Everyone has a choice,' Dakila said simply. The shadows stopped flowing forward, frozen mid-air, seeming to reform back to the shape of the man.

'My orders were to kill any threat to my master's life,' the Shadow said, voice low, voice weak, voice unconvincing.

'I am not a threat to our father's life. And neither are you,' Dakila said. The shadows flowed back into the man. 'The only threat to life here is him.'

The Shadow looked up, body back to flesh and bone again, staring suspiciously at Dakila, searching, asking for permission, for direction, for any word that may give him leave. But the look on Dakila's face must have set him off, for he transformed back into a cloud of smoke that rushed through the closed doors of the King's chambers, forcing it open as its metal parts rusted and its wood panels and stone bas relief withered, like the Shadow had been summoned to some place far away.

Dakila chased after the Shadow up the stairs, Maralita trailing behind, picking up his blade on the way. They didn't stop till Dakila was outside his father's chambers where two guards slumped on the sides of the door, life drained away

from them. Gritting his teeth, Dakila found the room empty
save for the bed by the window and the frail man lying there
looking barely alive.

The tip of a blade touched Dakila's neck from behind.

'What are you planning to do?' Maralita asked.

Dakila turned around to look at his lover's face, looking
hardened and betrayed. Had he really lost Maralita so easily?
Was duty more important to him than Dakila? Was everything
he shared with Maralita, was any of it real?

Love is weakness, his father said. Love ruined his mother
and pushed his brother to shun his duty. Was duty really
nothing without love?

'Nothing,' he answered, the word barely passing his lips
as a whisper.

'I don't believe you.'

Dakila gritted his teeth. 'There's nothing I can do.
You heard that Shadow. I'm nobody! I'm not even his
trueborn son!'

They stared at each other, their eyes prying at walls that
they'd pulled down for each other, the rubble at their feet, the air
clear and open and free between them. It was Maralita's hands
that trembled first, and he gritted his teeth as his face switched
from fury to betrayal to resignation to confusion, a painful
vicious cycle that sent Dakila spiralling into his own mind. He
knew that this would happen. He knew that the moment he let
this man in, he would open himself up to pain and betrayal.

But he loved this man, loved him like he had never
loved before.

This choice between duty and love, it was inevitable, but
Dakila knew then as he looked into Maralita's eyes that he
had made his decision long before this. He raised his chin

and closed his eyes, presenting himself to Maralita, all of him, body, mind, heart, and soul. He'd given him all of it the fateful moment he met this beautiful man.

'You're not a nobody,' Maralita said suddenly, putting down the blade. 'You're Dakila.'

Dakila's eyes shot open, knees almost buckling under him, the weight in his chest gone, the breath he was holding free, and he fell into Maralita's arms, crying into the crook of his neck. 'I thought I lost you.'

'I'm loyal to my country,' Maralita said, wrapping his own arms around Dakila. '*Ikaw ang aking bayan.*' He looked at Dakila's face and kissed him, deeply, honestly, fearlessly. 'Dakila, *you* are my country.' He wiped the tears on Dakila's face with the heel of his palm. The sound of more soldiers coming from their guard room down the hall echoed in the corridor. 'Promise me, no more secrets?'

'I'll tell you everything right now.'

'No, now you must face your father.'

ACT THREE

Chapter 18

Yin

A gilded cage was a cage nonetheless.

Yin was beginning to think that the seedgods must be toying with her life, throwing her from one cage to another, one small life after another, just for the heck of it.

Miya Dala was the Asinari's seat of power in the Maylaya ocean, just south of Castel and east of Masalanta, or so Kalem explained as they were led to their rooms. It was a palace, grander than any she has ever seen, granted the only gilded mansion she had ever known was the white mansion on Masalanta. She barely remembered Castel from her childhood.

Above the surface of the ocean, Miya Dala was an unassuming stone castle with minarets and spires dwarfed under the expanse of the sky that melted into waters in the horizon, but below the surface, the castle was a mountain of stone towers and buildings and pathways and pillars carved with iridescent and intricate bas reliefs and geometric patterns that seemed to glow where the light pierced through the water. The sprawling courtyard around it on the seafloor was a garden of colourful corals and marine life flitting about the castle the way rodents and tiny woodland creatures would in her sanctuary on Masalanta.

It was a beautiful palace for sure, irresistible to look at and maybe touch—save for Merfolk guards swimming around its perimeter above and underwater, holding tridents and spears, and looking menacingly at anyone and anything that might swim close to it.

Yin sat with her knees pressed up to her chest on the balcony of one the towers above the ocean, trying to make herself small, unassuming, unthreatening. An Asinari guard with violet and indigo scales stood at the door of her room, another swam in the water beyond the balcony.

Dian flew from the edge of her vision to hover in front of her face. *'When we left the island, I thought we'd go very far. We're barely over a couple of days away from it.'*

'There is no pleasing you, Dian,' she said, resting her chin on her knees, watching the water splash on the sides of the balcony below. *'Besides it's not like I could just get up and go.'* She gestured at the Asinari soldiers stalking beyond her balcony.

'Actually . . .'

'Shut it,' Yin said, knowing what he was about to say. *'I don't have anywhere else to go.'* And even if she did, it didn't feel right after what she'd done—twice—to Lutyo, who had asked her to run away with him.

'It's not so bad here, I guess.'

Yin raised an eyebrow at the bird as it perched on the balcony railing so that she was looking up at it, the morningstarlight piercing through it body. *'Are you sure you're all right?'*

'I am.'

'Why does it hurt when I touch Lutyo but not Kalem?'

'I assume it's because Sitan is of a different breed of god. I was born to be wonderful, a creature of growth and birth, and he was born to be a menace, a creature of death and decay.'

Frowning, she narrowed her eyes at Dian. *'You're making that up.'*

'How should I know? I don't even know where I came from or why I came here.' Dian swooped down to sit on her head, making a nest out of her hair, which did not move under its incorporeal form, but she felt its magic shift hers. **'Maybe like calls to like and opposites destroy each other.'**

She tilted her head up to look at the bird, who did not move from its comfortable spot. *'So gods of opposing magic negate each other, but gods of similar powers enhance?'*

'We're speculating. Ask the Kayuman. He seems to know this stuff.'

'I should ask him.'

She felt his magic shiver close to her own. *'But you won't?'*

'I'm not sure I trust him.'

'He saved you.'

'He did.' But *at what cost?* she added in her head. Yin leaned back, propping herself up with her arms, draping her legs off the side of the balcony so her toes were touching the water and allowing more of the sun to touch her skin and warm her. The heat at this time of day rarely bothered her. Had it been only six months ago when she wanted the Morningstar to burn her skin, hoping the beautiful boy noticed her? No matter how long she stayed under the sun, no matter how red

her skin becomes, it returned stubbornly to its pale shade as if it was correcting a wrong she did to herself.

Perhaps that was the problem. She was forcing herself to be anything but herself. She was born to a Dayo mother and a Kayuman father. She had been raised a slave; she had been told that she had a much more impressive heritage. She could fly, but she had told herself that she should not, that she should keep her feet firmly planted on the ground.

Now, that was all in the past. That part of her life was over. The island a distant dot memory against the infinite horizon. A new chapter had begun. Where would she go now?

She decided it didn't matter. She didn't care anymore where she belonged. She'd carve out a place for herself in the world if she had to. She was herself. That was what mattered.

She just thought she'd have Lutyo with her here when she did. He always did accept her as she was.

'Mayin?' a voice, gruff and clear at the same time, called her from the door.

She looked behind her and saw Dangal—her father—already making his way to the balcony.

She sat up straight when he took a seat next to her. She didn't know how to address him nor how she should act around him. This man was a stranger to her, though his blood ran through her veins. He looked at her squarely in the face, and she squirmed where she sat under his piercing gaze.

'How are you feeling?' Dangal asked. 'Are your . . . err accommodations to your liking?'

'I'm fine. I've never had a room all to myself, much less a room as grand as this one,' she said, fiddling with her fingers and then stopping abruptly, realizing just how stupid and awkward she felt around this man. She faced him and eyed him fiercely, impatient to get this part over with. 'Are you really my father?'

He blinked, both eyebrows shooting upward, surprised by her directness. The surprise quickly dissipated as a relieved smile bloomed on his face. 'I *am* your father, Mayin.'

Yin didn't expect that the man would match her own directness and suddenly she felt embarrassed for antagonizing him before he could get a word in. She looked down at her hands on her lap, fingers fidgeting awkwardly, unsure how to go forward from here.

'But I know I cannot claim to be your father. Not when you've only just met me.'

'Where were you?' It sounded like an accusation to Yin's ears, but it wasn't. She knew it wasn't. How could she accuse a man she barely knew, a man who claimed to be her father, of a sin that she didn't know had been committed against her until now? 'All those years that Nanay and I were on the run with a stranger? Why was it not you?'

Even so, the look on Dangal's face showed how much the question stung him. He took a deep breath in, averting his gaze from the girl. 'A datu that I admired once told me that duty without love is an empty promise. Love without duty is vanity.'

'I thought I knew what he meant when I first joined the Congress as young bannerman barely even out of Kolehiyo for our house. I loved my people and I loved my job to the point of working myself to the bone to prove my love and my commitment to my duty.

'The Congress of Datus, it's like a game of *sungka*, it's mind games and power plays, small sacrifices in exchange of big victories. It's a battlefield, albeit one that's fought with words as weapons and whispers in the shadows and veiled threats in the light of day.'

Yin could tell that he was oversimplifying what he had actually done. She'd overheard some of his conversations with Kalem about their new roles in Kayumalon's government, about Dangal's manoeuvres that had irked the King or the unusual secret alliances that Kalem's father had made in his time. She didn't understand any of it, but the way they talked, the way they argued about decisions that affected lesser people like her—people whose lives depend on the decisions and actions made by men like Dangal and Kalem behind closed doors, it made her feel like just a small piece, a weakness, a mistake, an accidental crack in a game that had been going on way before she was born.

'Why find me now? No one knew I was your daughter. You could simply deny I existed, and you'd still be playing in Congress.'

He smiled at her, looked her straight in the eyes with so much affection that it made Yin's insides warm. 'Love.' He took her hand in his. She kept her gaze far from him, but she didn't let go. 'Love without duty is an empty promise. Duty without love is vanity.' With his free hand, he gently pressed his thumb on her chin and made her look up at him. 'Daughter, I could never deny you. You gave me a reason for all this, for all that I have done in Congress, for all that I do. Without you, I'd have no legacy for the life I live. No one would remember me. No one would know that I ever existed. Life would not matter. Our children, they are traces of ourselves we leave behind when we go to Skyworld, clean slates to build a world better than the one we leave behind.'

She tilted her head, refusing these unusual affectations of a father that she never got from the man who stood as hers for as long as she could remember. 'You don't regret ever having me? Even just a little bit? Even now that I tell you that I don't know you. Even now that I say that all I have of you is your blood in my veins and nothing else. Even when you could have been king before your time?'

'Never. When you know what you want, you become wary of the things that pull you away from it. I wanted a family, a quiet home filled with kids, and the love of a good woman. I wanted a life, my dear, a full life, and if I couldn't have it, I would make the world the kind of place where you can have it—or anything else really that you want—freely.'

He seemed so earnest, so honest that Yin couldn't help being swept up, along with her suspicion and aggression and defences, in the tide of his affections. Is this what it was like to have a father who loved her? Is this what it was like to have a parent who wanted to give her a life? Is this really who her father was?

She was tempted to fall for all of it. Very tempted.

'I don't think this is the first time I've known you,' she said by way of apology, pulling her hand away and taking her knees up to her chest to rest her chin on top of them. She watched the sky over the seemingly endless Kayumalon sea. 'It's the very first memory I have of my life. A cloaked man in a noisy tavern, smiling too much and seeming too happy to see me.'

A smile bloomed on his face, followed by a hearty laugh. 'I remember the night I first held you in my arms. My wife, your mother, she gave birth to you in hiding. I was in the middle of a debate in Congress—for some such stupid thing as Masalanta seeddust allocation. I ran out of Congress in the middle of a speech. I barely made it in time. I had thought that I wouldn't make it, but I did, somehow I did. Thank the gods that I did. Because when the nursemaid placed you in my arms, I cried and laughed so hard, I wasn't sure I was ever that happy until then.'

'Tell me our story,' she said softly, curious now of the love and life that created her.

And so he told her their story, of how he fell in love with Caritas, his brother's nursemaid the first time she came to Maylakanon. Of why it was forbidden for Kayuman—especially for Kayuman of noble rank—to love Dayo or have children with them and how he still married her in secret. He told her about the day Caritas told him the news of her pregnancy and the twin panic and joy that had swept through him, about the day he sent them in hiding only to be found by his father again, about the man who was supposed to kill Yin and Caritas but didn't and who eventually spent the rest of his life protecting them from the King—and the sorry life that Dangal could have given them, about the day he found out that Yin was alive and Caritas had died before he could ever see her again.

He told her about the attack of Masalanta, an attack as much political as it was personal to his father. He told her about his misery when Caritas and Yin just disappeared as if into thin air and him turning a new leaf when he finally accepted that he could never have his family back. He dedicated his life in court to weakening the King's power, to making the country truly egalitarian. And he dropped it all when he found out that Yin was alive.

When he was done, a weight seemed to have lifted from his shoulders, and he looked at Yin as if apologizing for the life she had to live because of his mistakes. And then, he asked her about her life, her love, the things she was happy she did and the things she regretted. It was a bizarre experience, getting to know, for the first time, someone who should have been a part of her entire life, but she was happy that someone wanted to know her, to acknowledge her existence, her life.

She had never really good at being lost and alone. Maybe because she never was lost and alone. He knew she existed; he knew she there. It baffled her how this strange man could just pour out his soul to her, like she was the only good thing in his life, small as she was. It was much easier to lose things the closer they were to the end, he told her when she asked him why.

'If I had been born in a different life, if I had made different choices, you would have had a better life, the life you deserved. You're a princess, for seeds' sake,' he said, patting her hand momentarily then pulling back abruptly as if it had stung him. 'I'm sorry. I'm sorry for . . . everything.'

She took his hand back and kept it warm between her palms. The act seemed to take him by surprise, and it showed on his face.

A smile, brighter, less ridden with guilt now, blazed on his lined face. 'You won't be lost and alone again, daughter.'

She didn't want to believe him, afraid that if she accepted this, she'd have given herself another reason to keep her feet firmly planted to the ground.

And yet . . . it was a comforting thought to have an anchor, a home, a mountain to go back to whenever she let herself fly. She leaned into his shoulder, and he wrapped a comforting arm around her.

They stayed like that, watching the ebb and flow of the ocean beyond them, and in that brief moment, the world felt bigger and smaller at the same time.

Suddenly, she felt bigger than herself, bigger than the life she had lived. And it made her uncomfortable. She knew who she was. It was hard to believe herself to be the most important person in the country because her father was the most important man—when to her, he was simply her father. And she was simply herself.

Chapter 19

Kalem

The rigours of the past week had definitely taken a toll on Kalem. There were some wounds that didn't quite heal, and he was thankful for the three days of idle rest in Miya Dala. He felt like an empty bucket dipped into an infinite wellspring. Although, he suspected that he wouldn't be allowed to leave even if he wanted to. The Asinari queen needed him to stay, and whatever her reason was, he was sure it wasn't good. Especially for Dangal.

He fell back into his usual habits, seeking the comfort of libraries and books and pursuing knowledge with the desperation of a dehydrated man in the middle of the ocean.

That *phenomenon* he'd shared with Yin, it was unusual, to say the least. It was certainly not in any of the books on germachemy he'd ever read before, and he'd scoured the archives for anything and everything he could find about arcane seedmagic. The most he gleaned was mythologies and—being the pragmatic, judicious man that he was—that wouldn't do. There were noble seeds and common seeds, virgin seeds and sullied seeds, theochemy and germachemy.

That has been the perceived, accepted science behind magic. There must be a logical explanation to these *seedgods*, a way to quantify and categorize them that would make germachemical sense.

Many of his own inquiries could be answered if he would have time alone with Yin to interrogate her about their shared experience and be allowed to make a comparative study of their individual magics—which, he noted, couldn't be any more different in kind but were perhaps similar in structure.

That would have been possible if she hadn't been avoiding him, but he could tell that she, too, had questions for him. He'd spotted her peeking through slits between doors in rooms where he stayed, stealing glances at him in the hallway, and prowling near his bedchamber and outside his window. The moment he would look at her, she'd run away before he could even say a word.

One day, he was sitting, rather comfortably, in Miya Dala's vast library in the second tallest tower—the tallest one was reserved for an artificial arboretum—of the partially submerged Asinar palace. The Asinari archives looked nothing like Alaala. For one, the walls were made of limestone with shelves carved into them so that the books were crooked no matter how they were placed there. The windows were mere jagged holes in the walls, letting in morningstarlight and the ocean breeze. *It must be a nightmare for these books when storms pass by.* The collection here paled in comparison even to his personal collection in Castel, but he couldn't fault the merfolk for not keeping books and scrolls here where the salt air and harsh morningstarlight would all but ruin the books.

A thick tome on mythological gods of creation was perched on his lap. He wasn't sure what he was looking for, but he suspected he pulled this one particular book out because it was an abridged version of *Tales from the Skyworld Realms*—the rare unabridged version of which he had stolen from the High Master's collection.

Halfway through *The Great Skyworld Race*—half the gods of Skyworld, including the seven gods of light, had just emerged from the second trial and were now racing towards the third and last trials—he looked up from his book and saw Yin standing there at the doorway of the library, hands clenched at her side, lips pursed, eyes practically throwing daggers at him. His breath hitched in his throat as he just stared at her in clothes normally worn by Kayuman noblewomen. Her father had asked Datu Najima Malik to lend his daughter a lady's maid, but already Yin had practically dismantled the appearance she was expected to have. Her braided hair fell loose. Her clothes, a halter top and skin-tight trousers under a bahag in her father's red and gold patterns, were dishevelled. And she'd already lost her shoes. Her appearance reminded him of that night she taught him to fly, to listen to the songs of the winds, and to dance with them. It was the one time he wasn't thinking of a hundred different things at once. Just the winds and her, floating freely like a cloud on a cool summer's night.

He couldn't help smiling at her looking so hopelessly out of place and yet somehow so irreproachable that her very presence demanded that she be accepted as she were. He closed the book on his lap, stood up and approached her but the look on her face gave him pause, gaze looking beyond his shoulder before the winds whisked her away. Whatever was behind him scared her away, and he looked over his shoulder to see what—who it was.

'Datu Laya, please join me in the library,' Datu Najima Malik said, walking past him at the doorway and letting herself into the library.

He looked up and down the hall for Yin, but she was already gone. Sometimes, he could have sworn she was a cat, so elusive when they know you want something from them and yet so tenacious when they wanted something for themselves.

Sighing, he slipped back into the library and found the queen of the merfolk looking over the book he had just put down. The air seemed to hang thick around the Datu, from the unusual slump of her shoulders to her hands held tightly in front of her to the grief colouring her eyes, dark grey now compared to the shining obsidians when Kalem had seen her at the Datus' Ball, holding onto her husband. This was a lover in grief, a wife who had lost the light of her life, a woman who had lost the love of her life. The late Datu Sedhaj Malik may have had the reputation of a naive, hearty, cheerful fool at court, but he doubtlessly loved his wife and she loved him even in death.

'Light reading, Ginoo?' she said, voice sombre, wistful, yet affecting a cheerful tone. She flipped the pages. 'My husband insisted that Miya Dala should have a library. "A house without books is a puddle that thinks it's an ocean," he would say.' She sneered, but not in a way that made her husband seem inconsequential. 'My silly husband put so much value on things that were so easily lost to the tides.' She placed the book on the nearest table and faced him, her silver scales glossy in the morningstarlight streaming through the windows. 'My husband believed in your father, Datu Laya. Now he is gone.'

'I . . . offer my . . . condolences,' Kalem said, uncertain what to say or what the woman wanted him to say. He'd lost his father the same day she had lost her husband. Did she blame him for her loss? Did she want sympathy?

She cast him a wry smile, walking over to the crooked shelves and running her hand along the spines of books, many of which were thick, deformed, and yellowing from damage. 'It is disheartening to be told that you're strange in your own home country, Datu Laya. Strangelords, the Kayuman call us. My husband believed in equality, saw that it was his duty to make our country fit for his children to live in.'

'As did my father, Datu Malik,' Kalem said, watching her take slow, careful strides around the room, following a well-worn path that only she seemed to know. 'You know my father's politics better than I do, but I know him. My father was a paragon of duty. His duty was to his conscience.'

'Oh, I don't question your father's sense of duty.' She stopped and turned to face him from across the room. 'I question yours.'

He couldn't stifle the grimace his face must have made, and he cursed himself in his head for allowing his emotions to get ahead of him. He hadn't even thought of what that implied. He was Datu now, the new ruler of his father's house and datuship, which meant that his father was well and truly gone. The cold fear became a wave of sorrow so deep and cutting that the queen of the merfolk must have sensed it from across the room.

'Your father, he spoke very fondly of you, Kalem,' she said.

He noted the casual way she invoked his name, like she was family herself, and perhaps that too was his father's doing.

'By that, I would be very surprised, Datu Malik. I am sure I have not given my father reason to speak with any hint of fondness about me. Especially not to his peers,' Kalem said, resisting the urge to bite the inside of his cheek. 'I have not been the perfect son to my father nor prince to my datu.'

'Such are the trappings of being a parent, I'm afraid. The inability to see flaws in our own offspring.' She made her way back to his side of the room, eyes scanning the shelves, this time through seafolk history, as if taking stock of the tomes in her mind. 'But none of the southern lords saw it as weakness, especially not me or my husband.'

'Then what did you see it as?'

'The seeds of duty,' she said simply as she took the seat he had occupied before she came.

Now he was standing before her like a supplicant before a king, and he couldn't help thinking that she had meant to do this, to put him in his place. He didn't speak. He didn't answer, didn't so much as hint at any sort of reaction except to pull up the sleeves off his forearms to show his tattoos and fold his arms across his chest. She didn't seem to notice the subtle gesture of a challenge, or if she did, she didn't care. Only the Kayuman cared about the ink on a person's skin.

'Tell me, Kalem, what has driven you in your tireless pursuit of knowledge?' she said, leaning luxuriously against one arm of the chair. He raised an eyebrow at her, understanding this now to be a test, or a drawing of a line, or simply an alpha reinforcing her territory. How would his father have answered such a question like this? What had driven him in fulfilling his duty as datu to his people?

Despite his better judgment, he played her game. 'My father—' he began to say, but stopped abruptly, knowing that his answer fell short of what the truth was.

Like his father, he had tried to sidestep the duty he was born into by pursuing other goals. His father wanted to pilot a flying Dalaket ship; Kalem wanted nothing more than to find the limits of magic.

It was true that he had begun to take interest in his scholarship because of his father but having found true contentment in studying, he knew that he wanted nothing more than to live the rest of his life pursuing knowledge. He was so enamoured by it that it was almost an obsession.

It was then that the sorrow turned into grief and guilt combined. He abandoned his father long before the Day of The Bleeding Banners. He forgot why he pursued knowledge in the first place.

'Love, Datu Malik,' he said reluctantly. This time, he didn't feel the need to bite the inside of his cheek. 'I simply loved it.'

'Do you see my point, Kalem? Why I doubt you so?'

'Perhaps you can educate me. What drives you to do as you do?'

'The same answer, Datu Laya,' she said, standing up to her full height, looming over him. 'Love, for my husband and our children and our children's children.'

'Surely, you can't be implying that I love my father any less than you love your children. Let's skip the subtleties, Datu Najima Malik. You want me to abdicate my title. Is that it?'

'Between you and your detestable uncle, you would be the more prudent choice, inexperienced as you are. So no, but that isn't the inquiry I was trying to establish.'

'What is it then?'

'The south must secede from the crown.'

Kalem gaped at her, not surprised by the suggestion but more by his own inability to have perceived this. Of course, Najima would consider this solution and retribution. 'You want to know if Maylaya will follow. My father would not have wanted to break the country apart. That wasn't the point of his life's work. We have blood ties with the crown for seeds' sake.'

'And yet your province, your homeland, is set firmly in the south, Kalem. When it comes right down to it, where do your loyalties lie? Where have you planted the seeds of your duty?'

'You're making me pick between different sides of myself.'

'Something to think about then before the congregation of the southern datus and bannermen, or what's left of us, tomorrow.'

'My father would not have even suggested breaking our country apart, especially not now, during a time of unrest and war.'

'But you are not your father, are you? Can you say with absolute certainty that you share the same politics, the same conscience as him? Can you claim to be the perfect paragon of duty that you say he was?'

'I . . .' Kalem began to say, sifting through everything his father had tried to teach him about ruling a region, but his mind only went to that last day with him at Himagas, when he'd let his guard down for his son, the last time he had allowed himself to be just a father. 'I cannot.' Kalem felt a pang of pain in his chest at his admission. He was not his father, nor could he ever try to live up to the man that he was.

'I, too, do not feel the same obligation as my husband to fulfil his duty to this country. The day he died was the day my allegiance to the crown disappeared. How could I remain loyal when the throne that swore to protect me in exchange for my fealty had betrayed me and my own? We played our role, we played it well, and I must hand it to Datu Patas and Prince Dangal for trying to make us their equals in the eyes of the crown and the law, but their work has only taken us so far. Now, we take drastic measures. Tell me then, what drives you to take up the mantle of your father's duty?'

When he couldn't answer, she shook her head and made her way to the door. 'I imagine it must be hard for you, knowing that it is your own bloodline that has betrayed you.' She stopped at the doorway and looked over her shoulder. 'I hope you choose well, because once you do make a choice, I will hold you up to it, the same way your father did us. Tomorrow.' And she left him alone before he could finish saying, 'I am not my father.'

The truth of it a stabbed through his heart so deep that it broke the dam behind which he kept all the sorrow, the grief, and the pain he'd bottled up since the loss of his father.

He was not his father. His father was gone. And he hadn't mourned his father yet.

Chapter 20

Yin

The last few days had put far greater distance between the life she had lived, hiding up in the mountains, and the life she had now, looking out over the ocean from the highest tower of the most beautiful palace she'd ever seen. When did her life become about the *most* of things?

Her father assured her that they were safe here and that they won't have to stay here for long. He didn't say where they were to go next, but Yin got the impression that her father didn't intend to come back once—if they left.

But a part of her, the part that kept her alive in the mountain, the part with the intuition that told her to trust her gut feeling, the one that comes when something bad is about to happen, told her that she couldn't leave any time soon. Of course, the Asinari guards who followed her around the palace halls and grounds, who guarded her bedroom door and balcony, didn't help dispute her suspicion. She wasn't sure, though, if the guards were meant to keep her within the palace, or to protect her from danger, or to protect everyone else from her.

She'd been experimenting with the limits of their duty, to see how far she could go without getting in trouble within this gilded cage. They certainly didn't react when she left her room, didn't try to stop her when she went down to the kitchens and the cellars, didn't so much as say a word when she led them to the upper levels of the palace above the surface.

She'd been debating with herself if she could trust Kalem, this other vessel, this other seedgod who was not Lutyo, knowing now what they could do to help and hurt each other. Losing herself in favour of the whole. Pieces of a whole looking to become whole again. Under the pretence of exploring her new prison—she convinced herself that this was reconnaissance; feeling out a potential enemy the way one would feel out a sleeping snake in the grass—she searched for Kalem, only to change her mind when she caught glimpses of him in the halls and drawing rooms and libraries, talking with her father, his aide, the fish queen, and the grey-skinned creature that looked human but wasn't. She was afraid of Kalem, she had to admit that to herself. The connection that they had, that they shared, it was the same thing that she had with Lutyo. Two gods against one. And it made her think that perhaps Lutyo had actually meant to hurt her when Kalem couldn't. Didn't.

The mermaid queen seemed to think that she and Kalem were threats after witnessing three gods *dance*.

She didn't want to think of it as a fight. Lutyo couldn't have intentionally hurt her. But, even to herself, she couldn't say that with certainty. Lutyo had actually hurt her even after she had let him in.

She shook the thought out of her head. She had finally been reunited with her father. She had finally left her island. She was finally free from the tethers that held her down. This was the culmination of an entire life spent waiting for things to happen to her. She should be happy, but . . .

No, she refused to think about things that would break her heart.

'What's up there?' she asked the guards, turning to face them abruptly, pointing at a flight of crooked stairs that seemed to taper as it went up.

They stared at her blankly with black, beady eyes with silver rings on the outside—much like fish.

She folded her arms across her chest, waiting for either to say something. Neither did. So, without looking away from them, she took one step up the stairs, then another, then another. It was on the tenth step that they started following her.

She loomed over the two from the top of the stairs and with her hands on her waist, asked, 'Can you at least tell me what you're guarding me from? This seems excessive, don't you think?'

Still, neither answered, and she rolled her eyes and groaned. She walked on, peeking into rooms—a library in one, an empty bedroom in another, and, oddly, a pool with a fountain that fell off the side of this tower and all the way back down to the ocean.

Still, no Kalem. She was relieved.

The rest of the way, she walked at a leisurely pace, glancing out open windows that looked out at the ocean—the guards still tailing her. The scent of salt and brine permeated the air, but it wasn't the foul kind that wafts from markets at dusk. It was the scent of ocean water wetting the sand, lapping the shore at noon. It was the scent of summer, perpetually on the brink of warmth and too hot, when the promise of dark storm clouds seemed so far away that they were relegated to dreams and nightmares. It reminded her of Masalanta, not during harvest season, when ships came to the harbour and the villages set up a marketplace for the visitors at the docks, but in the calm between the harvest, after the festival and merrymaking, when there was nothing to do but wait for the next season to start. If she closed her eyes and focused on the scents, she could smell the scent of the flowers wafting in through the windows.

On a whim, she turned a corner and ran. The guards followed her, grunting harried breaths, webbed feet squishing on the slightly damp floor. Then, she stopped in front of an open window, allowing the guards to pass her by, and jumped out, calling to the winds to carry her upwards. The two guards leaned out of the window, watching her fly with equal parts awe and exasperation. She grinned at them and shot up to the highest tower. She vaulted over the railing and landed on a sprawling garden of *gumamela*, *kalachuchi*, lilies, chrysanthemums, roses, and *sampaguitas* surrounding a dwarfed fire tree with blue flowers. A man was leaning over the railings to one side.

She gasped where she landed, seeing Kalem there. Before she could run away again, he turned around, eyes wide with surprise, skin glowing indigo even under the waning Morningstar.

'Yin? How did you—' He looked out over the side and saw her guards looking in and out of the windows as they went up. 'You flew. Of course you flew.'

She swept her gaze around the garden, walking past him, feeling the air around the place being charged with magic, his magic. 'You made the flowers bloom?'

He smiled at her, though it didn't reach his eyes. 'A funeral of sorts.'

Her brows shot upwards, alarmed. 'Oh, sorry, I'll go . . .'

'No, no,' he said, waving his hands in front of him in a harried gesture meant to appease her. 'It's not a . . . My father . . . You're not . . . I'm not—' He cleared his throat, looking sheepish, hand stroking the back of his neck, face turning red.

They avoided each other's eyes, feigning interest in the garden that was exploding with colour. Then, as if regaining his footing over a precipice, Kalem spoke, 'You've been avoiding me.'

'I . . . have.' She didn't see the point of lying, but she hesitated to admit it.

Kalem's shoulders fell, and he bit the inside of his cheek. 'If it's the yellow, I promise I can control my baser impulses. I won't take advantage of you.'

Yin blinked and frowned, tilting her head to the side, thinking. She didn't know what to expect when she finally confronted him. His admission hadn't even occurred to her. 'No, it's not that. It's the Shadow—'

Kalem bristled at the mention of the Shadow, his jaw clenched and his teeth gritted, red fury, repressed and unbridled, burning on his face. 'We can kill that bastard together. I know that for sure even if I don't understand our magic. You don't have to worry about him if he comes again.'

She wrapped her arms over her chest, frowning, subtly widening the gap between them. The memory of Lutyo covered in blood came to her mind. *'I murdered an entire family,'* he had said. *'My master sent me to assassinate a political enemy. He'll likely send me to kill more.'*

'He killed your father,' she said, peering into his hard eyes, the veins around them still glowing indigo, the truth slipping past her lips seeming to soften the fury on his face. What replaced it troubled her because it was an all too familiar feeling: grief and guilt.

He tore his gaze away from her and leaned both elbows on the railing to look out at the ocean. 'He knew he was going to die soon, my father. He was sick. I spent most of my life away from him looking for a cure, and when I had finally had a breakthrough, the assassin killed him.' He pulled away from the railing and held onto it with a vice-like grip, his arms shaking. 'Everything I'd done, it was all for nothing. I couldn't save him.' He pressed the heels of his palm against his eyes. 'I even left him for dead in the end.'

She watched him warily and with a curiosity that felt intrusive. It was so easy for him to pour his soul out to her, so easy for him to trust her with this side of him, so vulnerable, so afraid, so utterly heartbroken. This was a man who still lived in the past. She couldn't fault him for trying to find kinship with her. She couldn't very well reject him when he likely felt so alone. He wasn't very good at being alone either, it seemed, and something told her that this man had not been given time to mourn till now.

Nothing she could say would make the grief any less painful. So, she held her tongue.

She took the spot next to him, leaning back against the railing and watching the wind rustle the flowers in the tree; the petals fell like rain and were carried by a swirling gust of wind that took them to the ocean. She didn't say anything, didn't do anything. She let the air between them carry their grief for all that they had lost, let their breaths mingle with the winds that carried away the flower petals across to Skyworld. Grief was a kind of loneliness that people learned to live with, a tether that held them back so long as they held onto it.

He faced her fully, and she felt the pulse of magic flow between them along with something else entirely. Acting on instinct or intuition or maybe even the gut feeling that had kept her alive this long, she took his hand in hers and squeezed it reassuringly.

And she knew that was all they both needed.

Chapter 21

Kalem

Grief was an open wound that refused to heal. Sometimes, Kalem truly believed that it was a wound that would never heal. Grief, after all, was love staying alive after death.

He was not his father. His father was gone. All that was left of him was his son, his legacy, and the aftermath of those two things being forced to mingle with each other. It wasn't a promising marriage.

His father was a bigger man than him, a far better man than he could ever hope to be. The queen of the merfolk couldn't have said it better. He was not his father, and he could never live up to his father's legacy.

But his father's loss hadn't truly settled into Kalem's mind and heart until that talk with Datu Najima Malik. Already, the wheels of life had begun to turn, leaving behind the dead and the past and all things that tethered mortals to the ground. Life had left his father behind. It felt like a betrayal, like Kalem leaving his father for dead again at the arena. It felt unfair that Kalem got to move on.

Yin's hand was a comfortable anchor in his, a tether that kept his feet to the ground. Even when he told himself that it was her magic that made him feel this way about her, that made him feel better, he let himself fall into her. An indulgence, he was sure, but a welcome one when the agony of grief and loss and loneliness felt all too harrowing to carry alone. A hand to hold, a friend, was what he needed now. It amazed him how she could have known that her hand was what he wanted before he knew it, that a reliable anchor was what he craved for at this time. She was intuition incarnate, it seemed. He was envious and in awe of that kind of stable footing in the world.

He couldn't tell if it was skill, magic, or an innate intuition that made her that way, but he decided he didn't care. He wouldn't want to ruin the magic that was her by rationalizing her, forcing her into quantifiable morsels to analyse later. He wasn't stupid enough to try such a thing—just stupid enough to consider it.

It reminded him of what his father truly stood for and the seeds of his own duty.

He watched her marvel at the moonslight over the garden he had made for his father, a supposed funeral that looked too alive to be one, the riot of flowers and plants and life refusing to acknowledge death. She fit seamlessly in this garden, her veins glowing slightly golden with magic, even under the rising moons that painted the garden with the varying colours of seven lights. She was beautiful and lively and so very lovely right here, right now.

If he stayed a moment longer, he'd lean into her and start to believe the lie.

He'd begin to ignore the truth.

His father's legacy hung in the balance and fell into Kalem's clumsy, inadequate hands.

So, he took his hand from hers and walked away.

* * *

'Our country is broken,' Kalem said without preamble as he barged into Dangal's room. 'And it's your fault.'

Dangal looked up from a letter he was reading, raised an eyebrow, and then exchanged looks with Panday who was leaning casually against the doorframe behind Kalem.

'I take it Najima talked to you about the south seceding from the empire,' he said, putting down the letter and leaning back into his chair. 'Your father always did say that she was the most likely to cause problems in the south.'

'You knew about her plans?' Kalem said, slamming his palms on the table between them.

'Datu Patas made her promises,' Dangal said. He interlaced his fingers over his torso, looking at Kalem with generous understanding. This irritated him. 'She came here before she accosted you—'

'Came with a trident and sword, too. Thrashed the room, she did,' Panday spoke up. 'Got in a few good jabs at his majesty over there.'

It was only then did Kalem notice the state the room was in. Pieces of furniture were upturned. Carved out pieces of limestone littered the floor close to the walls they'd fallen from. The floor itself was slightly damp, and walls under the windows were wet with dribbles of seawater. Even Dangal's chair and table were wobbling from damage. He turned to Panday, who he now realized was probably guarding the door in case the queen of the merfolk returned.

'She blames me for the Day of Bleeding Banners,' Dangal said, moving a hand reflexively to massage his torso.

'What did my father promise her?' Kalem narrowed his eyes at Dangal. 'What did you?'

'Patas promised to force the King off the throne and install a more *democratic* government through the Congress.' He rolled his shoulders as Kalem raised an eyebrow, encouraging him to elucidate. 'I made no such promise. You father wants a united country, and I only want to be free of my father. But the means to our ends were the same. We both want the King off the throne no matter the outcome. Men like Duma shouldn't be given that much power to begin with. No man should be given that much power.'

'And you abandoned my father at the last minute. It's no wonder Datu Malik blames you,' Kalem hissed.

'I finally knew where my lost daughter was—but I knew because the King knew. My informants said as much,' Dangal snarled. 'The attack of Masalanta was my father's retribution to great houses that had fallen out of his favour. I risked losing my daughter, too, if I supported Patas openly.' He waved a hand dismissively at Kalem. 'And what of you, Datu Laya? You're why your father began all this.'

Kalem glared at him and slammed both palms on the table again, shaking it so that it almost buckled under his weight. 'You pin the blame on me? I was in Kolehiyo the whole time!'

'Exactly.'

Kalem drew away and paced, lips pressed into a thin line. Dangal was right, of course. How dare he turn the tables on Kalem? He wasn't born with the burden of ruling an empire of broken kingdoms. Kalem was not his father. He was a scholar of magic, lording over his books and laboratories and experiments—

He had no right to blame Dangal. Kalem was born into duty, too, and his father had tried to take that burden off his shoulders, had allowed him his indulgences for as long as he could. *'Your father didn't die for him; he lived for you,'* Panday had said that night they had fled Castel and Kalem had left his father for dead.

Panday's face was unreadable save for the simmering rage and irritation that coloured his brown cheeks red as he watched Kalem and Dangal talk.

Maybe the problem was he'd been indulging, ignoring the duty he was born into, duty that was borne from his father's love. His father didn't die for a stranger. He lived for his son.

Kalem stopped pacing, took in a deep breath, trying to maintain his composure. 'Isn't this what you wanted, Dangal? You have your daughter now. You can turn away from all this, and no one would know any better.' This went without saying and articulating it wasn't helpful. But there were some things that needed to be said out loud for them to become true or at least believable. It seemed to rile up not only Dangal but also Panday.

Dangal frowned, eyeing him with equal parts suspicion and derision as if he was looking at a man whose mere existence was offensive. 'Isn't this what *you* want? Abandoning your duty so you can sulk back into your books?'

Kalem opened his mouth to say, 'You should have known better than to marry a Dayo!' but was interrupted.

'That's it!' Panday forced Kalem to face him. 'I've had it with you two selfish idiots pushing the blame back and forth on each other.' He faced Kalem. 'Your uncle, that royal bootlicker, holds the seat of Maylaya.' He jabbed a finger at Dangal. 'And you? Leaving right now? After dividing the country? After dismantling the monarchy that holds the country together? Right when invaders are at our borders?' He took out a blade and stabbed the letter that Dangal was reading. 'How dare you two play with people's lives because they inconvenienced you!' He raised his arms in frustration. 'Maybe this only shows that you two idiots aren't fit for your duty. But you know what? No one else is in a better position to do it than you two! Maybe the strangelords should break away before idiots like you break them, too. Maybe our country is actually doomed! Let it all burn!'

Panday paused to catch his breath, staring at the blade that had stabbed the letter on the table. He was breathing hard, his chest rising and falling rapidly—more from the fury than his outburst.

'My sister, my father, my mother, they died because they were *inconveniences*. I wanted nothing more than to burn our country down even if it meant I burn with it.' He drew in a breath as he touched the scar on his face and then looked Kalem in the eye. 'Your father talked me out of it, gave me a reason to live, showed me a better, more potent way to exact my revenge. If there's anything I learned from your father, it's this: We're stronger together than apart. So, tell me, what is love if you ignore your duty to it? What is duty if it's not borne out of love?'

Kalem watched Panday the entire time. He hadn't considered running away like Dangal, but he'd ignored his duty for years or pretended that he wasn't beholden to any duty other than his scholarship. He wasn't like his father, who planted his seeds of duty so deep that they bled into Kalem's life. Love without duty is an empty promise, words spoken to imitate depth. It didn't matter. Duty without love is vanity, a chore that demands to be done, however unwanted or unpleasant it is to do. And he realized he wasn't even thinking of running away, only trying to get a lay of his land to see the problems wholly, from the lens of a scholar in the throes of a breakthrough in an experiment—albeit in the most annoyingly theatrical and melodramatic way.

Panday lost everything because some all-powerful man deemed his family, him, inconvenient if allowed to stay alive. Still, here he stood, alive and well and strong, determined to wake up each day to sow his seeds of duty and patiently wait for harvest season. How had Kalem dared to undermine his life?

He stared into Panday's eyes, raging with passion and fire and maybe even divine retribution, but his face softened at Kalem's subtle nod. 'You're not out of the job yet, Panday Talim.'

Panday sighed with relief, patting Kalem's shoulder. 'You, I wasn't all that worried about,' he said, comfortably slipping back into his accent.

They both looked at Dangal who sat there watching them, waiting, presumably, for his turn to speak. 'What do you two idiots expect me to do? I'm the most hated man in the south.'

'And the north. And among the strangelords. By everyone, really.' Panday pointed his thumb at Kalem. 'He, on the other hand, is your cousin, second in line to the Maragtas throne now that the Payapas are gone and Dakila is serving in the Kalasag. And he's a son of the south.' He pulled his blade out of the crack he had made in the table, looking over the letter. He raised his eyebrows as he read it but didn't ask anything about it. 'There's an easy solution to your problems, don't you see? You have a daughter—whose skin, I might add, will bristle some feathers at court but will calm the Dayo rebels. And my boy here has the hots for her. Solves lots of problems right there,' Panday said.

'Don't bring her into this!' Kalem said just as Dangal glared at him.

Dangal stood up and loomed over Kalem. 'What did he say?' he snarled. 'You have the hots for my daughter?'

Kalem backed away from the man, fury rising off him like heat coming off the ground in the summer, veins lighting red with magic. 'He's joking, Dangal!' Kalem said, scrambling for an explanation when Dangal would not relent, seemingly egged on by the flustered look on Kalem's face. Kalem swallowed. 'Even if I did like her that way—' Dangal raised a fist up to Kalem's face. '—I wouldn't force her to do anything she doesn't want. It's not up to me.' He raised both arms to shield his face from the incoming fist. 'It's up to her! Her choice!'

The punch didn't land on his face like he expected it to, but Kalem waited, just in case Dangal changed his mind. A cool draft carrying the scent of flowers and mangoes drifted through the windows, and Kalem was forced to look up at Dangal who was just standing there and looking out the window like he'd seen a ghost.

Kalem turned around to see what Dangal was looking at, but it was gone the moment his eyes fell on it, the winds carrying away the scent. He faced Dangal again whose glare had softened, grown weary, grown ashamed.

'I don't want Mayin involved in this,' Dangal said, sitting back down in his chair, eyes on the letter. 'She's the one thing I can't have ruined by this.' He sighed, shoulders sinking lower. 'But it is clear to me that if I am to protect her, I'm going to have to stay involved myself.' He raised the letter to Kalem. 'If we're to continue the work your father and I have done in Congress, we need to put our houses in order first.'

Kalem took the letter from Dangal and read it.

'My brother has sent his aide to make his case to the southern lords. Maralita should be here by tomorrow night,' Dangal said, rubbing his eyes with his thumb and index finger.

'We have our work cut out for us then,' Kalem said, sighing and looking to Panday and then to Dangal. Grief wasn't the only thing that emerged from the ashes of death. Life went on anyway. 'I don't know how I'll sway the southern lords. I have a plan . . .'

Panday grunted. 'You don't sound so sure.'

'I have part of a plan,' Kalem added with a feigned, dismissive shrug that didn't at all reflect how inadequate he felt. 'I have the notion of a plan.' Panday and Dangal exchanged looks. Kalem sighed, sensing what could only be wavering confidence. 'I'm not my father.'

'Neither of us are our fathers, Kalem.' Dangal shook his head. 'Unfortunately, you'll have to do.'

Chapter 22

Yin

Life flourished where Kalem was. Yin watched him walk away with equal measures of awe and resentment as he left her alone in that garden after sharing a . . . moment. Was that a moment? Where he passed, flowers bloomed so that the air was heavy and heady with a sweet, floral, nectarine scent. Her mind reminded her of that night with Lutyo, the night that tasted of his blood, rot, and the subtle tones of life beginning to bloom from his decay. Life led to death, but life was born from death. Two sides of a wheel spinning endlessly, a cycle of grief and joy, birth and decay. And she couldn't help feeling like she was a spoke forced to spin with two opposing forces, never really given a clear direction, not even an escape route.

Yin stood alone in the garden, watching the moons race across the sky in pursuit of the Morningstar.

'You've made a new friend, little bird.'

Yin spun and came face to face with Lutyo standing under the fire tree. Blue petals fell over him, many turning black and then to ash where they touched the dark cloud that was reshaping into Lutyo's human form.

'Don't forget that I found you first,' he said, grinning at her so casually that fury flared in her.

'Lutyo,' she said, her pounding heart rising up to a drumming in her temples. For the first time, she was at a loss for words around him.

'You should be mad at me,' he said, tentative. Smoke rolled and curled into his dark cloak behind him, bristling with the energy of a storm cloud resisting its own rain and lightning and thunder.

The furrow between her brows deepened, her breath coming out as cold, steamy clouds through her lips. 'Don't tell me how I'm supposed to feel.'

He folded his arms across his chest and leaned casually into the tree trunk. 'What do you feel then?'

One heavy footfall after another and she found herself standing before him, looking up at his cool, calm face as if that dreadful last week hadn't happened. How could he act this way? So casually cruel, the torment of a stranger who was once not? 'You lied to me, Lutyo.'

A flicker of doubt flashed across his face, but it was gone before she could pin it down. 'I did tell you not to trust anyone who tries to tie you down.' He grinned at her, but it didn't reach his eyes.

'Why are you here, Lutyo?'

He pressed his lips into a thin line. 'My master finally decided on what to do with you.'

'Your master is the King himself,' she said, a question, an intuition, phrased as the truth. She still hoped that he'd deny it, tell her that it wasn't true. 'You've known all along who I was.'

He ran a gloved hand through his hair. 'I have.'

'Is that why you came to Masalanta?'

'Yes. He sent me to look for you.' He straightened up so that he was looming over her. 'For my master.' He gestured at her blade. 'He didn't want to kill you just yet, so I took a chance.'

'You took a chance on this thing stabbing me so I can get its power. Why?'

'An act of defiance maybe . . .' he said with an unintentional shrug. She knew that wasn't the only reason, and she waited for him to elaborate. A small smile crept on his face, a smile that felt all too eerily familiar to Yin. 'Access to more magic, more control. At the very least, it's why I can't kill you even if I were ordered to do so. The magic protects your life from me, but that does not mean I can't hurt your mortal body. It's because our magic equals and negates each other that we can't defeat each other.'

Yin frowned.

'It's like you want to kill me.'

That wiped the smile off his face. 'Of course I don't, Yin. Do you think I wanted to run away from you on that last night together? I wanted *you*.' He pressed his forehead to hers but pulled back almost immediately after their skins touched. 'You're the only reason I have left to live.' He watched the black veins dissipate from her skin. 'And I can't even touch you without hurting you.'

She pressed her palms to his chest, wanting so much to lean into him, wanting him so much that it hurt. But he terrified her now, now that she knew what he was capable of doing, knew what he'd done at the behest of his master, knew the cost and limits of his tether. If she dug deeper, let herself wonder about him, about the inner workings of his mind, she was afraid to find that a part of him had condoned—wanted, even—the horrible things he'd done for her grandfather. She couldn't look him in the eyes when she asked, 'The others, the Masalanta villagers, your master's political enemies, the Day of Bleeding Banners, Kalem's father . . . Did you want to kill them all?'

He turned away and walked over to the railings to look out over the ocean. 'Death becomes easier to swallow the more you see of it.' He looked over his shoulder at her. 'You're afraid of me, and you're afraid that I kill for sport not because I am commanded to do so.' He shook his head, avoiding her curious, prying eyes when she joined him where he stood. 'The truth is much more horrifying. I simply don't care about all those people I kill. With every death, I am rewarded a few moments of freedom to do whatever I want, be whoever I want, go wherever I want . . . be with whoever I want.'

Her knuckles were turning white from her tightening grip on the railings. 'Don't blame me for the things you've done, Lutyo.' She didn't mean to lace her tone with spite, but the casual and cruel way she said it stung them both.

He gritted his teeth and pulled her into an embrace, burying his face into the crook of her neck. 'I don't, but love is a choice. I choose you.' His breath, his lips, his skin on hers felt like sharp daggers under her skin, like live lightning shooting through her veins. 'I can't sacrifice you, Yin,' he said against her skin. 'I would destroy myself first before I could ever hurt you again.'

She wrapped her arms around him, trying her best to ignore the lighting, the shot of pain rippling from his skin to hers. 'But don't you see, Lutyo? You already did, but I chose you anyway. I chose the pain that came with wanting you.'

He pushed her away abruptly, almost a little violently, his face a painting of horror and terror upon seeing her, her pale skin webbed with black veins. 'You don't understand. I came here so you could use your dagger to take my magic from me.'

'But you said that would kill you.'

He gave her a sad, pained smile. That was exactly what he wanted.

'I won't do it. You can't make me.'

'But Yin—'

She pressed her fingers to his lips, her veins turning black at the touch. 'There's a way around this—' she raised a hand to stop him from interrupting her, '—one where neither you nor my father will have to die. There must be a way.'

'There is one way. Take my dagger back from him.' He pushed her hand away before it turned all black. The yellow pushed away the black and returned her skin to its normal pale tone. He watched her, at once looking pensive and determined, and the moment reminded her of that first time they'd met. Two lonely gods who didn't want to be lost and alone anymore.

'There's still the danger to my father. "Kill my son," you had said. I assume the command cannot be immediately enacted, seeing that you're here,' she repeated under her breath, pacing before Lutyo as her mind worked.

'I can't do anything to hurt myself directly, which includes enacting commands stupidly,' Lutyo said, but Yin was already deep in her thoughts. 'Vessels cannot harm themselves while they carry gods. Nor can we do anything to cause harm directly to ourselves or our wielders.'

Maybe she could ask Kalem to help. He would have a solution to this if he was actually the seedmagic expert that he said he was. He would have already turned the puzzle in his head a million times and found a solution. Kalem who was life and Lutyo who was death. The contrast astounded her, confused her. She had a moment with Kalem . . . But she had Lutyo. She shouldn't be confused by this.

No. Not now. She can't think about that now. Not while Lutyo was looking to her so expectantly, fearfully.

Lutyo's master had ordered her dead but because her magic equalled Lutyo's, he couldn't kill her so easily. Her magic negated his magic and the order to kill her. 'Does the King have other sons?'

'He does. Me,' he said, his face brightening momentarily at the thought.

Yin didn't know how to react to this revelation. Lutyo was essentially related to her by blood. Lutyo, whom she loved, had dropped this information without so much as blinking an eye. Like he didn't care at all that this was a fact about their true relationship to each other. Yin didn't know what to make of this. Lutyo's nonchalance made her question the intensity of her reaction. He seemed to treat it as a non-issue and saying something might make things awkward. *Anyway, it's not like I grew up with Lutyo as family*, she reasoned. The thought still made her cringe. Unwilling to confront this further, she turned her mind back to their conversation.

'And you can't kill yourself. Vessels can't harm themselves while they carry gods, you said. So, that must negate the order?'

'You're bending the rules.'

'How do you know if it doesn't work?'

'Regardless of which son my master ordered dead, he still has my blade. When he finds out that you and your father are still alive, he can simply amend the command. Taking my magic away is the one thing that could prevent that.'

She frowned, closing the gap between them so that she could feel his breath on her cheek. 'Don't you want to be with me?'

He drew away, but Yin pulled him back by his collar. 'I don't want to hurt you.'

'I don't believe you.' She pushed him away and jabbed her finger at his chest accusingly with every succeeding question. 'You know what I think? You're afraid of what we could have. I think you didn't actually mean it when you said that you wanted me, that you chose me.'

He grabbed her by her shoulders again. 'I want to be free, Yin. I want to die on my own terms.'

'You're not dying by my hands. I'll fly to him right now and take your dagger back if I have to—'

Before she could finish talking, he forced his lips on hers, reigniting their connection, reigniting the magic in their veins. She felt their magic mingling, two turbulent oceans meeting at a strait, dancing, fighting, pushing and pulling for dominion over the other. She knew better now, knew to expect the pain that came with the pleasure, and he matched his force with hers, two opposing ends spinning and spinning like a wheel. She knew better. She knew him. She knew the pain he'd inflict, the magic that came in waves to mix with her own and the aftereffects of his curse trying to kill her mortal body. This was a connection tainted by his poison, and she wanted it, all of it, all of him, magic and curse alike.

In the back of her mind, she asked herself, shouldn't the connection be easy, painless, unwrinkled? Like with Kalem.

He pushed her away when she responded to him too willingly, giving into him more than taking from him. 'We can't be together! Don't you get it, Yin? I love you, but I can't love you without hurting you. I can't live like this.' He fell to his knees. 'I don't want to live knowing that *I* can't make you happy. I don't want to live knowing that my entire life is meant to hurt and kill. Please, for once listen to me, Yin. I have made my choice. Use your dagger. Free me.'

Yin backed away from him, her hand falling on the blade's hilt hanging from her belt. Love is a choice, and he'd made his. He was choosing this. Instead of her.

She shook her head and said, 'No,' before a gust of wind carried her off into the night.

This wasn't her choice.

Chapter 23

Kalem

Kalem was beginning to think that his notion of a plan was actually wishful thinking, and he felt silly now, standing before a council of southern lords sitting at a round table and eyeing him with caution and a hint of distrust. In the heat of the moment, while explaining his dumb plan, he had risen to his feet. Now, he felt like a naive idiot.

The southern lords were debating the fate of the entire country, whether to break away from it or to fight the duplicitous King or to take back lost parts of the country that didn't even fall within their purview—the south was too far from the northern lands for the coming of the Tukikuni to matter. Maylaya lands straddled north and south, providing a natural bridge between these two major regions of the country and between the crown and the southern lords. Perhaps that was why Maylaya's datus had historically held such crucial positions of power at court.

However, Kalem's plan hinged on him being Datu of his father's house, something he hadn't thought was in question till now.

'Masterrrrrr Laya,' the grey-skinned Asuwan lord, Datu Truben Natera of Olimawi, began, his accent rolling the r of the title he deliberately used for Kalem and extending the last note airily like he was constantly chasing after his exhaled breath. He leaned casually on the armrest of his chair, his grey wiry hair falling stiffly on his hollowed cheeks, his patterns fitting snugly over his bony body. His black eyes were opals in his skull-shaped head. 'Your uncle hasss all but declarrrred you dead.'

'His uncle is not the rightful heir.' A young man, younger than Kalem even, barely out of Kolehiyo, leaned his elbows on the table, levelling Kalem with a piercing, almost angry gaze that Kalem mistook as actual anger. Kalem's jaw dropped, meeting the boy's eyes with a spark of recognition. This had once been one of the blank faces that stared back at him in Kolehiyo. Mapalad Layag of the Maragtas Isles, a datu now, no doubt after the death of his father during the Bleeding Banners. 'Master Laya—Datu Laya, we find ourselves in the same circumstance so you must understand, too, why I have chosen to be here,' Mapalad said, the same determined air that he'd always displayed in class surfacing, albeit more refined, more focused, more aware of his naivete. 'You do not truly believe that the King would step down so easily—by simply asking—not after what he's done at Congress.' He flicked his chin up, his boyish face hardening as his eyes flicked to Dangal who was sitting next to Kalem at the table. 'The age of the Maragtas kings is at an end, Master. His house ensured that.'

Najima was staring thoughtfully at Kalem, elbows on the table, hands clasped in front of her, chin and thin lips pressing against her fingers. She didn't say anything, didn't defend him, didn't antagonize him like he expected her to. Though he felt like she was piercing into him like a needle burying into his skin.

Kalem's plan was to rally the northern lords against the King to force him to abdicate in favour of his son Dangal. The northern lords needed military support in the war against the Tukikuni. The southern lords needed votes in Congress not only to reformat the government and spread out power but to also relegate the crown to a more ceremonial title. It was a compromise that certainly didn't completely satisfy everyone. But the fact that no one was happy meant that at least they all had equal measures of gain and loss.

He did not take into account the fractured mess that the south had turned into after the Bleeding Banners. Without his father providing an anchor to unite them to a common cause, every southern lord had much more egocentric— bordering on mercenary—goals coming into this meeting; far beyond just seceding from the crown. They were less disappointed by him not easily falling into the same duty as his father and more by him trying to wrest control from their new de facto leader, Najima. Regardless, the hard, hurtful implication of all this was that Kalem was not his father.

Dangal spoke up. 'I am not my father. I'm on your side.' He was sitting comfortably in his chair, fingers steepled in front of him, pressed up to his lips, arms propped on the armrest of his chair. 'Remember that *I* stopped the King from placing one of his cronies into the Lakantabi seat. All this would be moot without that.'

'At the cost of angering the King and pushing him to wipe out dissenting houses,' Natera said. 'Including your own cousins, I might add, Master Dangal. The remaining datus are already at odds with each other, and the King is egging it on.'

'Not to mention, this rift among us datus will fracture the country's military power at a time of war against the Tukikuni,' Layag added unhelpfully, disdainfully. He had no respect for the son of the man who had killed his family.

Dangal looked up at Kalem who was still on his feet. 'You need assurances that I will not try to take back absolute power when I take the Maragtas throne.' He sat straighter, leaning forward as if to divulge a secret conspiracy that needed to be said in hushed tones. 'My daughter is half Dayo.' If any of the southern lords had any violent reactions to that, none deigned to show it. It was an admission of a scandal that had long plagued his reputation. An heir with questionable pedigree was always a stain on any house's record, no matter how high the house was in the social hierarchy.

Dangal was well aware of this and knew the ways of the court—a skill that Kalem was lacking—well enough to leverage his weaknesses in his favour. He eyed each of them warily. 'I do not intend to sire any other heirs. I do not intend to pass on this burden to her, nor do I expect you to accept her as if she were entirely Kayuman.' He looked straight at Najima, knowing full well her politics, her motivations. 'I only wish to give her a home that will not persecute her for what she is. I care not for the title I hold, only that it is a tool that I use to protect her.'

Najima and Dangal stared at each other, an entire conversation seeming happen pass between them, perhaps a debate or a negotiation. Dangal had the same seeds of duty as Najima. Children. A legacy passed on by blood.

He certainly knew how to play into Najima's good graces, and she seemed aware of what he was trying to do. Kalem should learn from that.

The Asuwan lord spoke up, 'That's all well and good, Master Maylakan, but perhaps you should focus on fixing your house's affairs rather than meddling in ours.'

'Hold on, Datu Natera,' Datu Layag said. 'Perhaps it is fortunate that he is here. It is the prince's job to offer tie-breaker votes. Seeing that Master Kalem is unsure yet where his loyalties lie, we may need him.'

'Do not let your schoolmate sway you, Datu Layag.' The Asuwan lord leaned back into his chair. 'His position here is tenuous at best, now, with Maylaya in the hands of Lord Batas Laya.'

'I know where my loyalties lie, my seeds of duty, as Datu Malik calls it,' Kalem said. 'It's in protecting my father's legacy. Even from me if I have to. He would not want us to break apart from Kayumalon, not in this new age of conquest. Divided, we are weak. The choice is either to do our duty to our country and be the masters of our fate or do nothing and let the world decide what becomes of the broken pieces of us.'

Najima broke her silence, Natera, Layag, Dangal, and Kalem shooting curious and surprised looks at her. 'So you would vote not to break away from Kayumalon? That is your choice, Datu Laya?'

'If my country breaks apart, it would not be by my hands or by my word,' Kalem said, tapping his chest as he spoke. 'Every balangay has reaped both boon and loss in this country but that is the price we pay for our freedom—a freedom, I might add, that remains intact so long as it does not impede on another's. Together we are stronger, the strongest, the most powerful country in the world. Divided the rest of the world will flock like vultures to peck at our remains. Our children will not stand a chance when we are gone.'

'I refuse to subject myself or my people to another Maragtas king. Not again.' Datu Layag was gritting his teeth, fists clenched on the table before him, body trembling. Fury marred his young face, grief dulled his eyes.

'Be reasonable, Layag. All of us Kayuman, even you, are of the Maragtas bloodline,' Kalem said, slipping into a teacher's tone used for students. Mapalad Layag had been one of the good students during his years in Kolehiyo, diligent, industrious, patient but prone to bursts of passions, which the masters had to tame in class on more than one occasion. 'Taking out a sitting ruler would effectively take out an entire country during a time of invasion. Rebuilding the government will require time and the promise of stability—'

'A king with southern roots then,' Najima said in an offhand way that threw them all off. Kalem met her eyes, which had an almost mischievous glint in them. The corners of her mouth twitched as if resisting a self-satisfied smile from forming on her face. Even sitting down, her tall frame loomed over the rest of them. 'One who will ensure a more . . . egalitarian government.'

Kalem and Dangal exchanged looks, understanding the implication of what she had just said. She wanted assurance that the reign of Maragtas kings would end in her lifetime, but even if Dangal abdicated to allow Kalem to sit on the Maragtas throne, a descendant of the Maragtas bloodline would still become ruler. She needed to weaken the Maragtas bloodline's hold over the throne so as to completely relegate it to a ceremonial role or even to eradicate completely the need for the position in the future.

The best she could hope for was Kalem and all succeeding Maragtas descendants abdicating their titles and their claim to the throne, but the most she could get without causing all-out war amid the warring provinces of Kayumalon was for Kalem, the next in-line to the throne with unquestionable bloodlines, to sire descendants with questionable bloodlines. She needed the next Maragtas king to produce heirs of questionable pedigree. She meant to use Yin to her advantage.

'Keep my daughter out of this,' Dangal said, understanding what the queen of the merfolk was trying to drive at. He rose to his feet, eyes darting from Najima to Layag to Kalem. 'I did not bring her back to be used as a pawn at court.'

Najima rose to her feet, arms folded across her chest. 'Install a southerner on the Maragtas throne, you get our armies and our continuing allegiance to this country. This is our condition.'

'You dare give me an ultimatum?' Dangal said, the words coming out almost as a growl.

'Not an ultimatum. You have the freedom to pick between Layag and Laya,' Najima said smugly, like she's just outplayed a master at the game.

'Her life is not ours, Najima,' Kalem said. 'Do not make decisions for her.'

'I do not like the idea of marrying a Dayo, Datu Malik, even if she is a Maylakan princess,' Layag said.

'But you would be king, Layag. I imagine that would make the agreement more . . . palatable. A southerner as king and an outsider as queen,' Datu Natera said.

Dangal raised his voice this time. 'She was not born for Kayumalon court. She does not belong at court.'

The hall echoed with their debates, disagreements, and arguments. No word was spoken without being interrupted. No point was made without emotions flaring. No explanation was offered without the talk devolving into fight. All of it forced to end only when a powerful gust of wind blew through the open arches and a girl landed in the middle of the table with a loud thud.

'Kalem is right. My life is my own. I make my own decisions,' Yin said, earning a collective gasp around the room. She kept the winds circling the room lightly as the datus talked among themselves. This was the woman who gave the Berdugo the push they needed to rebel. This was the woman who had the winds at her beck and call, and the air they breathe in this room was the reminder and announcement of that—that she was a goddess.

'A Dayo doesn't get to decide the fate of this country,' Layag said.

'You don't get to decide what I do with my life,' Yin snapped back.

'Daughter, you don't have to do this. This shouldn't concern you,' Dangal said.

'No, Father, it concerns me that decisions are being made for me and how I live my life. People have been making decisions for me all my life. Let me make my own this time,' she said. 'I will marry Kalem Laya if he'll have me, but you, queen of the merfolk and the rest of you strangelords, must follow him and my father wherever they need you to go—be it war or victory or ruin. You will protect him and my father from everything that would cause them harm.'

Najima smiled, victorious, smug, her eyes darting to Kalem who stared in astonishment at Yin. She raised an eyebrow at him as if to ask 'So? What'll it be?'

'I've made my choice,' Yin said, noticing with rising annoyance the silent exchange between Kalem and Najima.

'Well, Datu Laya?' Najima said, smugly ignoring the girl with the tempestuous temper.

Kalem's mind went to the memory of his father in Castel. Not in the chaos of the Bleeding Banners, but in the quiet comfort of the Himagas. His father had said, *Men like us aren't afforded the luxury of pursuing our dreams, not with the weight of duty bearing down our shoulders. Leave or stay, our people's blood will be on our hands.*

Kalem had expected that he'd be married off to a Kayuman noblewoman who could offer his house the most advantage, but the freedom to love was the least that his father could give him when he couldn't have everything else he wanted. It was the one indulgence he was allowed to have. But looking at Yin, he wondered if he loved her, the pressure to understand how he felt for her—if it was magic or biology or something else entirely—weighed down on him like a boulder. Did it matter what he wanted? Did it matter if it was magic or not if he made a decision now? Did it matter once he's made a choice? She chose him—was choosing him now. Did he matter?

He was not his father. This was the only value he brought to the table. A pawn. Not a datu. Not a king. Not himself.

But he would be king in name. He wondered if it was worth everything he would lose.

Dangal and Yin glared at him, daring him to take the other's side.

Kalem nodded, his lips parting to voice out his agreement when a black cloud of death swept into the room.

Chapter 24

Yin

The shadow of death that Yin knew all too well swirled over them, datus and Dayos alike.

There was a mechanical attribute to the way Lutyo moved, his form swirling downwards and reshaping into a pair of feet, legs, torso, arms, neck, and head, his cloak billowing out behind him, part smoke, part fabric. His blank gaze fell on Dangal, who grabbed Yin off the table and drew her to the back of the room, toward the hall's closed double doors, which slammed open to let in Asinari soldiers led by Panday, going straight for Kalem. The other datus and their aides and bodyguards scrambled away from the table and toward the door at one end of the room, weapons drawn and ready to face the Shadow. He disintegrated the table and the chairs with his smoke, clearing the space of obstacles leading to his prey standing ready to fight at the exit.

Layag's face turned pale white at the sight of Lutyo, and he was surrounded by his own guards who backed him away from the Shadow. Najima took a spear from one of her soldiers and Natera prepared to fight, protracting black claws from his fingers and toes, elongating the teeth from his lower jaw.

Kalem stepped ahead of them, his veins lighting up Indigo, his stance ready to attack. 'Shadow God,' he snarled as he raised a hand up at Lutyo, 'you shouldn't have come here.'

Yin's father pushed her down by the door, wary. 'Run and hide, Yin!' he said, before turning to return to the fight.

She ran after him and grabbed his arm. 'No, he's here to kill you!'

The billowing black cloud descended, swirling and curling fingers of black smoke reaching for them, eroding stone and wood and paper and what little flesh it touched. He went after the closest Asinari soldier, whose body disintegrated to dust as the cloud touched him. Then, he chased Najima, Layag, Natera, and Dangal, tendrils of smoke sliding over their weapons and limbs when he could get close enough.

'Stay back!' Kalem yelled at the rest of them. A cloud of indigo mist burst out of him, surrounding him and those around him, meeting the Shadow like oil and water. Yin pushed past her father, summoning the winds to contain the smoke, her veins lighting up yellow as she joined Kalem where he stood.

'Lutyo!' Yin called, arms circling in front of her, commanding her winds to flow this way and that and forming a whirlwind within which the Shadow was contained. Lutyo stood at the bottom, in the eye of her storm, seeming unbothered by her magic.

Kalem grabbed one of her hands, igniting their divine connection, combining their magic, indigo swirling with yellow under their veins. She shot him a surprised look, but his eyes were only on Lutyo, murderous, vengeful, furious. Yin pulled back from him, ending their connection abruptly, turning off the magic they had already summoned. They fell backward from the impact.

Lutyo used the momentary distraction to scan the room. His gaze fell directly on the people behind them, whimpering and hissing in fear. He glided forward, feet turning to smoke underneath him.

It was Kalem who scrambled back up to his feet first, chasing after Lutyo, reigniting the divine indigo, which pushed at the black cloud as if pushing at a wall.

'You killed my father!' Kalem said, tone laced with fury, his magic sparking static where it met the smoke, which didn't budge despite his efforts, nor did his magic pull back from the smoke. A stalemate between two equal gods.

'"Kill my son," my master ordered,' Lutyo said, repeating the order blankly, eyes focused on Dangal standing at the doorway. The next sequence of events happened so quickly that Yin had hardly gotten up to her feet before the stalemate was broken, and she was calling out her father's name and calling forth the winds to protect her and her own. Lutyo pulled his shadows from his fight with Kalem and shot all of them, as much as he could summon to slam into Dangal. Kalem's magic, in turn, fell like a wall, shooting toward Lutyo and sending him sprawling on the floor.

Yin turned away from them and ran to her father, still engulfed in the black death, mouthing her name over and over. The winds swooped ahead of her, glowing, glinting golden with her magic, cutting a pathway toward Dangal who had fallen to his knees, his skin webbed with black veins.

His eyes fell on her as she tried to pull him up to his feet, away from the cloud, and toward the doorway. Her veins blinked yellow and black as her magic fought against Lutyo's. Yin felt the black magic pull away suddenly from them, a gasp escaping her lips from the surprise. She fell to her knees, dropping her father to the ground. He didn't stand back up.

She raised his head so that he was lying on her lap. He stared blankly at her face, the black veins spreading the colour across his skin, seeping into the black tattoos. She brushed the hair off his face. 'Father, Father, Father . . .' Tears stung her eyes. She was losing another father. She felt him drifting off, his life like sand in the palm of her hand. She looked up desperately for help. The datus and their guards and soldiers stood at the doorway with horrified looks on their faces, fearing the decay that had befallen the room and people that Lutyo's cloud had managed to reach. Lutyo and Kalem were fighting endlessly, mists of black and indigo around their bodies, sparking where their magic touched, like lightning enveloped by storm clouds at dusk. Never besting the other. Never losing to the other. Their magic, that of life and death, too similar, too equal, too complimentary to ever defeat the other.

'Kalem!' she called desperately, but though he looked at her, he could not very well pull away from the fight without risking a final, fatal blow to his body from Lutyo.

Her father's trembling fingers rose to touch her face only to fall back down limply, the black turning into ash and white as his body disintegrated in her arms. She looked back down at him, pulling him closer to her, taking his ruined hands to touch her face like he had wanted. He mouthed her name,

'Mayin,' soundless, breathless, lifeless. His eyes rolled back into his head, and black gave way to ash, the fragmented remains of her father drifting with the winds till she held nothing but her own hands, her own skin, the blade hanging from the belt around her waist.

Her body, trembling. Her mind, hazy. Her eyes, tear-stained and staring straight at two gods. She stood up slowly, drew her black blade, and walked up to them. Lutyo was the first to notice, and the first to let his magic fall. Kalem's magic tossed him back almost violently, slamming him against a wall, his body sliding back down.

She stepped past Kalem, blade in hand, and stood over Lutyo, who only looked up at her as if he had been expecting—wanting—this from her all along—the sweet release of death. She raised the blade, her magic flowing throughout her veins and into the black metal that turned transparent, like glass glowing golden from within, the runes on its body blinking, the magic swirling within the spherical pommel. The corners of Lutyo's lips pulled up slyly into that casual, cool grin that she knew so well—the one he gave her when he knew he'd won their little game that day—when his eyes met hers. Then, he closed his eyes and bowed his head to her in submission.

She loved him. She chose him. She wanted him. And here he was, submitting himself to her. The Death God who had found her when she thought herself lost and alone. He had fulfilled his master's command. He was free from the tether for now. He was free to run.

Even here, now, asking for death, she was not being given a choice.

She lowered her blade. 'Go,' she said under her breath.

Kalem pulled at her shoulder, forcing her to look at him, glaring at her, eyes asking why she was changing her mind now. And she matched his glare with her own, daring him to try and stop her. He gritted his teeth, veins still lit indigo, hers still yellow. 'You want to set the Death God free?' he said, outraged, a colour that she had never seen on the mild-mannered man she knew.

Lutyo's eyes shot open and switched glances between Yin and Kalem.

'Run away, Lutyo,' she repeated without breaking eye contact with Kalem, her blade poised to stab him instead, to take his magic if he tried to stop Lutyo.

Magic sparked tempestuously between the three of them. Black, yellow, indigo. Raven, maya, turtle. Death, love, and life. Three gods of equal might at a stalemate.

The Death God was the first to flee.

Chapter 25

Kalem

The girl intended to kill a god, and her blade was not pointed at the Death God.

Kalem didn't turn away from her when the Shadow fled from them, not even when she lowered her blade.

'He killed your father and mine, and you let him escape,' Kalem said disbelievingly.

'You do not blame the blade for what its wielder has done,' she said.

'He was complicit!' he said, raising his voice.

That gave her pause, but it wasn't long, her face turning from defensive to pitiful. 'You do not know the limits of our magic, do you? You don't know the price of our power.'

Kalem felt like a fool, and he did not like the idea of her thinking him that. He was a germachemist. An expert seedmage. The best of his generation. But this seedgod, this power he had stumbled into, he did not understand it.

'I do not,' he admitted, gritting his teeth. 'And I assume you think you understand it more than I do?' he asked that last part spitefully, pridefully.

'I know enough to kill our kind,' she said, her grip on the dagger's hilt tightening.

'Should I take this to mean that you intend to kill the Shadow yourself? Or do you intend to kill me instead?'

She pressed her lips into a thin line. 'I will not enact your vengeance, Kalem.'

'My vengeance? He killed your father!'

'Lutyo is not my enemy,' she said, her jaw clenching. 'His will is not his own.'

He was taken aback by the admission, and he gritted his teeth knowing that he had been taken for a fool this whole time. 'You know this Shadow?'

'I do.'

There was an abrupt end to the way she answered, one that Kalem sensed had broached a rather painful topic. Still, she faced him with that same determined face he knew from when they had first met. The demeanour that asserted she knew her place, that carved out a place for her where she might not belong.

'I have not forgiven him for what he's done, complicit or not,' Kalem said.

'Neither have I,' she said firmly. 'But it's not up to you, whatever I do next. I'm done waiting to be rescued. Whatever I do now, I do for myself.'

'I know,' Kalem said, softly, bitterly understanding full well what a life dictated by others felt like, understanding the choice she was making now—it wasn't him she was choosing. 'How will you kill a god?' he said, choking back the lump in his throat.

'This.' She raised the blade up between them, presenting the metal that had turned back to black. 'Our own blades can siphon the magic of other seedgods. But these blades are also tethers that hold us back and control us if they fall into the wrong hands.' She lowered her blade, sensing the eyes watching them in the ruined room. He followed her gaze to see Najima, Mapalad, Natera, and Panday with their guards and soldiers crowding one side of the room, eyeing them both reverently and fearfully.

Kalem ignored them. 'That is what you intend to do? Siphon his god?'

'I intend to free him,' she said.

'That is not the answer to that question.'

They stared at each other, trying to put the pieces of the other back together, trying to place each other in their memories, that first time they met, that time they danced in the sky, that time they flew together. They crossed a threshold, a line that defined their borders and determined where they stood in each other's lives. It was not hard to tell that she had feelings for this Shadow, that the Shadow held her heart even as it pained her to let him go. But here and now, Kalem had chosen her and, for a short time, she had chosen Kalem. It wasn't love. It wasn't magic. It wasn't anything abstract or divine or unknowable that informed their choice.

It was duty.

And what was duty if it wasn't born from love?

The winds picked up around the tower, blowing into the wide open windows where a small, flying Dalaket ship hovered, a gangplank bridging the gap between the tower and deck, from where a man in rumpled Crimson Guard uniform crossed over.

Kalem levelled Yin one last, longing look, biting his lower lip and the inside of his cheek as the thoughts raced in his mind. 'Do what you must, Yin. Your life is yours.' That last one was a thinly-veiled desperate plea for her to stay, to choose him. Of course, he wouldn't ask it of her, he couldn't do that to her. But that seemed to have struck her hard, like he had slapped her across the face, from the way she looked. He had made her choice even as she made hers.

He walked away from her before she could allow herself to be persuaded by him, before he could persuade himself to kneel before her and beg, leaving her confused. Did he expect her to honour their betrothal? Did he expect her to return to him? To choose him again after she'd settled things between her and the Shadow? He hated to admit that he did, but as he stood now, facing his peers, datus, soldiers, and statesmen alike, he knew that his duty to her was a necessary choice. The fulfilment of the one indulgence his father had allowed him to have: Love. So, she would be free of him because of love and duty in equal measure even if she never chose him again.

He didn't watch her take to the skies, instead focusing on his peers, the other datus looking distraught and astonished by him and her, two gods coming to a silent agreement even as they came to power. Duty must take precedence for now.

'What has happened, Maralita?' It was Panday who addressed the newcomer first as he joined them at the doorway.

'Elevendsende will fall—has likely fallen by now—to the Tukikuni,' Maralita said, gravely. 'The King is indisposed. In the absence of Congress and in the interest of expediency, Dangal must call to arms the rest of the country before the Tukikuni takes Kahinbuwan and the three veins of power that connect all our lands.'

'The crown prince is dead.' It was Najima who broke the silence first, taking Maralita by surprise. 'Datu Kalem Laya is next in line.'

Suffocated, Kalem walked out the room, another necessary choice lest he look back and continue to hope that Yin had chosen to stay. The other datus followed him, including Panday and Maralita.

'What do we do, Mas—your highness,' Layag asked, sounding like the boy that he had been back in Kolehiyo.

'Datu Layaaaaaa, the sssssouth standssss with you,' Natera said in that upsetting accent of his.

Najima walked up to his side, following him wordlessly in her own palace. How quick they were to submit to him now that he had power, title, position, legitimacy, divine magic. They got exactly what they wanted. One of them, sitting on the Maragtas Throne.

He stopped to face them, making sure he met the eyes of each one as he swept his gaze over them. He held Panday's gaze the longest, his most loyal friend expecting an answer. The Crimson Guard soldier standing next to him bearing the same expectation, forgetting for a moment what Dangal's death meant for him, for this war, for the whole country. The lot of them seemed to have forgotten it to make way for other, much more pressing concerns.

'Kalem?' Panday asked. A worried inquiry about his friend's health and current disposition.

'War,' Kalem began, hesitating at first, remembering who he was, what he was. He was not his father. But who he was now had the magic of a god and had catapulted him to the Maragtas Throne. He was his father's son, but he still was his own man. So, in one grave breath, one that breathed in the last of the fading nectarine-scented winds, he continued, 'We go to war.'

Epilogue

Jinwun

The Spider Empress was a merciless master, but she was generous when rewarding her most faithful servants.

Every time JinWun pleased the Empress, her one reward was an entire day with her husband within the confines of the Spider Empress's palace in Jjada City, capital of the Tukikuni Empire. But this wasn't a reward. It was a reminder of what JinWun would lose if she disobeyed the Empress.

She didn't wear her armour today and chose, instead, a robe painted with green flowers and studded with jade. She let her dark brown shoulder-length hair down and even wore a flower in it. Despite the cold, she bathed that morning to wash off the grime of death.

She sat on a stone bench under a cherry tree in an enclosed private space of the sprawling palace garden, watching the koi fish swim lazily in the pond. Flowers and trees dotted the land surrounding the palace structures, its eight black towers topped with sweeping pagoda roofs tapering as they reached up to the spring sky. The winter cold took its time leaving Tukikuni, but it wasn't unbearably cold.

Her seedgod, Yeou, bounded up to her in the green misty form of a fox, skipping over the surface of the water and blithely circling her on the bench. *'When you get far enough from the spider, maybe the blade won't work anymore. Maybe she can't compel you to do her bidding anymore. Then maybe we can both run away.'*

'I can't leave, Yeou.' JinWun watched the doorway to the garden, her heart pounding in her chest, her mind, a hand fidgeting over the skin on her cheek, hoping to erase the vein stains there at least.

'Why?'

JinWun stood when a man in a ragged grey tunic, trousers, and chains around his wrists and ankles was delivered to the garden by two soldiers who were standing guard over him. The fire spread in her chest, and she ran to him, desperate and crying for his warmth. She wrapped her arms around him and he wrapped her around his. His jet black hair fell over his shoulders and his overgrown beard covered his once clear, beautiful face. She stood on her tiptoes and kissed him deeply, passionately, hungrily.

He pulled away and placed both palms on her cheeks, eyes searching hers, emotion swelling from longing to joy to concern to rage. 'She hurt you again.'

JinWun turned her head away, self-consciously covering her face with her hands and her hair. With GonChun, she allowed herself to soften, to show the parts of herself that would never survive war. She wasn't a soldier or a godvessel or the spider's most favoured servant. She was simply GonChun's wife. 'It was my fault.'

Sighing, Jin GonChun gently took her hand away from her face. 'Let me see you, JinWun. Please.'

JinWun looked up, a hand on his chest, the other on his cheek. He'd lost more weight since she last saw him. Gone was the muscle mass he'd gained from hours of military training and hard labour. Gone were the supple cheeks that dimpled when he smiled and laughed. Gone was the fire in his almond-shaped eyes, now caged by crow's feet. Only her reflection was left in them, a dying ember fighting for life, fighting for her. He'd aged considerably since they had first met while her magic maintained her youth. How long had it been since the spider put him in his prison? How many years had passed since she'd fallen in love with him? What had they done to him, her wonderful, beautiful, vibrant GonChun? She blamed herself. She blamed her failure. She blamed her weakness. The man she loved was wasting away in a cell, and everything that made him *him*, was withering away piece by piece at the spider's whim.

'Have they been starving you again?' She pulled away partly to speak with the guard and more to hide the tears that threatened to fall down her face. 'I'll talk to the—'

GonChun held her firmly and pulled her back into his arms. 'Stay,' he whispered into her ear. 'Please stay.' He kissed her cheeks, her neck, her chest, her hands, everywhere. He made her whole again, he made her feel like herself again, the girl he had fallen in love with all those years ago.

At her touch, he felt alive again, her touch felt warm and inviting, it felt like home. He had been her fire during that long, cruel winter all those years ago, and she'd clung to him for dear life.

She lay on top of his frail body on the grass, holding him close, afraid they'd take him away from her so soon.

She listened to his heart beat in his chest, a crescendo falling back into gentler tones and rhythms. Her heart danced to his tune. He stroked her hair, running his slender fingers through it, warming her scalp and neck where his fingertips touched her. They stayed like that, thinking, longing, wanting, holding each other, listening to each other's breaths and heartbeat, memorizing every bit of this moment so that it would remain etched in their heads when they were forced to part again.

'You will never be free. And there's nothing I can do while I'm in here,' GonChun muttered, his eyes staring up at the sky, at the clouds drifting past the Morningstar and ushering in the first moons of the night.

JinWun propped herself up on her elbows to look at GonChun's face. 'What are you thinking?' she asked, suspicious of the way he said those words.

GonChun shook his head and kissed the top of her head. 'I'm thinking that you make me so happy. You're the only thing in this world that brings me joy.'

She rested her chin on his chest. 'I might not see you again for a long time, my love.'

'She's sending you away?'

She nodded. 'South. To another war.'

'How long?'

'I don't know, but the spider is determined to take Kayumalon soon. She knows she has the power to win. She's been waiting for this provocation.'

'Maybe you don't have to.'

'What?' she said, suddenly outraged.

'What if you don't have to leave?' He sat up abruptly, pushing her off his body. He held her and made her look at his face. It was the face he made when he had brought home three dead rats after charging into a snowstorm to find food that day many years ago when they tried to run away. Stupid and proud children they were. 'What if she can't compel you to do her bidding anymore?'

She pulled herself from his grip and narrowed her eyes at her husband. 'I don't like where this conversation is going, GonChun.'

He smiled a small, almost muted smile, the stupid look gone, but she could tell that the idea was still there. He pulled her back to his body. 'All right. The conversation won't go there.'

She placed her forehead on his chest. 'You're the only reason I have left for living, GonChun. Don't do anything stupid while I'm away.'

When he didn't speak, she glared at him and spoke with as much conviction she could muster. 'Don't do anything stupid while I'm away, GonChun.'

'All right. All right,' he said with a half-hearted laugh. 'I won't do anything stupid while you're on your campaign, my love.'

She searched his eyes for broken promises and empty words. A feeling deep inside her told her this was not the end of it, but she could tell he was being truthful. 'I love you, GonChun.'

'I love you, Woon.' He placed a palm on her cheek, gently stroking her magic-stained skin with his thumb. 'When do you leave?'

'The day after tomorrow. At dawn.'

'We'll have to make the most of the time we've got left then.' He embraced her again, warming the parts of her that had been frozen in ice.

Acknowledgments

It takes a lot of balls for a writer to think, 'Hey, I'm going to write a novel for the first time, and I'm going to write epic fantasy!' That thought would be akin to an indoor kitty-cat thinking it can take on a Bengal tiger in a fight. But it was the middle of the lockdown, and I had a lot of time on my hands. Fortunately (or perhaps unfortunately), I literally don't have the balls, and it only took me three long years, thirty-seven drafts, obsessive worldbuilding painstakingly handwritten in piles and piles of notebooks, and literally over a million words discarded to get to the manuscript that I finally pitched to publishers. Even then, I knew *Winds Of War* wasn't ready for the world to see. It took so much faith and patience for this book to come to fruition—not just from my part. I don't have the gall to say that I did it all alone. I have so many people to thank, it just might take another half a million words just to express my gratitude, and even then it might not be enough. Fortunately, I have the girl guts to try anyway.

Nora Nazarene Abu Bakar, publisher of Penguin Random House SEA, you were the first to take a chance on me and my stories. I daresay you had more faith in *Winds of War* than I ever did, and for that, I am so very thankful.

I hope my stories could live up—are living up—to the level of faith you had in me.

Thatchaayanie Renganathan, my wonderful, patient, and persistent structural editor, oh my god, I've made you so miserable these last few months. Where editing *Love on the Second Read* felt like a walk on the beach, editing *Winds of War* felt like climbing a mountain with three peaks in the dead of night in the middle of a typhoon with no flashlight. Thank you, thank you, thank you so much for not giving up on me or my books. Thank you for staying with me till the third and last book in this trilogy. This trilogy would have still been a hot mess without you. I might stick to romance for the foreseeable future—or maybe not. Let's see where my writing takes me next. Haha!

Chaitanya Srivastava, my publicist and best cheerleader and social media marketing genius, I will never forget that you called me in the middle of the night when I was in the middle of a panic attack (because I had just had my heart broken and I couldn't eat and I was out of prescription meds—it's a whole other thing) even when you weren't feeling so good yourself. Thank you so much for everything you've done for my books. We wouldn't be here without you. My books (and I!) would have faded into obscurity had you not dragged me out of the dark night of my soul.

Garima Bhatt, my digital media marketer, and Almira Ebio Manduriao, head of sales, thank you so, so, so much for all you do to get my books to bookstores and in readers' hands. I would have hoarded all my books with myself if you hadn't done what you've done.

Sneha Bhagwat, my copyeditor, wow, you've somehow made the editing process so much easier. Thank you for taking on this mammoth book. Of all the novels that I have written, this one has made me doubt myself the most. Seeing your edits, seeing this draft, the way you just understood everything I was trying to do and helped me improve it, I feel so grateful. Thank you so much!

Swadha Singh, who handled *Love on the Second Read* and *Winds of War*, you made so many of my wildest fantasies come true. I could never have imagined me becoming an author of a book with a fantasy map! I'm sorry for the hot mess that my map doodle and worldbuilding were but thank you so much for pushing through and making it the stunning book that it is!

Divya Gaur and Trisha Udumudi, who have designed and made the artwork for the books so far in the Seedmage Cycle, thank you for such stunning covers you've made. Even though it's difficult for me to tell apart shades of blue (the making of this book cover really was an inconvenient time for me to find out that I can't see the color indigo! So sorry for that!), you got my vision. Oh my goodness, it just blows my mind how much you get me. Not only do you get me, you elevate my vision to a level even I can't imagine. I can't wait for the next book and to see all three together!

Divya Aggarwal, Ishani Bhattacharya, and everyone who worked behind the scenes of making my books, hello again! I know what it's like to work in the background of making books, and sometimes, I feel like my part of the job doesn't matter because it's not glitzy and nobody knows I was ever part of the project. Just know that I see you! I know you're there! I will always remember that my books wouldn't exist without the hard work and love and patience you put into them. Thank you for all you do. We wouldn't be here without you.

Mom, Dad, Jem, Jas, Lolamommy, Tita Jane, and my entire family, thank you for supporting my dream and for understanding when I act like an ogre and smash my keyboard to get in my daily word count goal. I hope you're proud of me.

Koko, June, James, Lio, Gem, Marc, Ela, Bea, Ms Dina, Ms Lotte, Ms Rose, Ms Jen, thank you for leaving me alone after I clock out so I can write my books (haha!). It means so much to me that you give me room to pursue my passions outside of the day job that I also love so much.

Mrs Emerita Tagal, my favourite high school English teacher who tolerated my twenty-page essays for homework, can you believe that this is my third book? This wouldn't have happened if you didn't believe I could write back when I actually couldn't write. Thank you for pushing me to pursue a career in writing even when the world told me to pursue math instead.

The entire book community, bookstragrammers, booktokers, book bloggers, and bookworms everywhere, you have been so generous and kind and loving and patient with me since my first book. Thank you for making all of those fun posts and for promoting my books on your platforms. Thank you for the time you put into reading, reviewing, commenting, and making posts!

And you, dear reader. It takes a lot of faith to pick up a book by a nobody from nowhere and read it through to the end. At the heart of the Seedmage Cycle is an unabashed faith in love and in people's capacity to do everything in the name of love. It would then take real girl guts for me to say that it must be love that brought you here because it was also an act of love that led me here to you. And in case you need to hear it now, I'll say it here: I love you. May your life be lived in love.